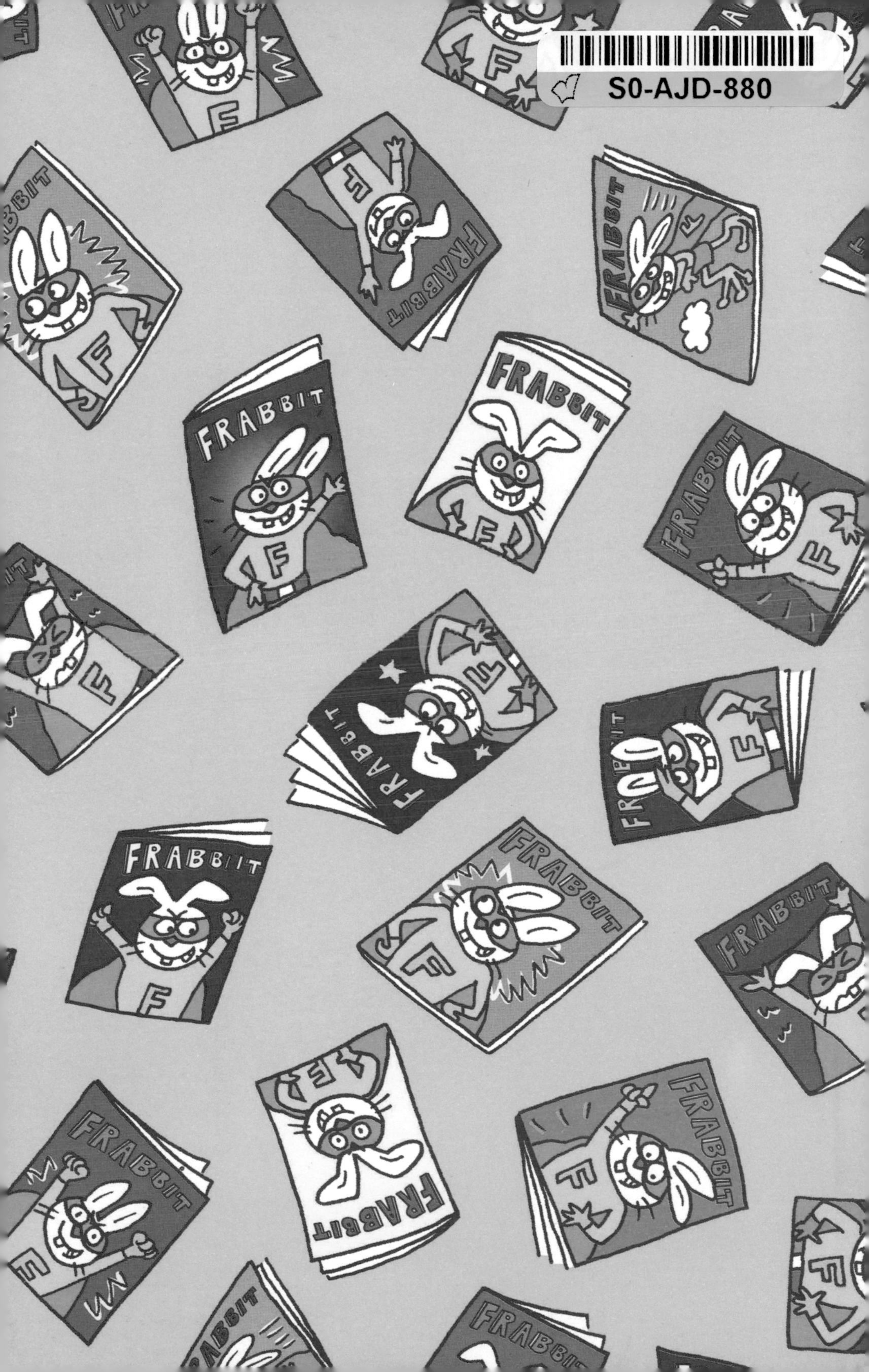
FRABBIT
FRABBIT
FRABBIT
FRABBIT
FRABBIT
FRABBIT
FRABBIT
FRABBIT
FRABBIT
FRABBIT
FRABBIT
FRABBIT
FRABBIT

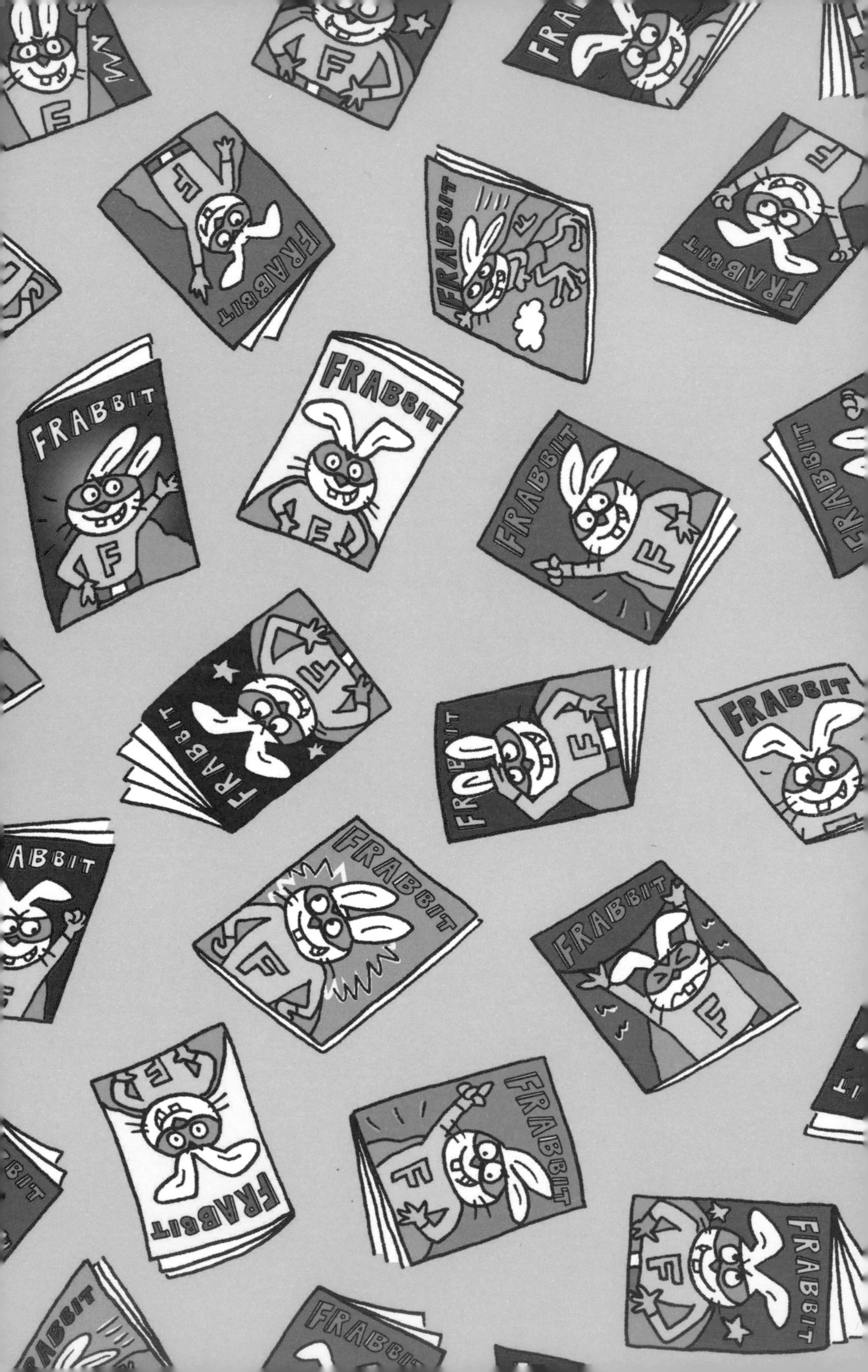
FRABBIT
FRABBIT
FRABBIT
FRABBIT
FRABBIT
FRABBIT
FRABBIT
FRABBIT
FRABBIT
FRABBIT
FRABBIT
FRABBIT
FRABBIT
FRABBIT

# The Bumble Brothers
## Crazy for Comics!

Written by Steve Metzger
Illustrated by Brian Schatell
*With color by Gary Fields*

FRABBIT
F
WOW!
FRABBIT
FRABBIT
FRABBIT

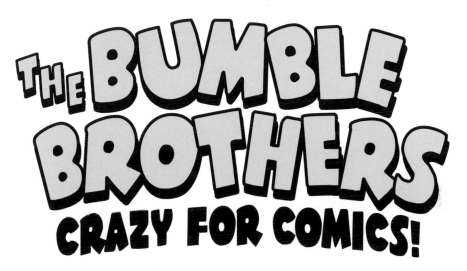

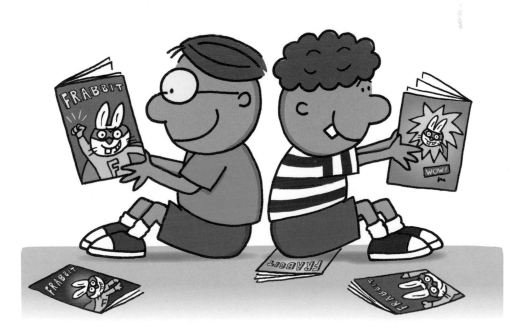

Reycraft Books
55 Fifth Avenue
New York, NY 10003

Reycraftbooks.com

Reycraft Books is a trade imprint and trademark of Newmark Learning, LLC.

Text © 2022 Steve Metzger
Illustrations © 2022 Brian Schatell

Educators and Librarians: Our books may be purchased in bulk for promotional, educational, or business use. Please contact sales@reycraftbooks.com.

Library of Congress Control Number: 2022903719

ISBN: 978-1-4788-7583-3

Author photo: Courtesy of Rob DeSantos Jr.
Illustrator photo: Courtesy of Jane E. Gerver

Printed in Dongguan, China. 8557/0522/19073

10 9 8 7 6 5 4 3 2 1

First Edition Hardcover published by Reycraft Books 2022.

# Meet The Bumbles

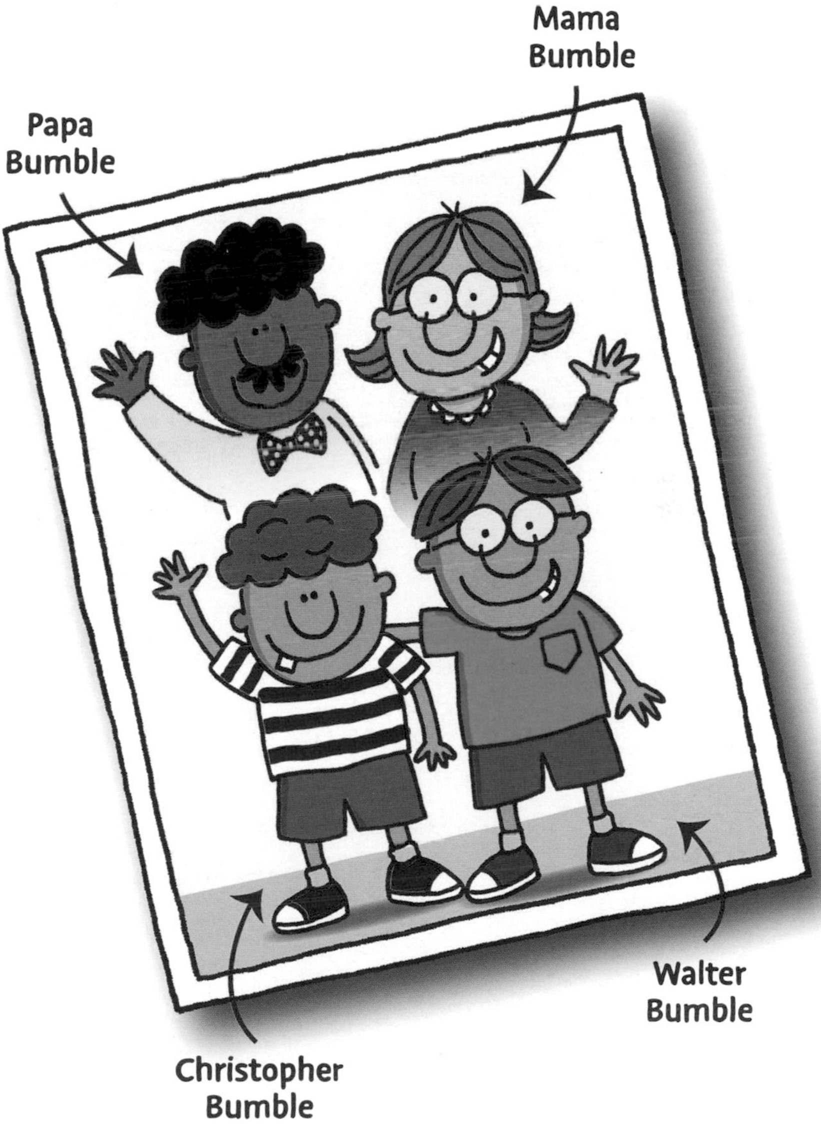
Mama Bumble
Papa Bumble
Walter Bumble
Christopher Bumble

To Steve Kriegsman, who was there from the very beginning.

- S.M.


For Lynn Bacharach.

- B.S.

# CHAPTER 1 - WAKE UP!

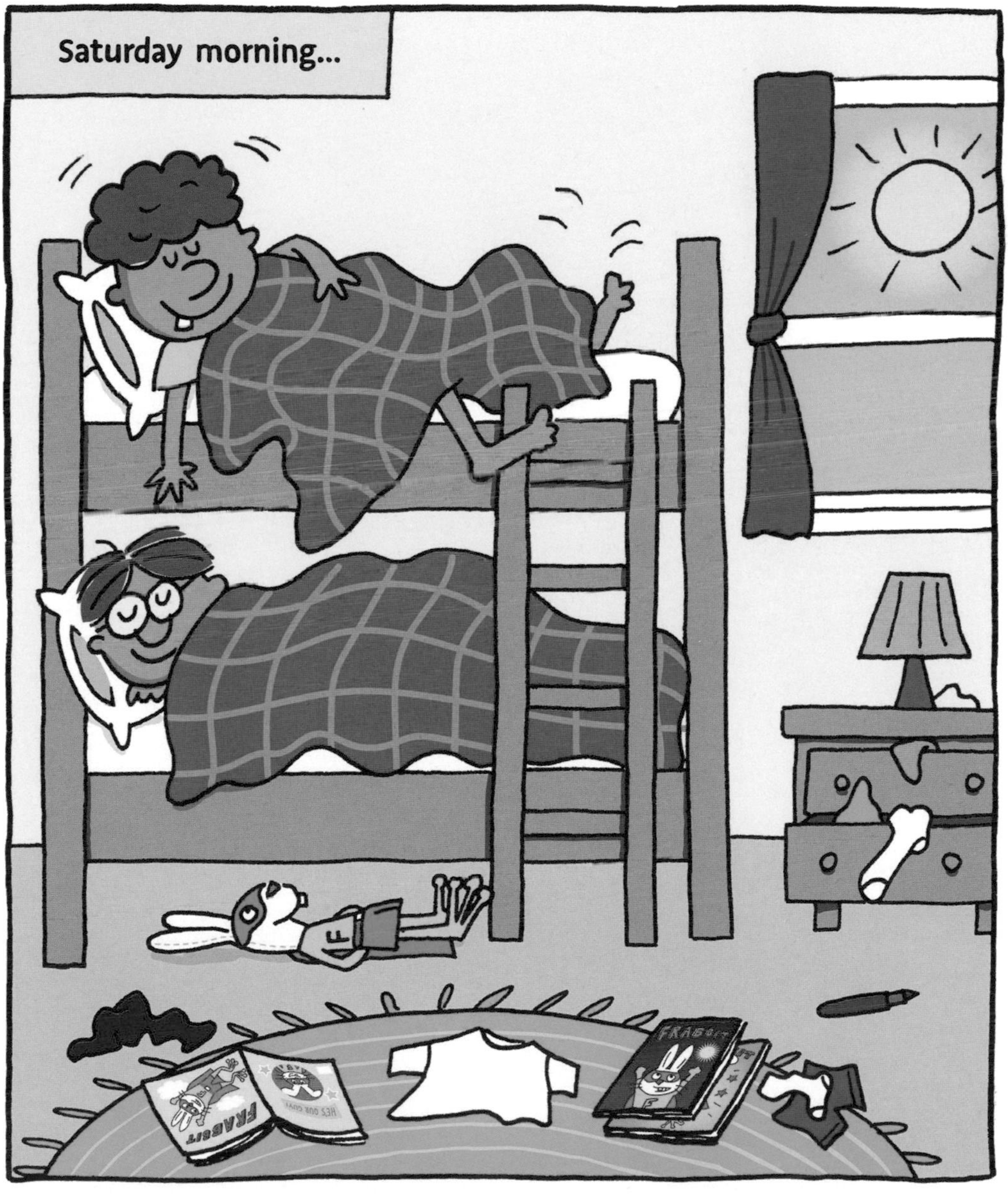
Saturday morning...

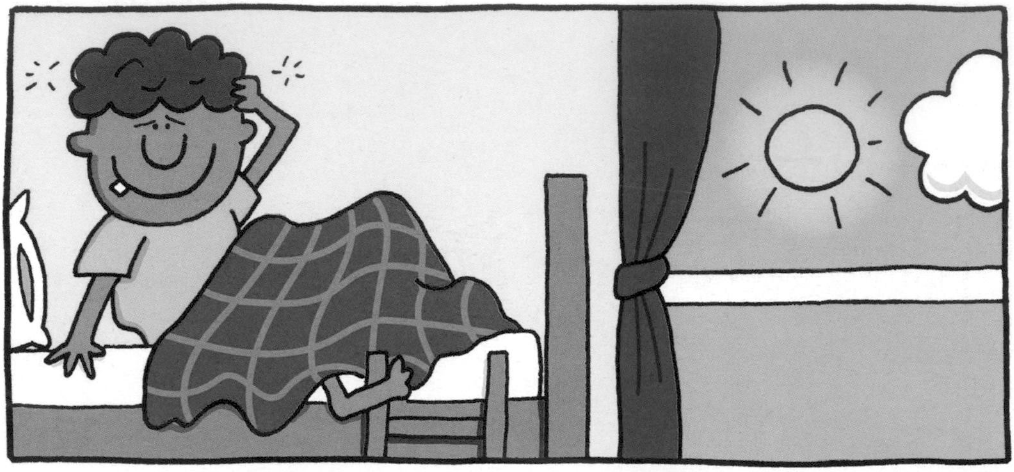

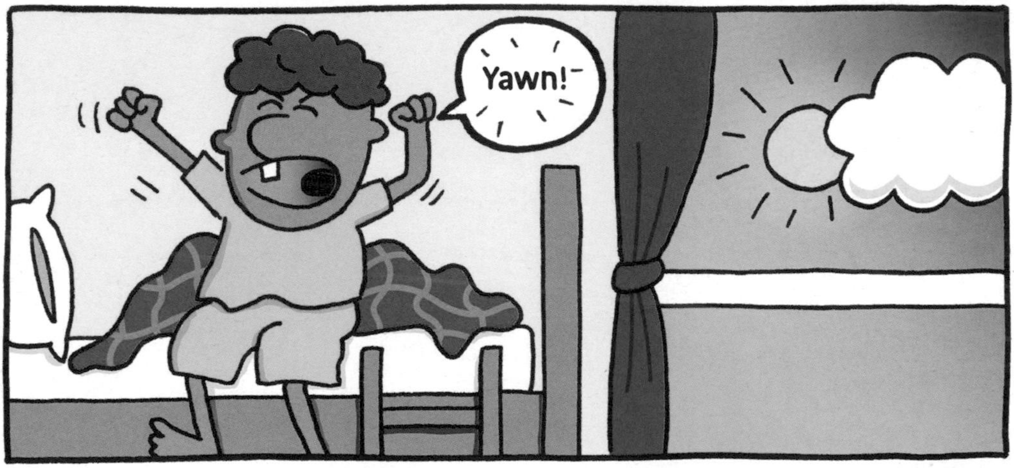
Yawn!

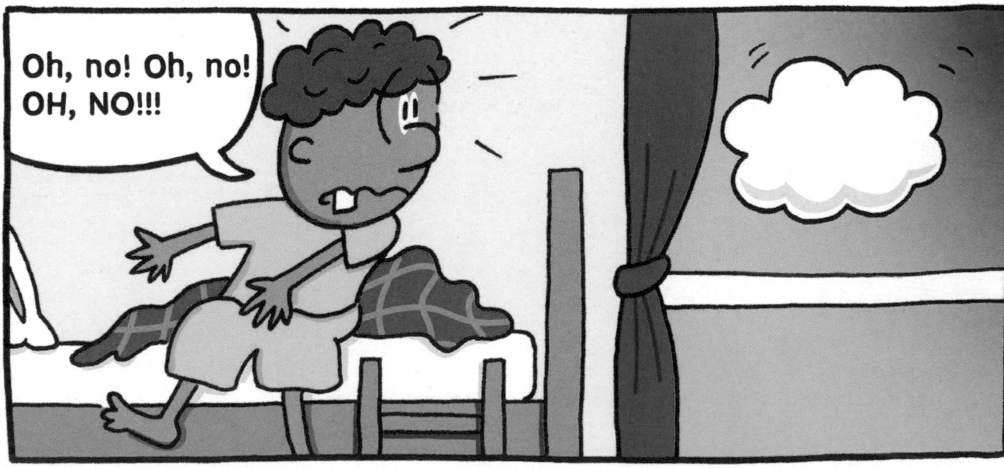
Oh, no! Oh, no!
OH, NO!!!

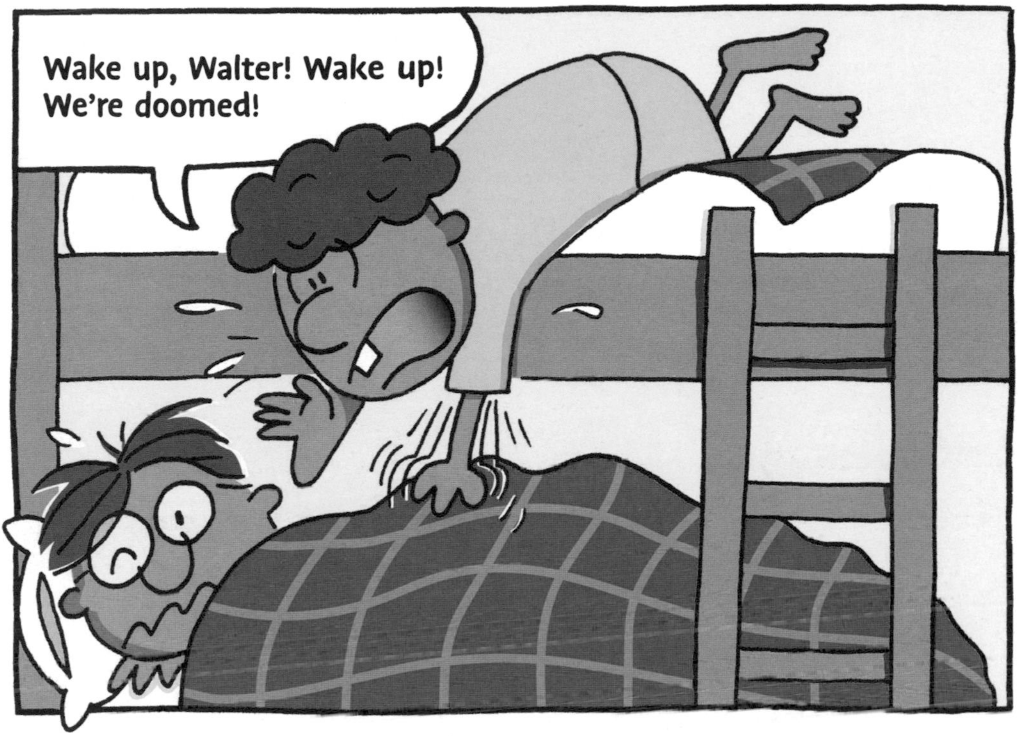
Wake up, Walter! Wake up!
We're doomed!

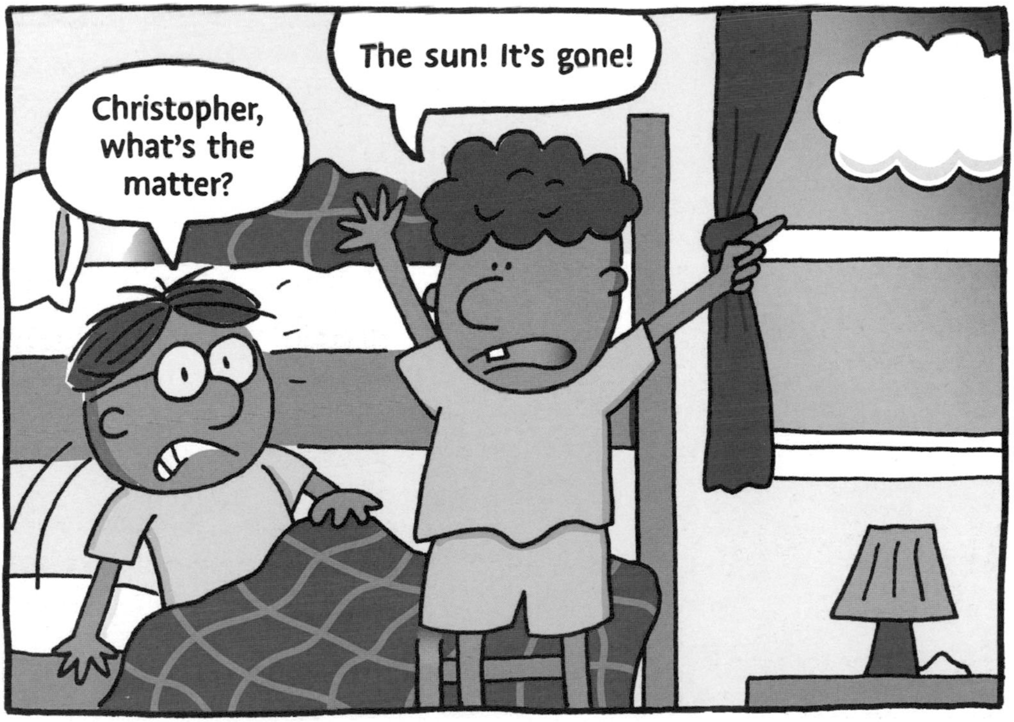
The sun! It's gone!
Christopher, what's the matter?

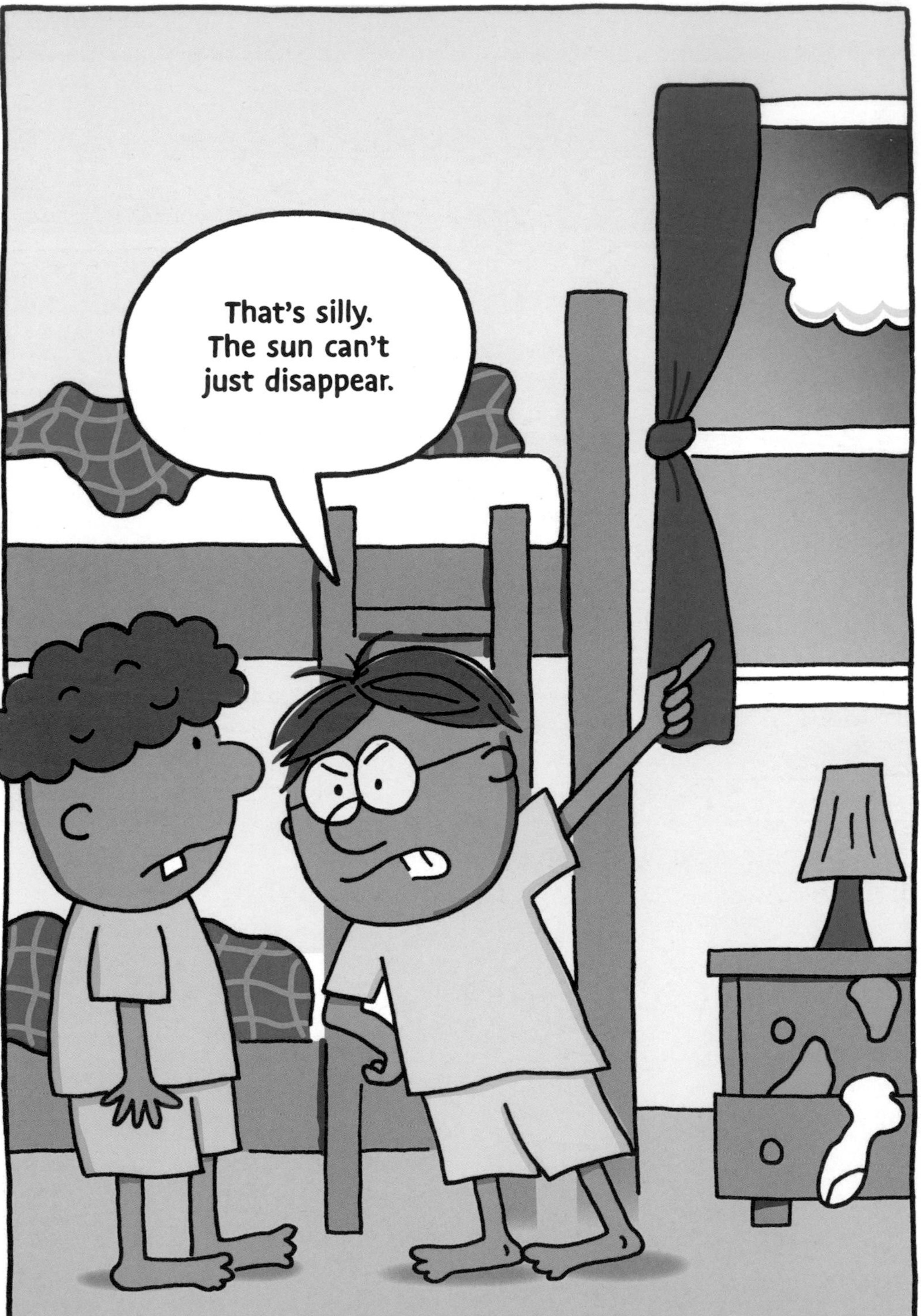
That's silly.
The sun can't
just disappear.

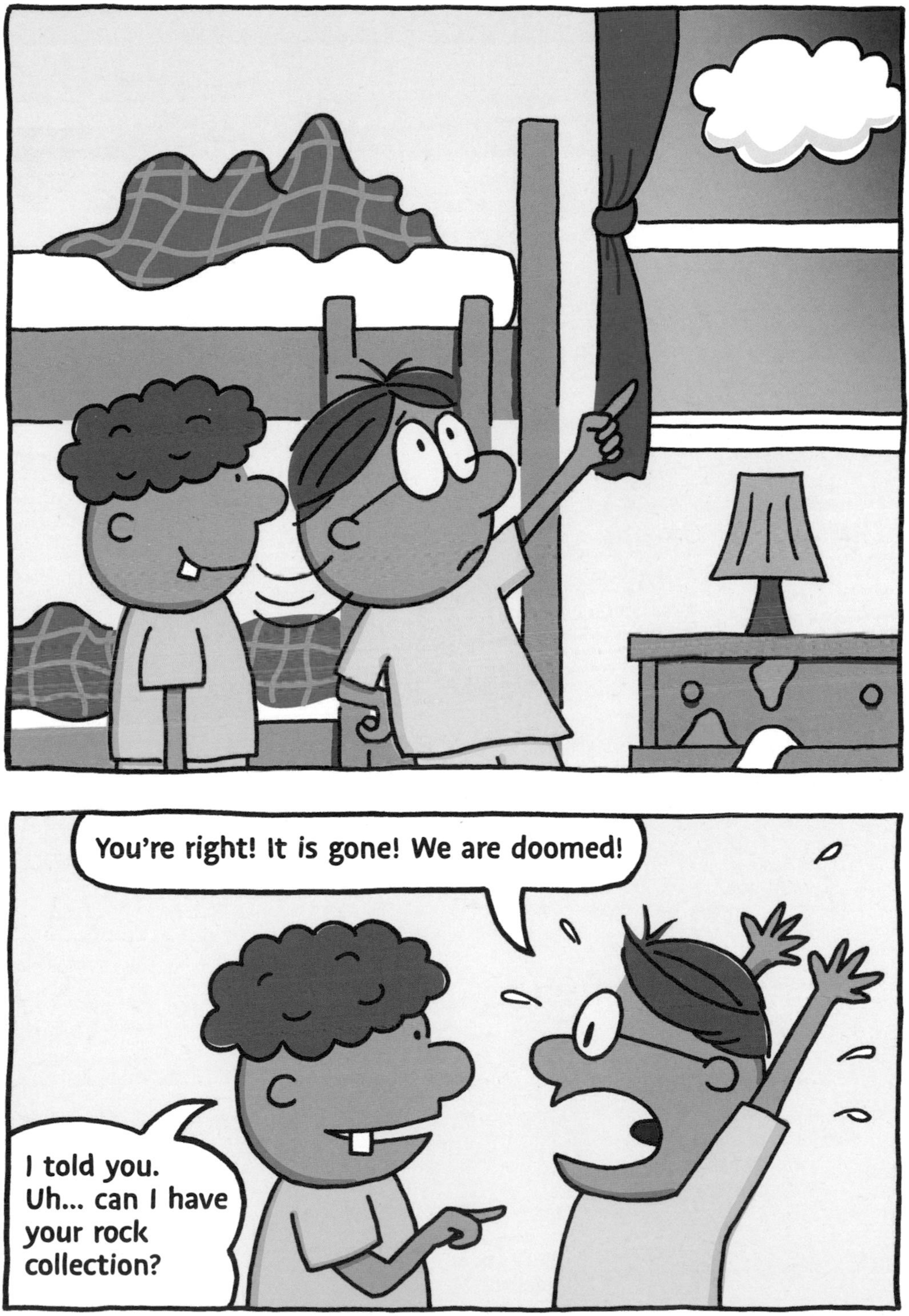
You're right! It is gone! We are doomed!
I told you. Uh... can I have your rock collection?

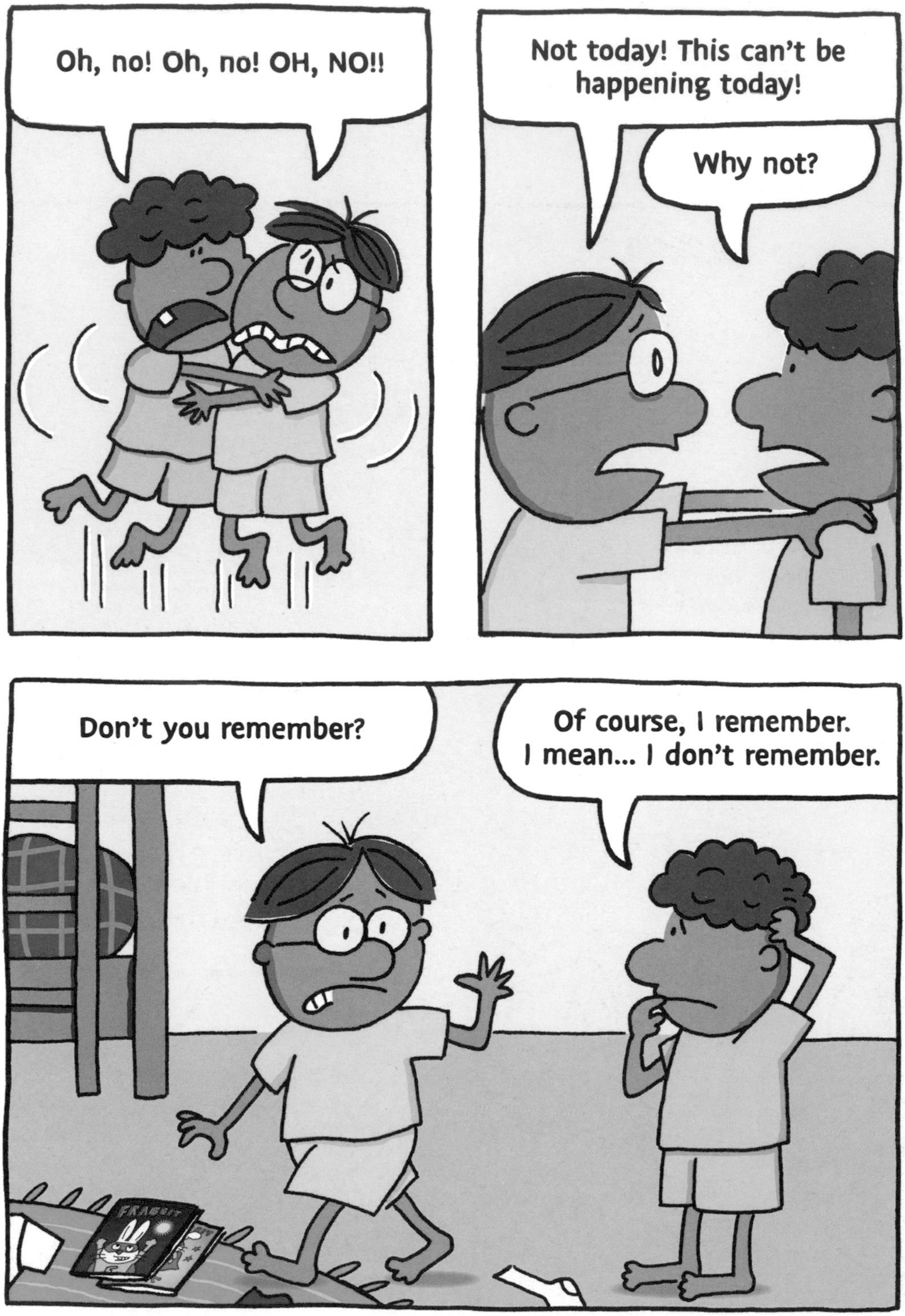
Oh, no! Oh, no! OH, NO!!
Not today! This can't be happening today!
Why not?
Don't you remember?
Of course, I remember. I mean... I don't remember.

# CHAPTER 2 - FRABBIT AND WORMO!

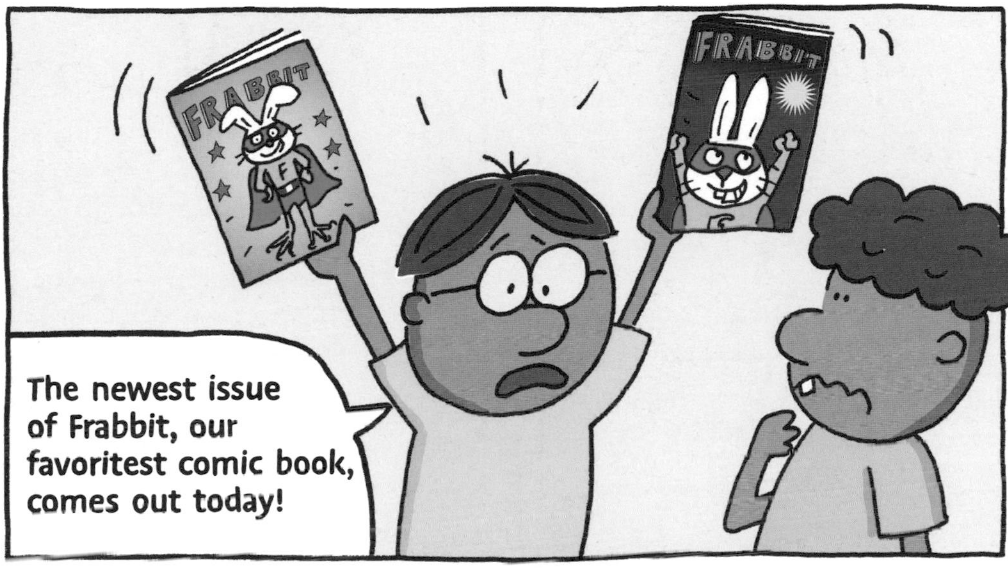
FRABBIT
FRABBIT
The newest issue of Frabbit, our favoritest comic book, comes out today!

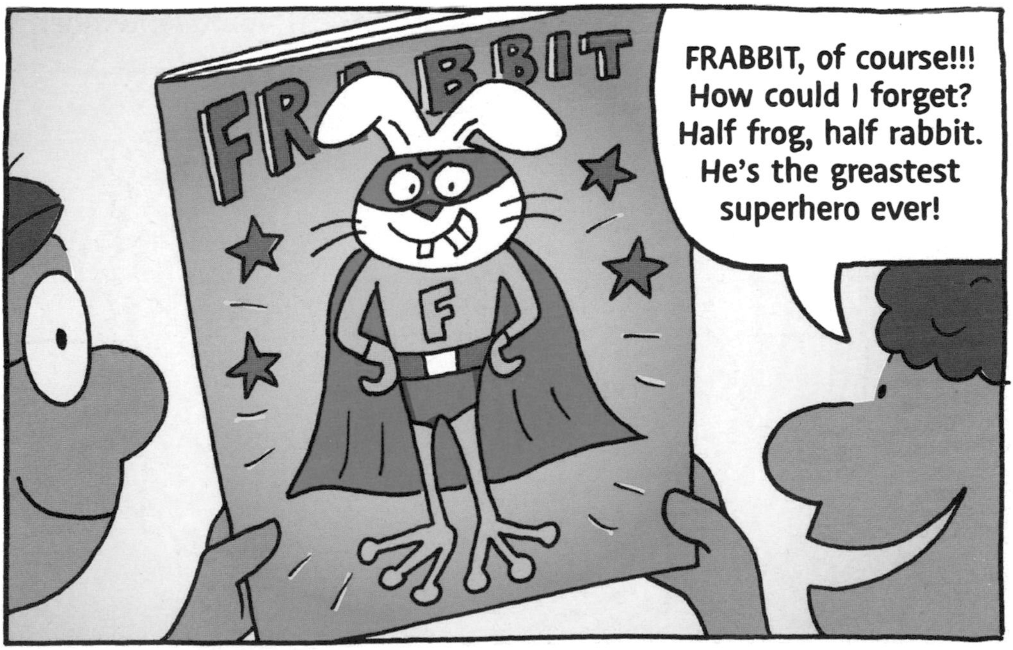
FRABBIT
FRABBIT, of course!!! How could I forget? Half frog, half rabbit. He's the greastest superhero ever!

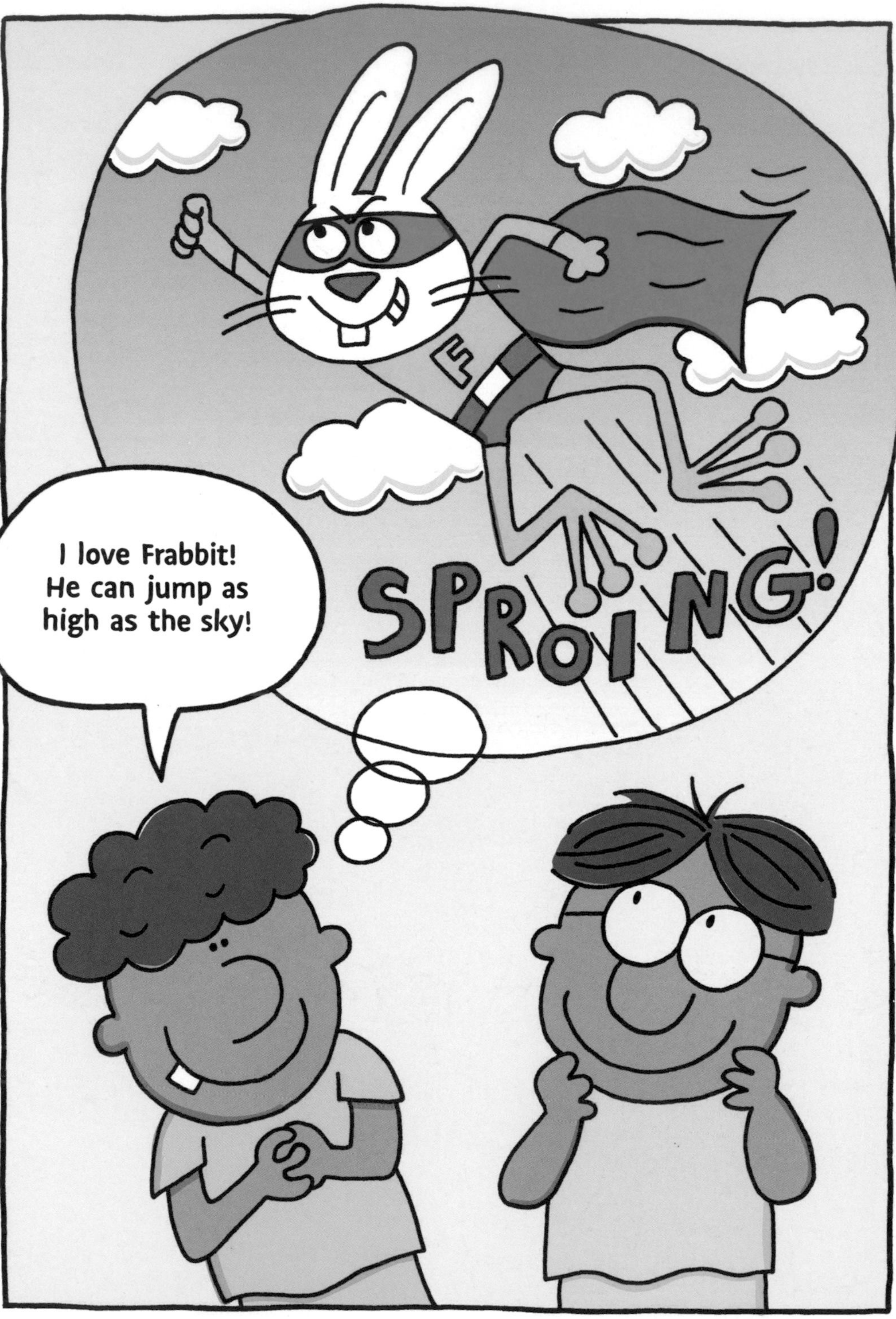
I love Frabbit! He can jump as high as the sky!
SPROING!

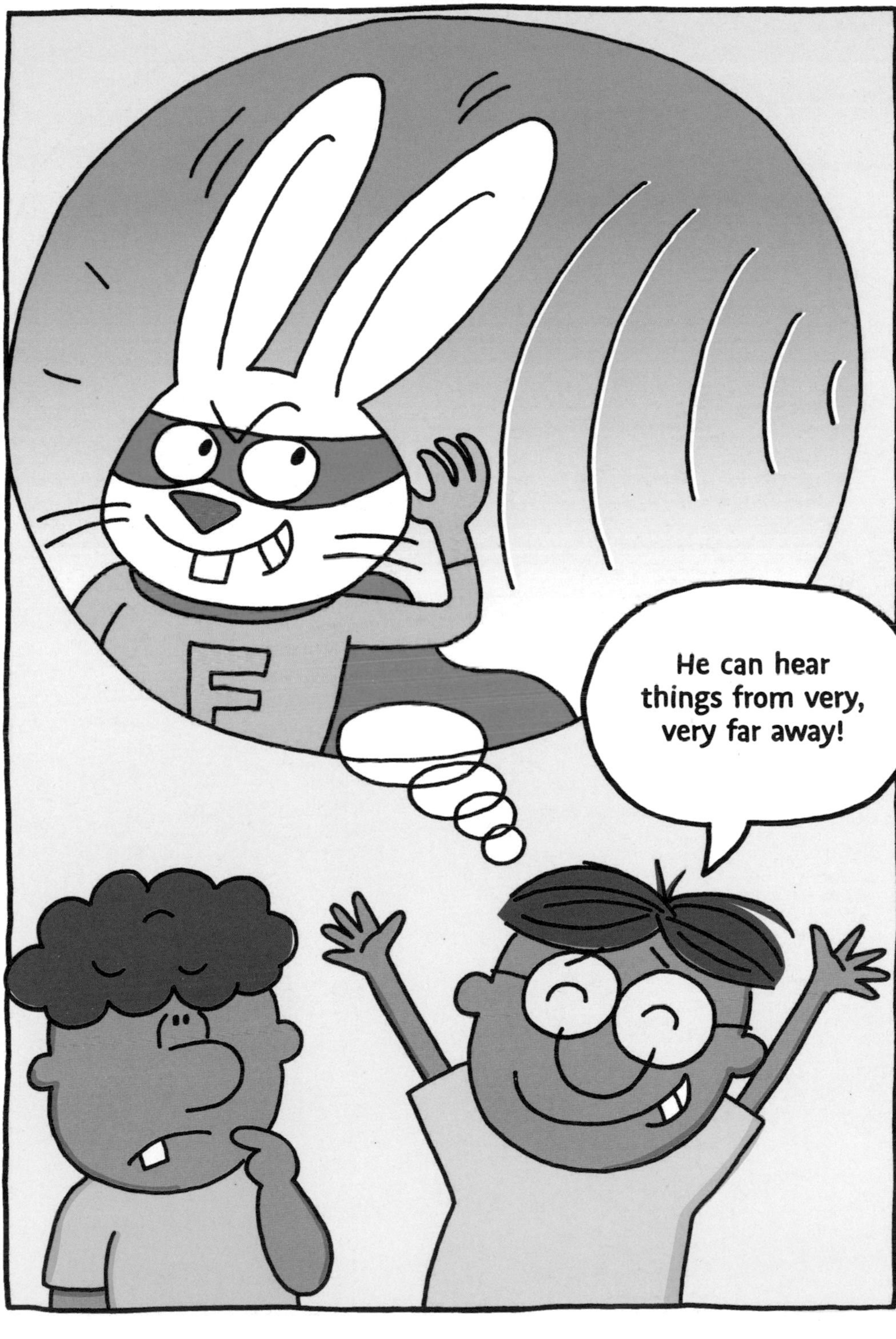
He can hear things from very, very far away!

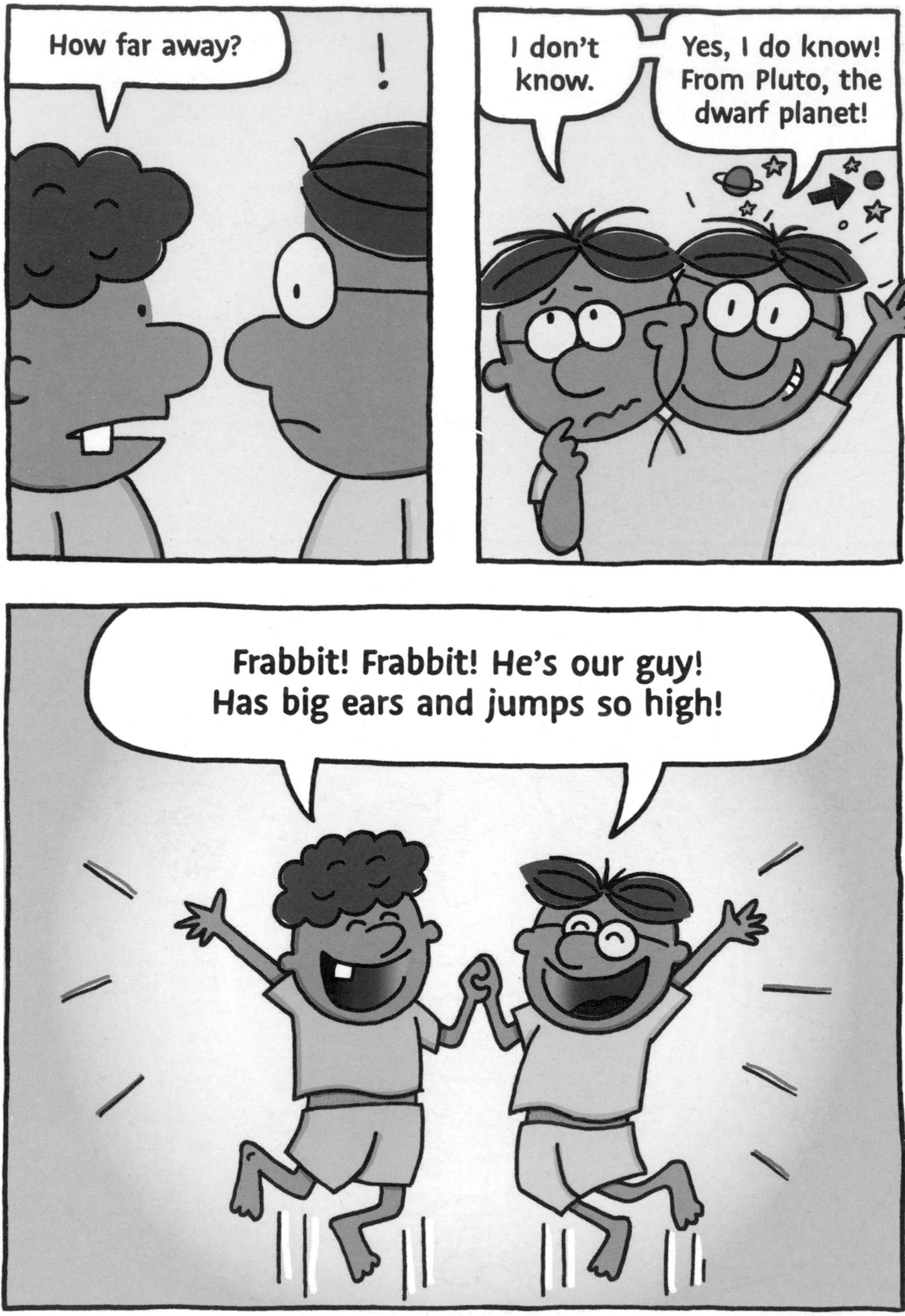
How far away?
!
I don't know.
Yes, I do know! From Pluto, the dwarf planet!
Frabbit! Frabbit! He's our guy! Has big ears and jumps so high!

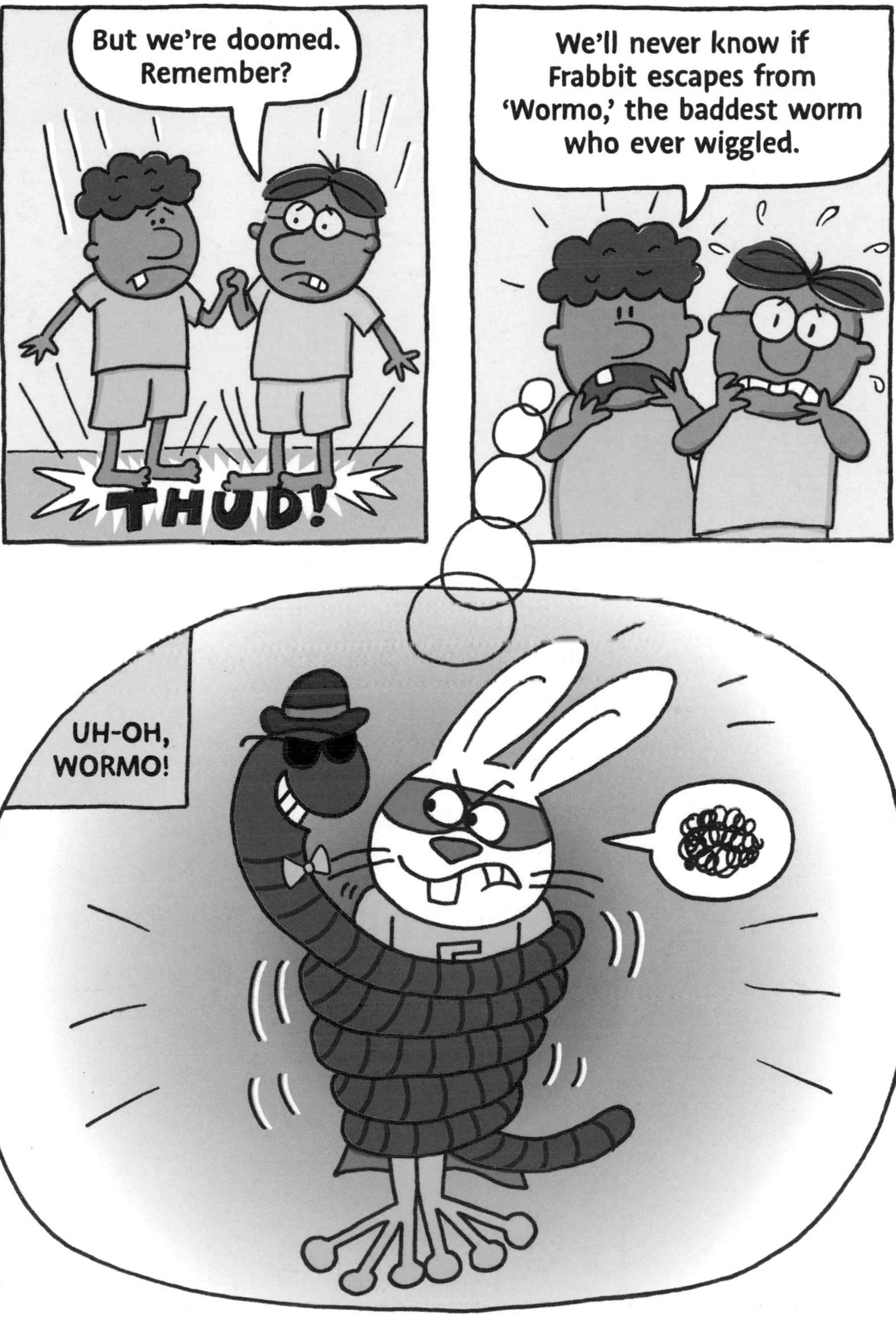
But we're doomed. Remember?
THUD!
We'll never know if Frabbit escapes from 'Wormo,' the baddest worm who ever wiggled.
UH-OH, WORMO!

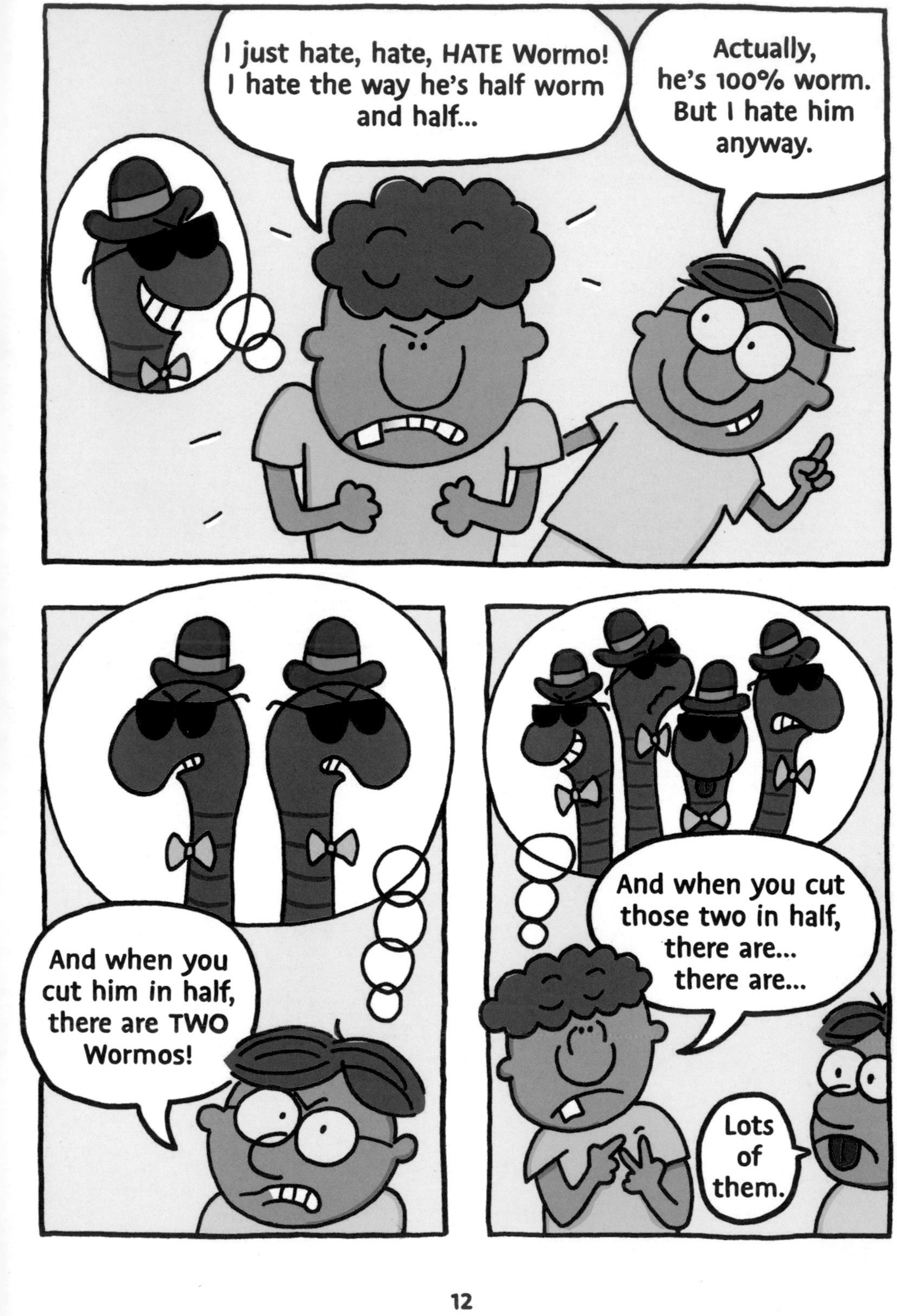
I just hate, hate, HATE Wormo! I hate the way he's half worm and half...
Actually, he's 100% worm. But I hate him anyway.
And when you cut him in half, there are TWO Wormos!
And when you cut those two in half, there are... there are...
Lots of them.

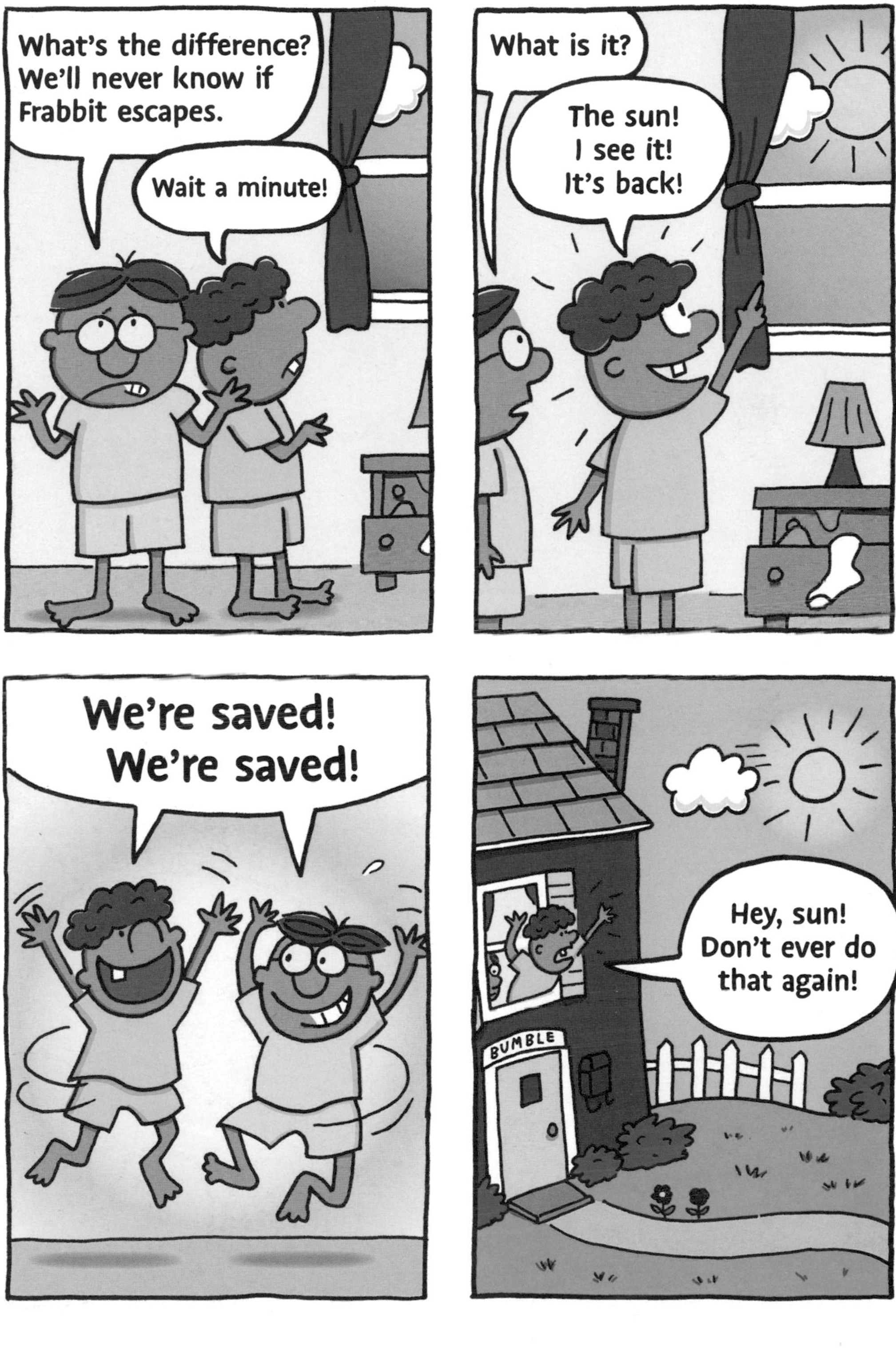
What's the difference? We'll never know if Frabbit escapes.
Wait a minute!
What is it?
The sun! I see it! It's back!
We're saved! We're saved!
BUMBLE
Hey, sun! Don't ever do that again!

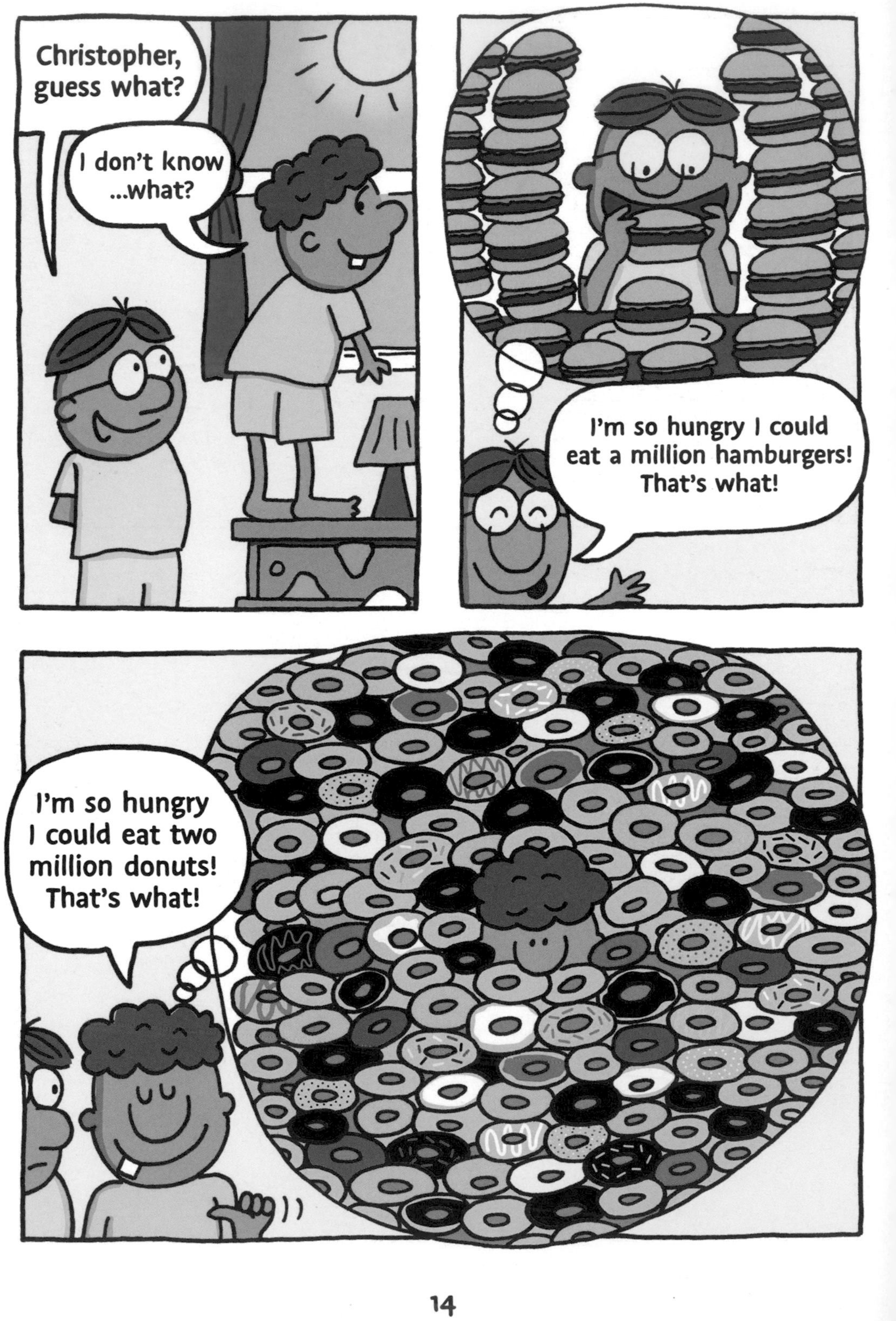
Christopher, guess what?
I don't know ...what?
I'm so hungry I could eat a million hamburgers! That's what!
I'm so hungry I could eat two million donuts! That's what!

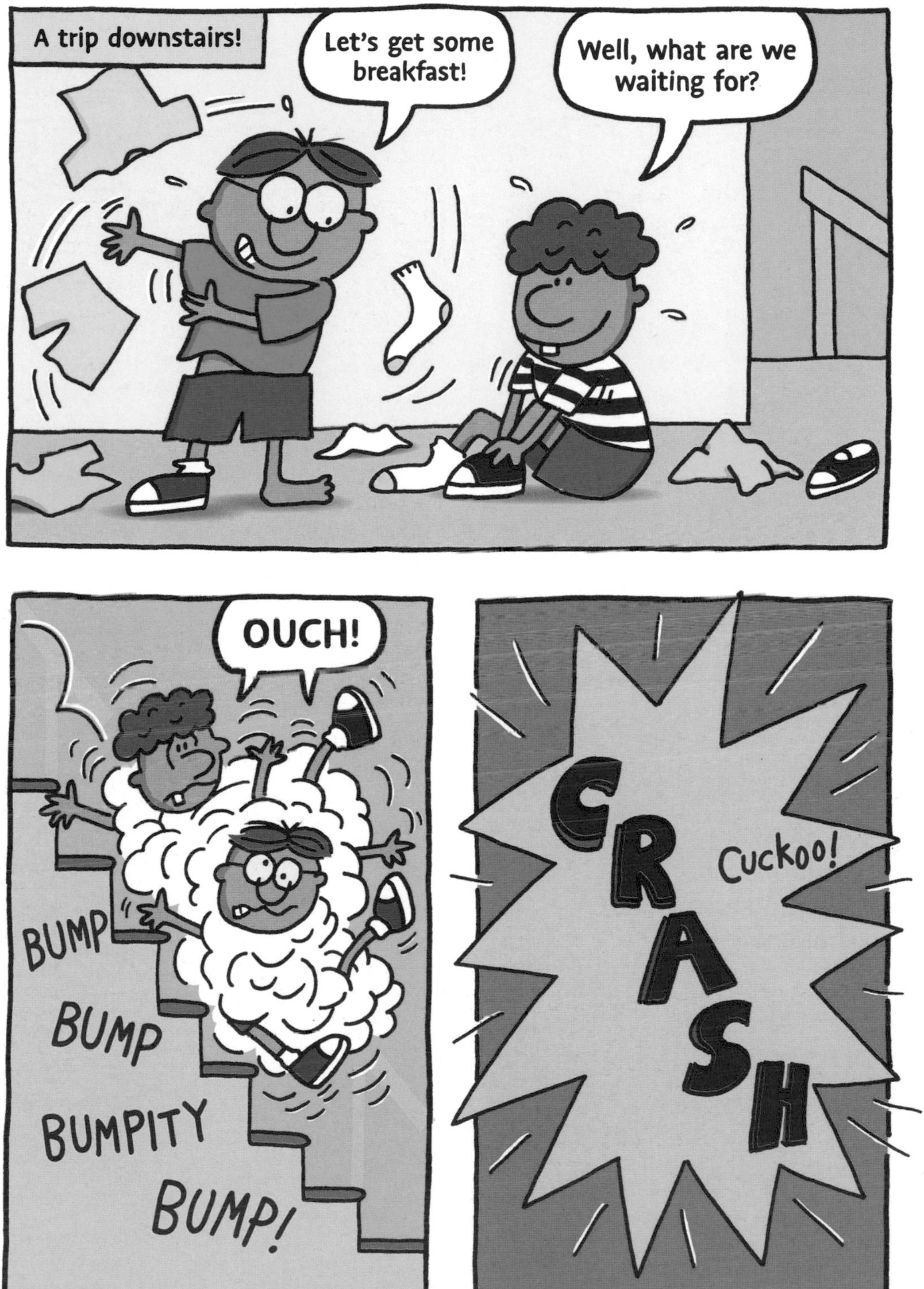
A trip downstairs!
Let's get some breakfast!
Well, what are we waiting for?
OUCH!
BUMP
BUMP
BUMPITY
BUMP!
CRASH
Cuckoo!

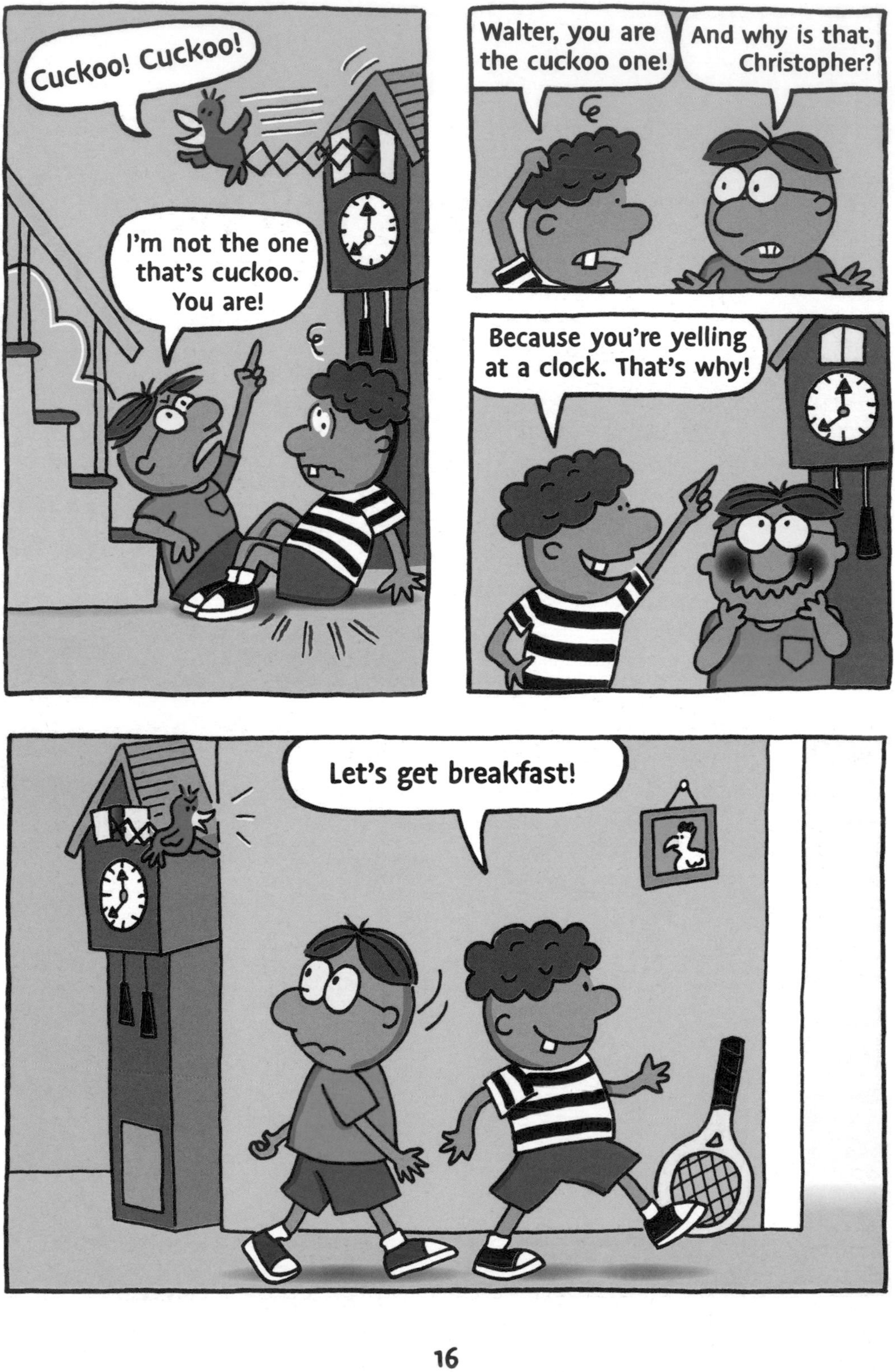
Cuckoo! Cuckoo!
I'm not the one that's cuckoo. You are!
Walter, you are the cuckoo one!
And why is that, Christopher?
Because you're yelling at a clock. That's why!
Let's get breakfast!

# CHAPTER 3 - BREAKFAST WITH ALIENS

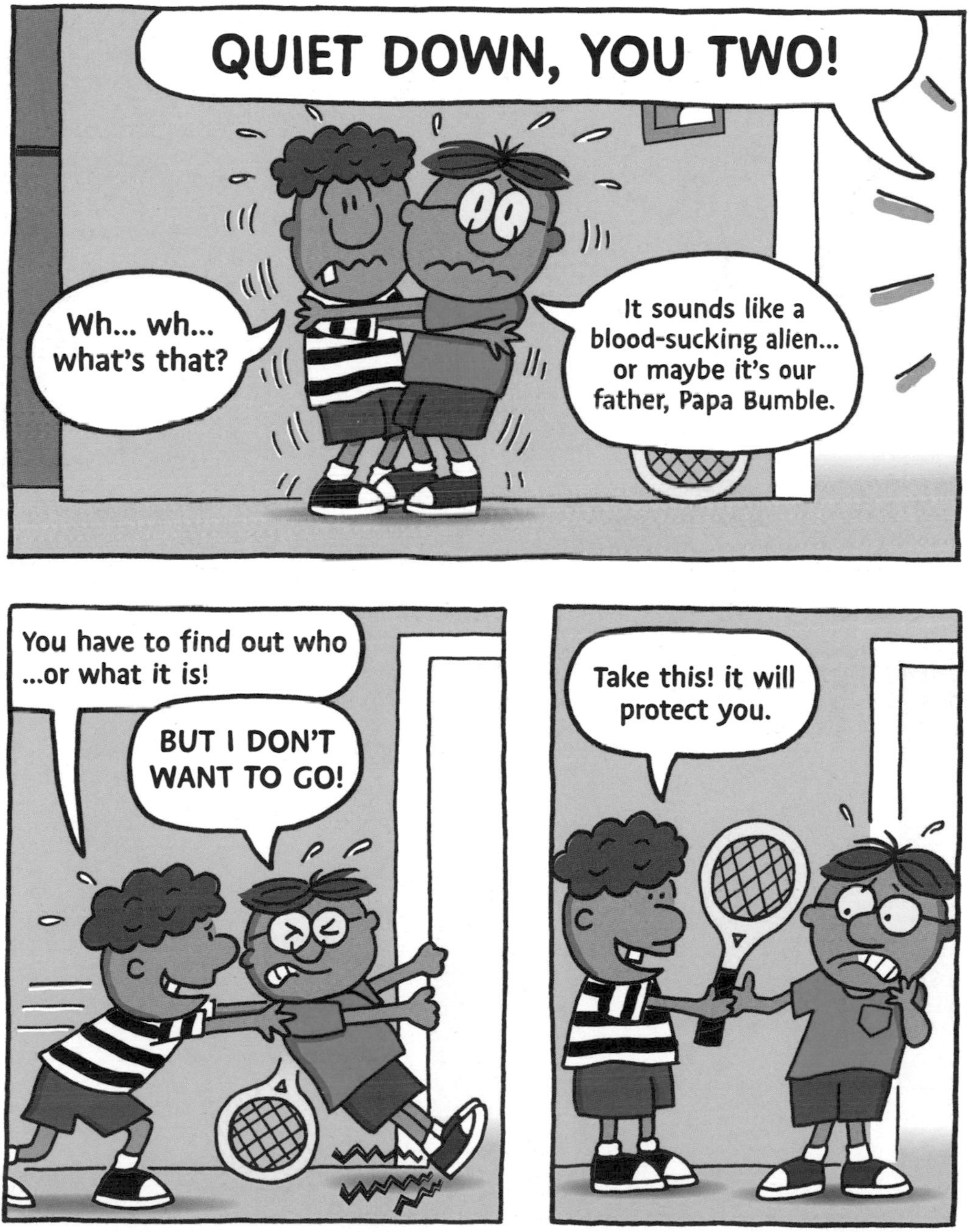
QUIET DOWN, YOU TWO!
Wh... wh... what's that?
It sounds like a blood-sucking alien... or maybe it's our father, Papa Bumble.
You have to find out who ...or what it is!
BUT I DON'T WANT TO GO!
Take this! it will protect you.

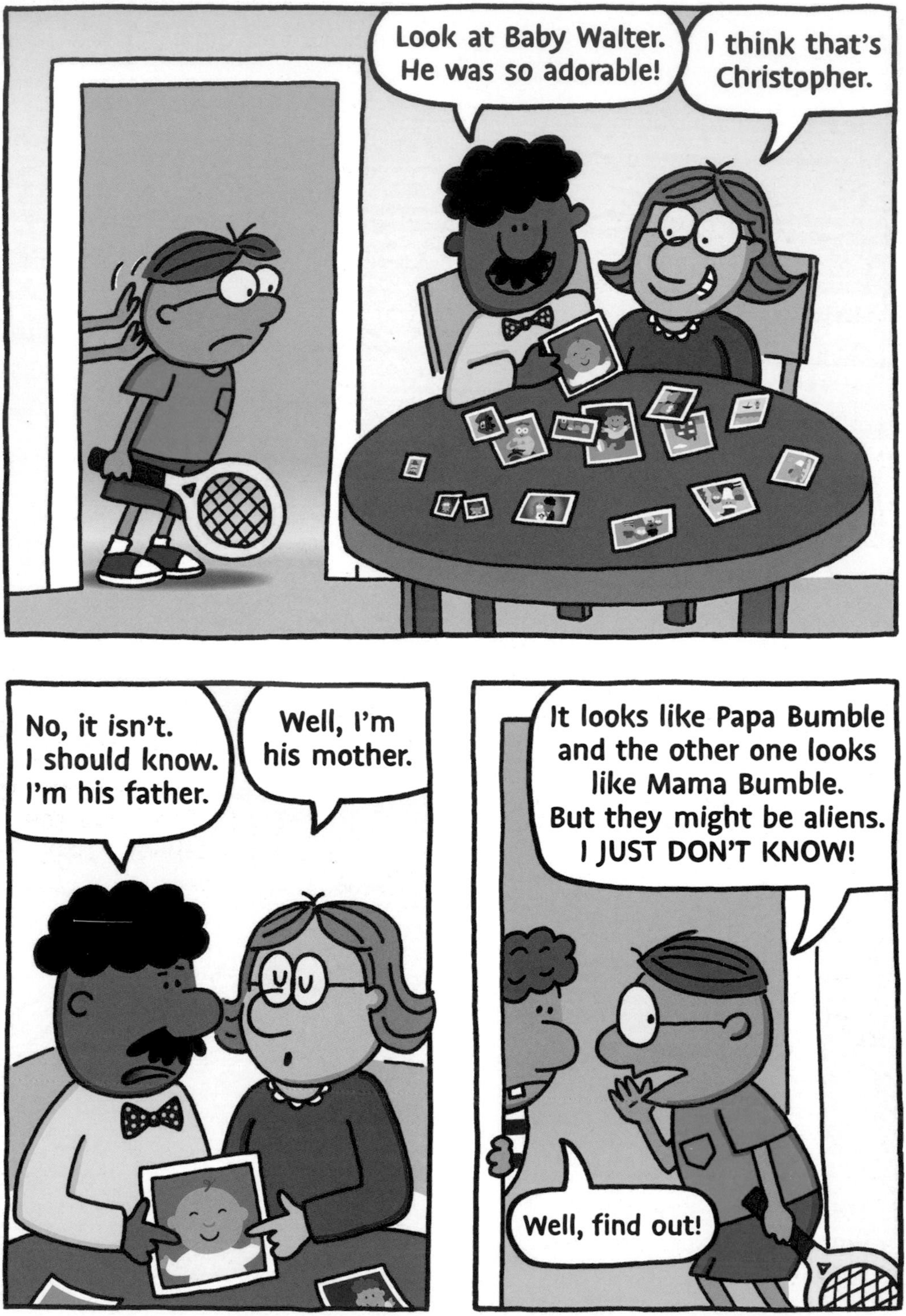
Look at Baby Walter. He was so adorable!
I think that's Christopher.
No, it isn't. I should know. I'm his father.
Well, I'm his mother.
It looks like Papa Bumble and the other one looks like Mama Bumble. But they might be aliens. I JUST DON'T KNOW!
Well, find out!

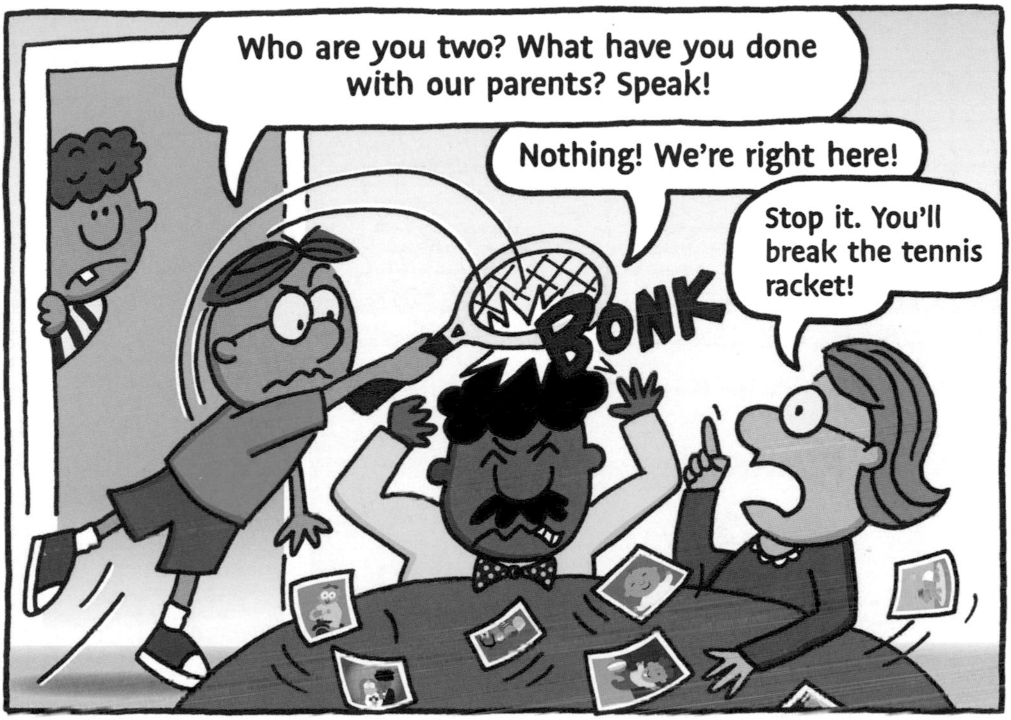
Who are you two? What have you done with our parents? Speak!
Nothing! We're right here!
Stop it. You'll break the tennis racket!
BONK

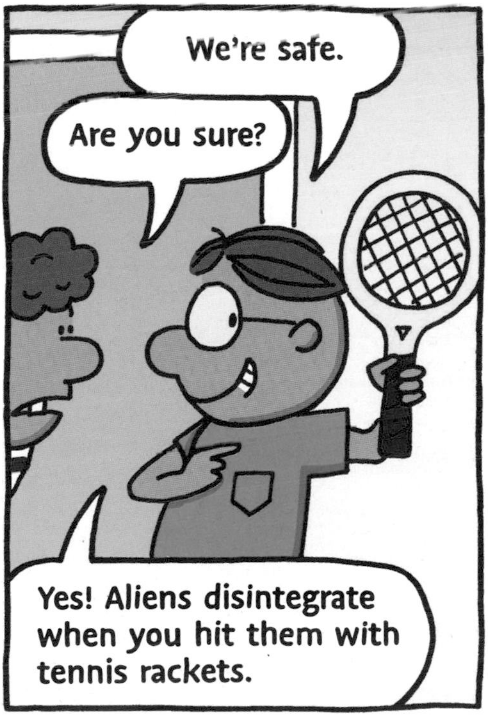
We're safe.
Are you sure?
Yes! Aliens disintegrate when you hit them with tennis rackets.

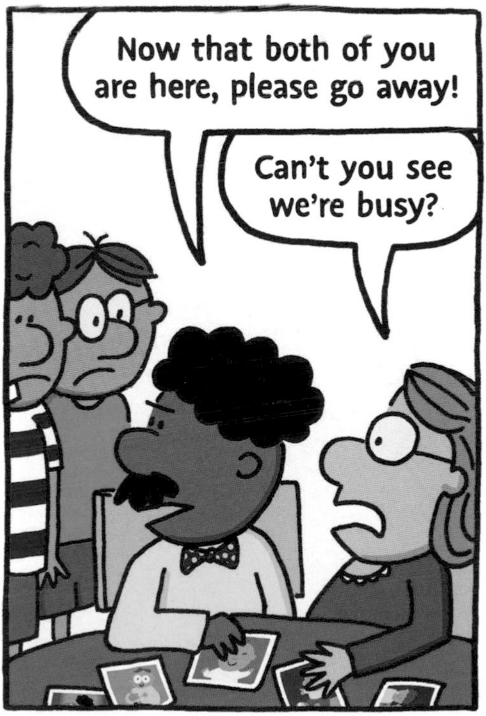
Now that both of you are here, please go away!
Can't you see we're busy?

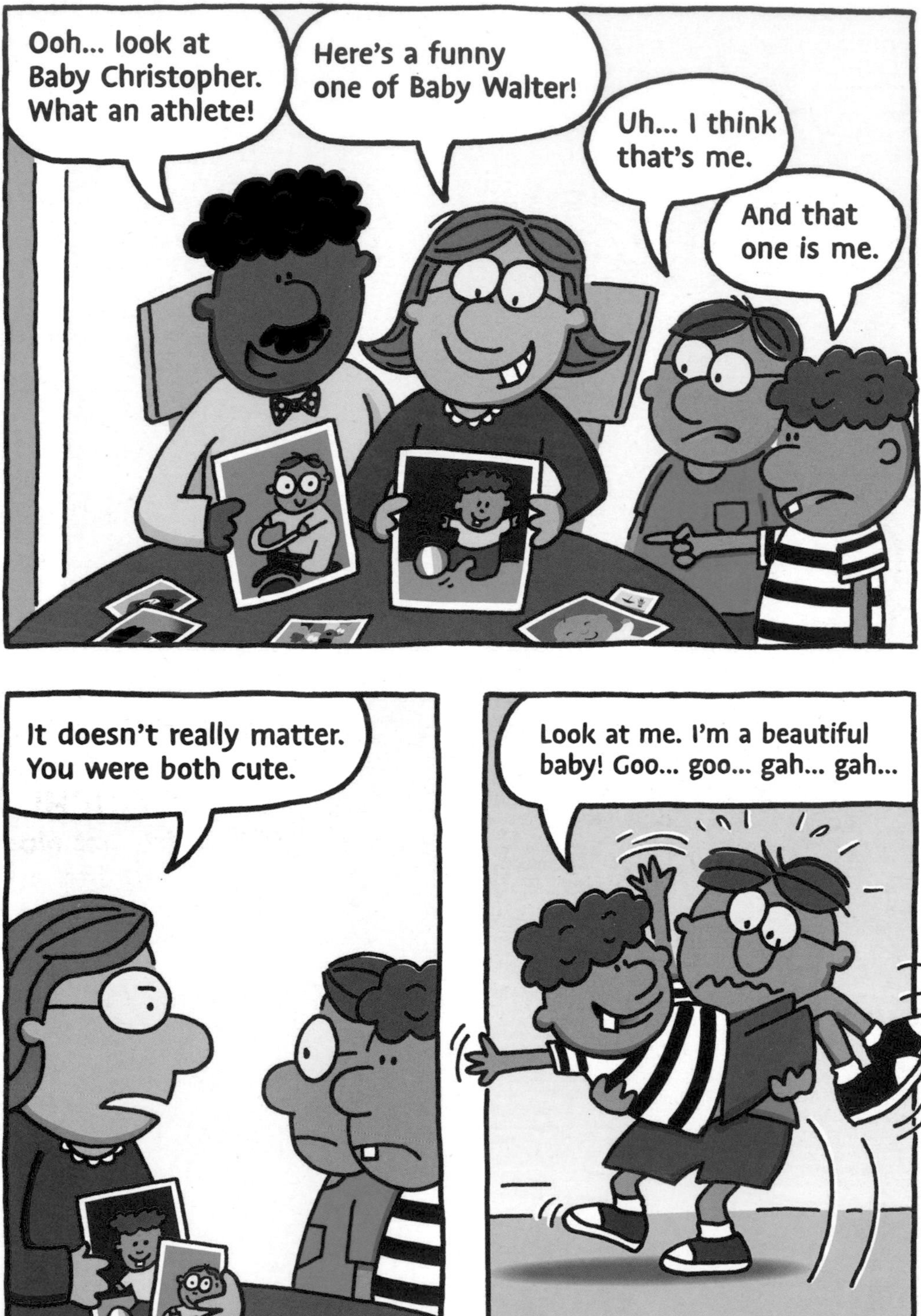
Ooh... look at Baby Christopher. What an athlete!
Here's a funny one of Baby Walter!
Uh... I think that's me.
And that one is me.
It doesn't really matter. You were both cute.
Look at me. I'm a beautiful baby! Goo... goo... gah... gah...

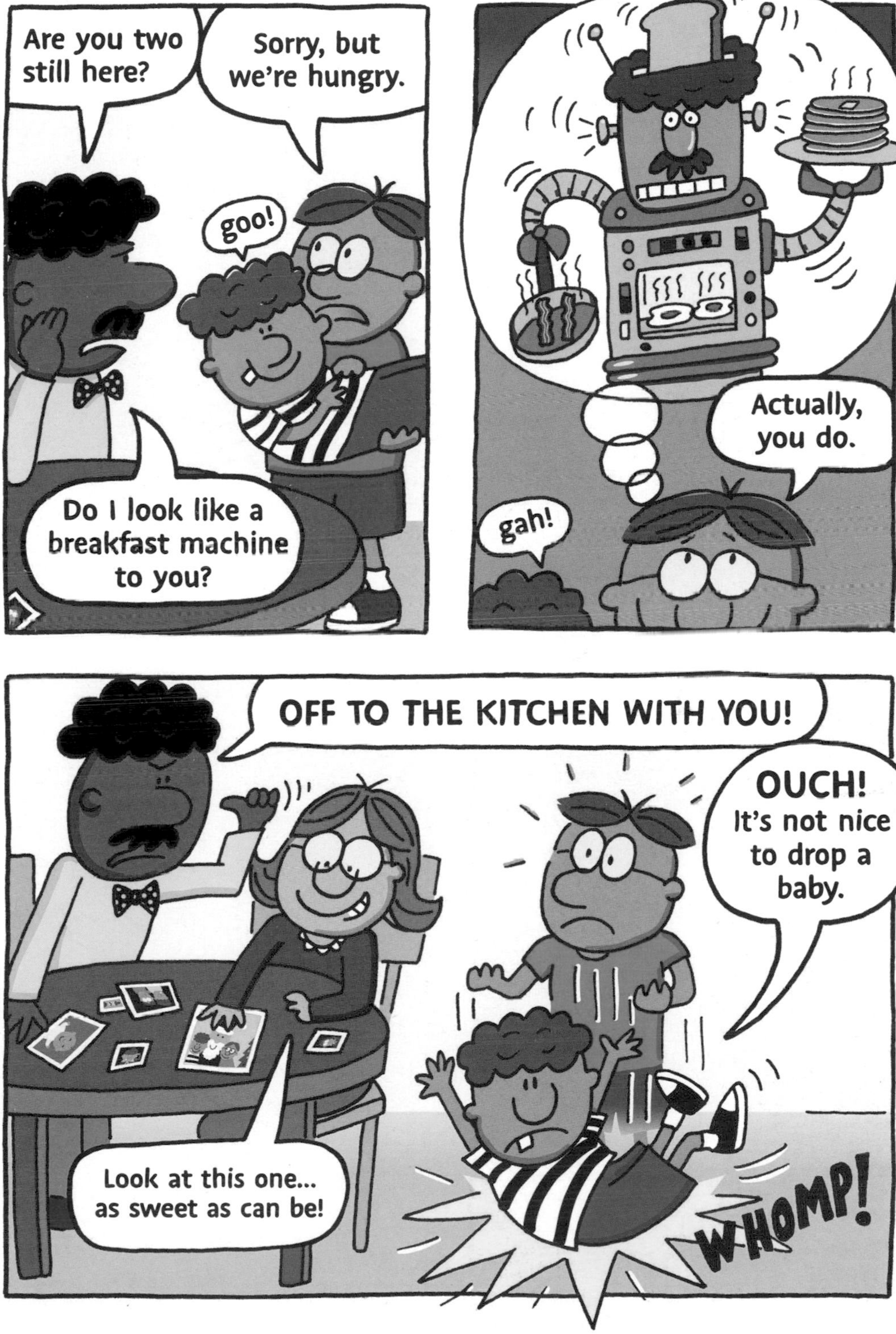
Are you two still here?
Sorry, but we're hungry.
goo!
Do I look like a breakfast machine to you?
Actually, you do.
gah!
OFF TO THE KITCHEN WITH YOU!
Look at this one... as sweet as can be!
OUCH! It's not nice to drop a baby.
WHOMP!

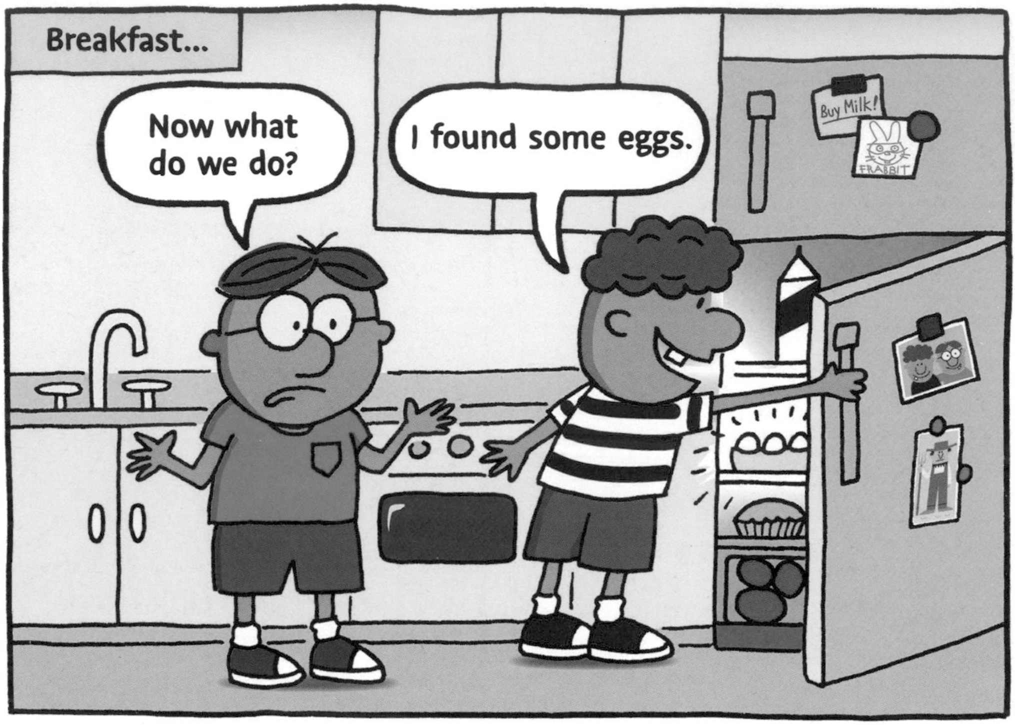
Breakfast...
Now what do we do?
I found some eggs.
Buy Milk!
FRABBIT

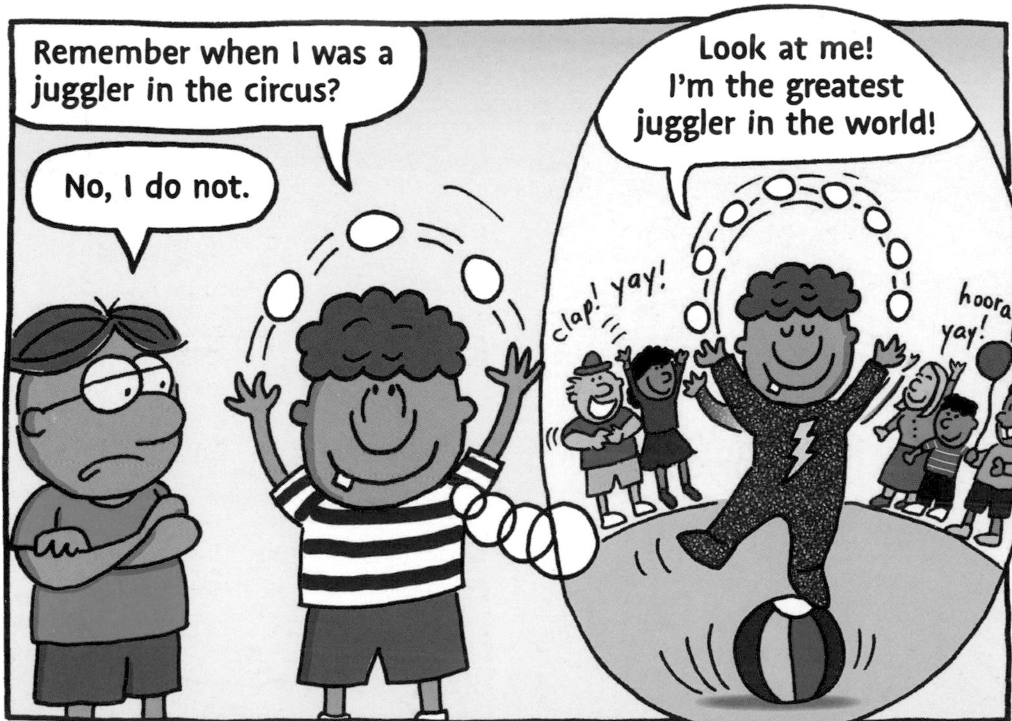
Remember when I was a juggler in the circus?
No, I do not.
Look at me! I'm the greatest juggler in the world!
clap!
yay!
hooray
yay!

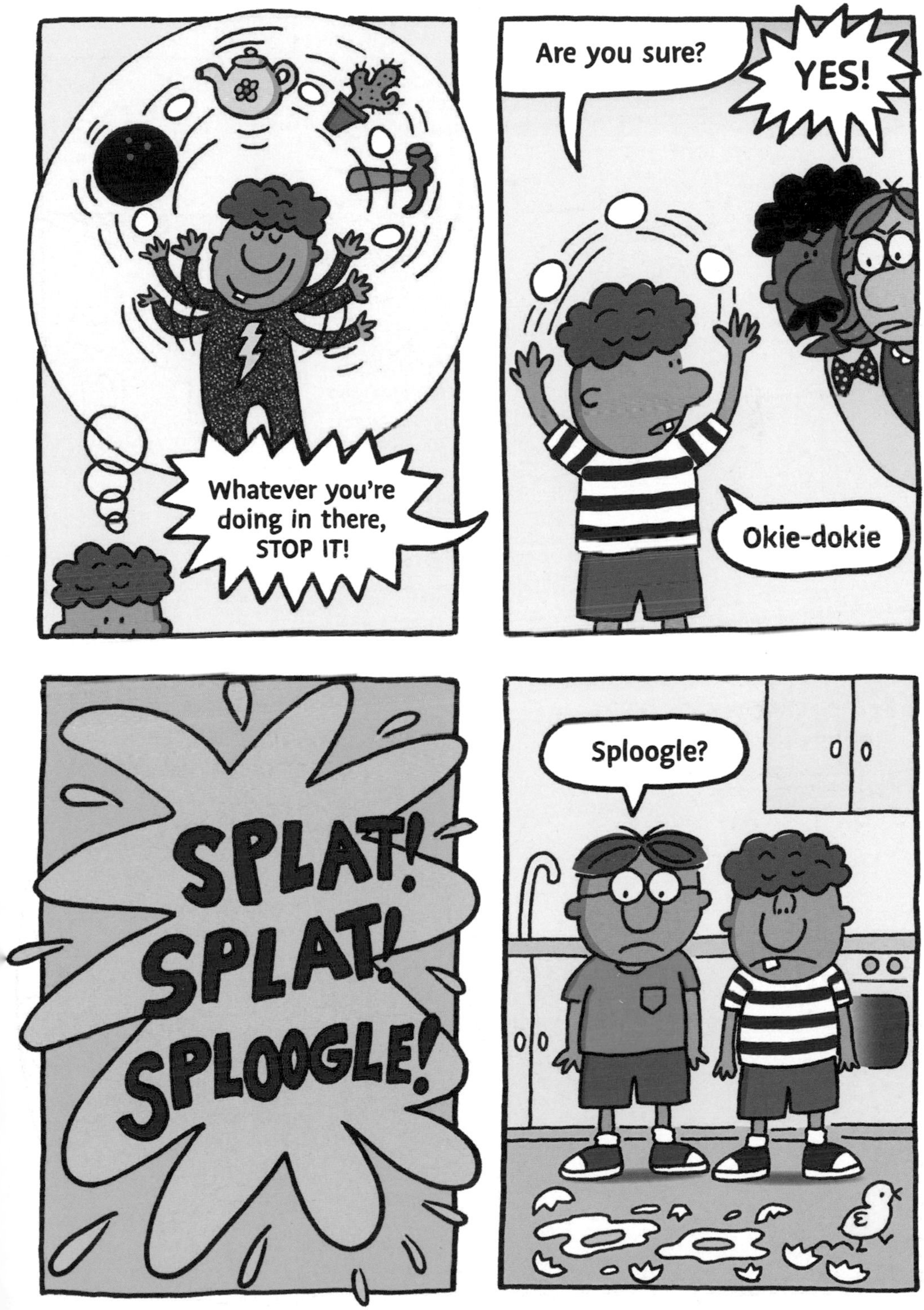
Whatever you're doing in there, STOP IT!
Are you sure?
YES!
Okie-dokie
SPLAT! SPLAT! SPLOOGLE!
Sploogle?

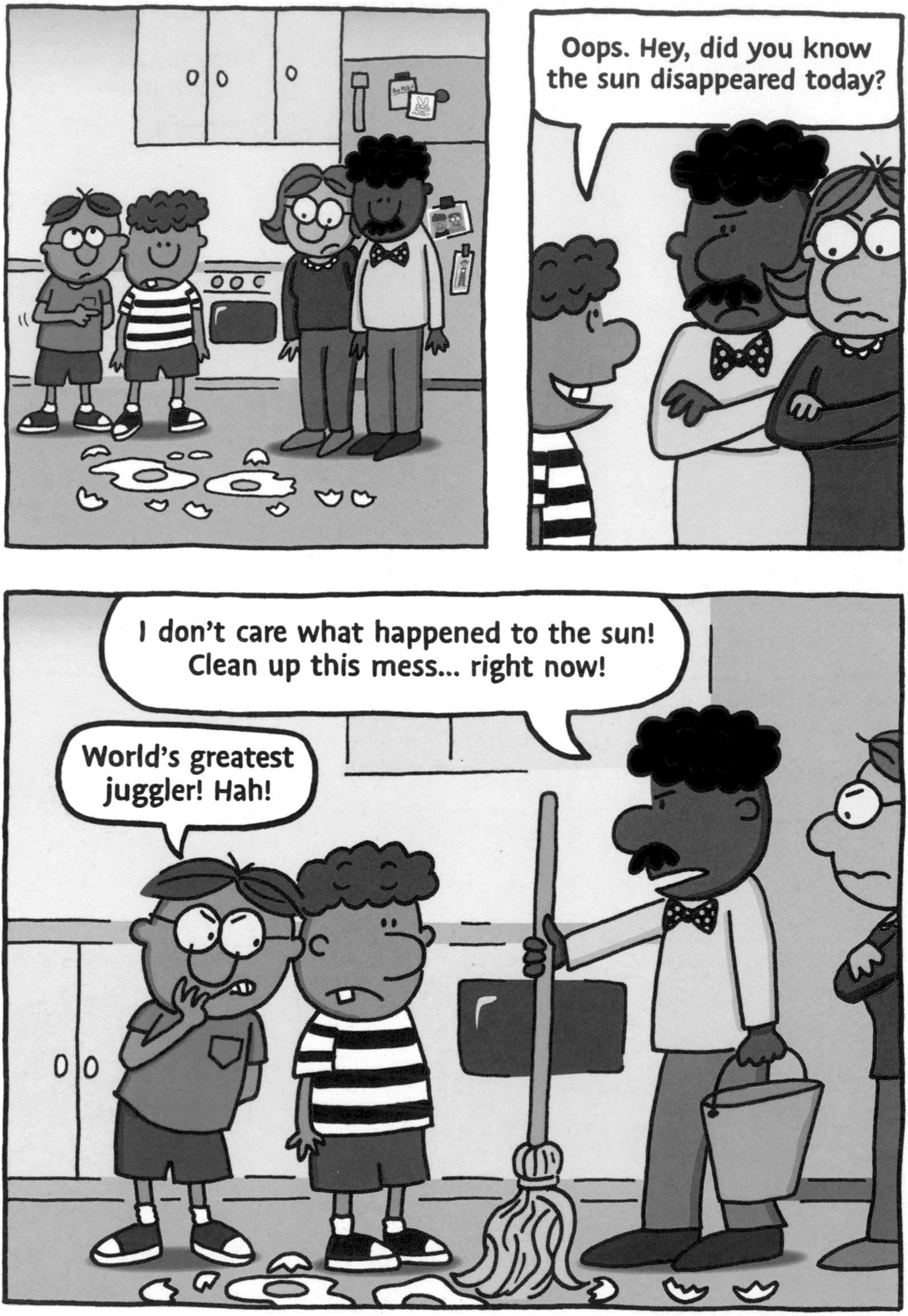
Oops. Hey, did you know the sun disappeared today?
I don't care what happened to the sun! Clean up this mess... right now!
World's greatest juggler! Hah!

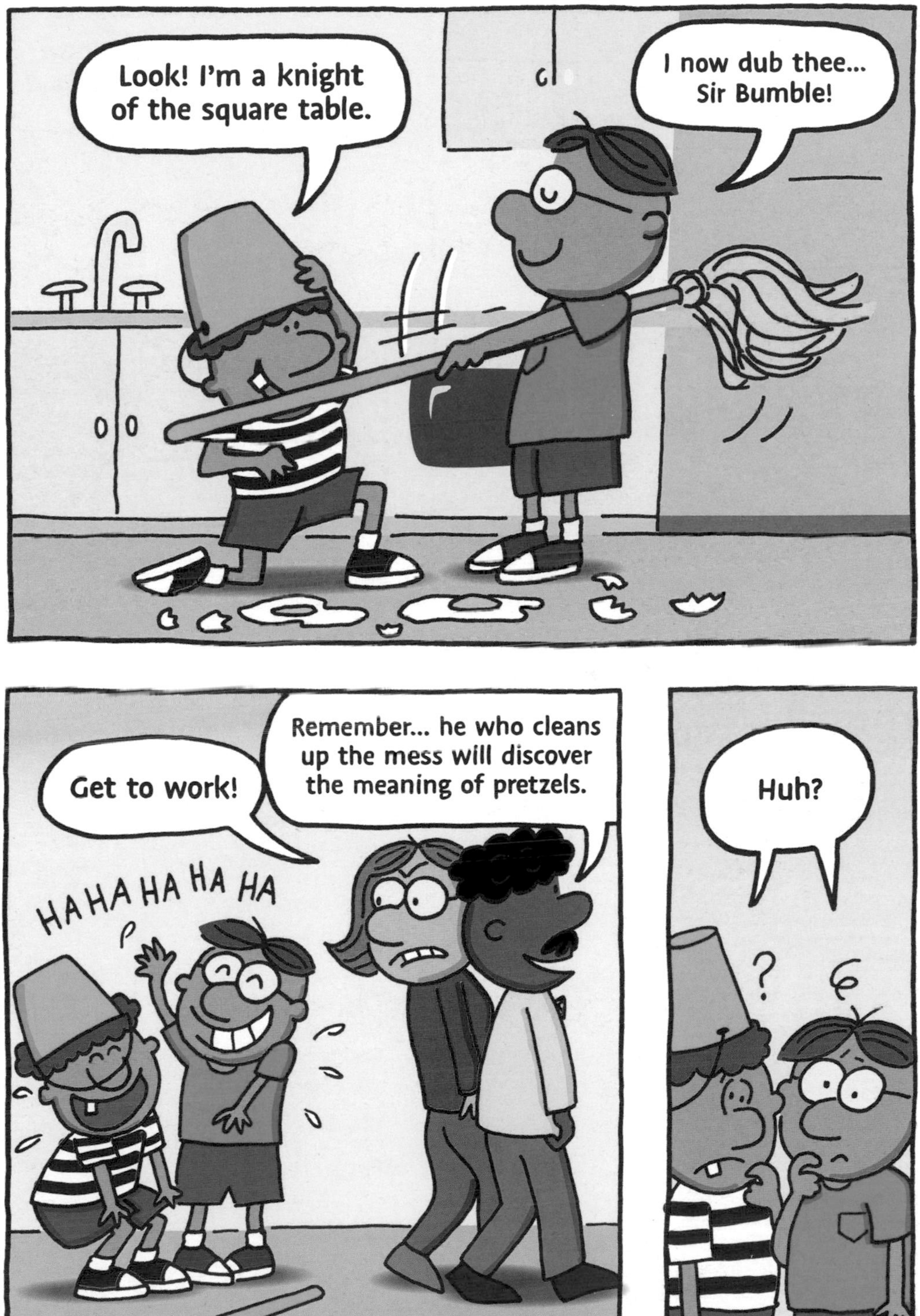
Look! I'm a knight of the square table.
I now dub thee... Sir Bumble!
Get to work!
Remember... he who cleans up the mess will discover the meaning of pretzels.
HA HA HA HA HA HA
Huh?

# CHAPTER 4 - NO MORE MILK!

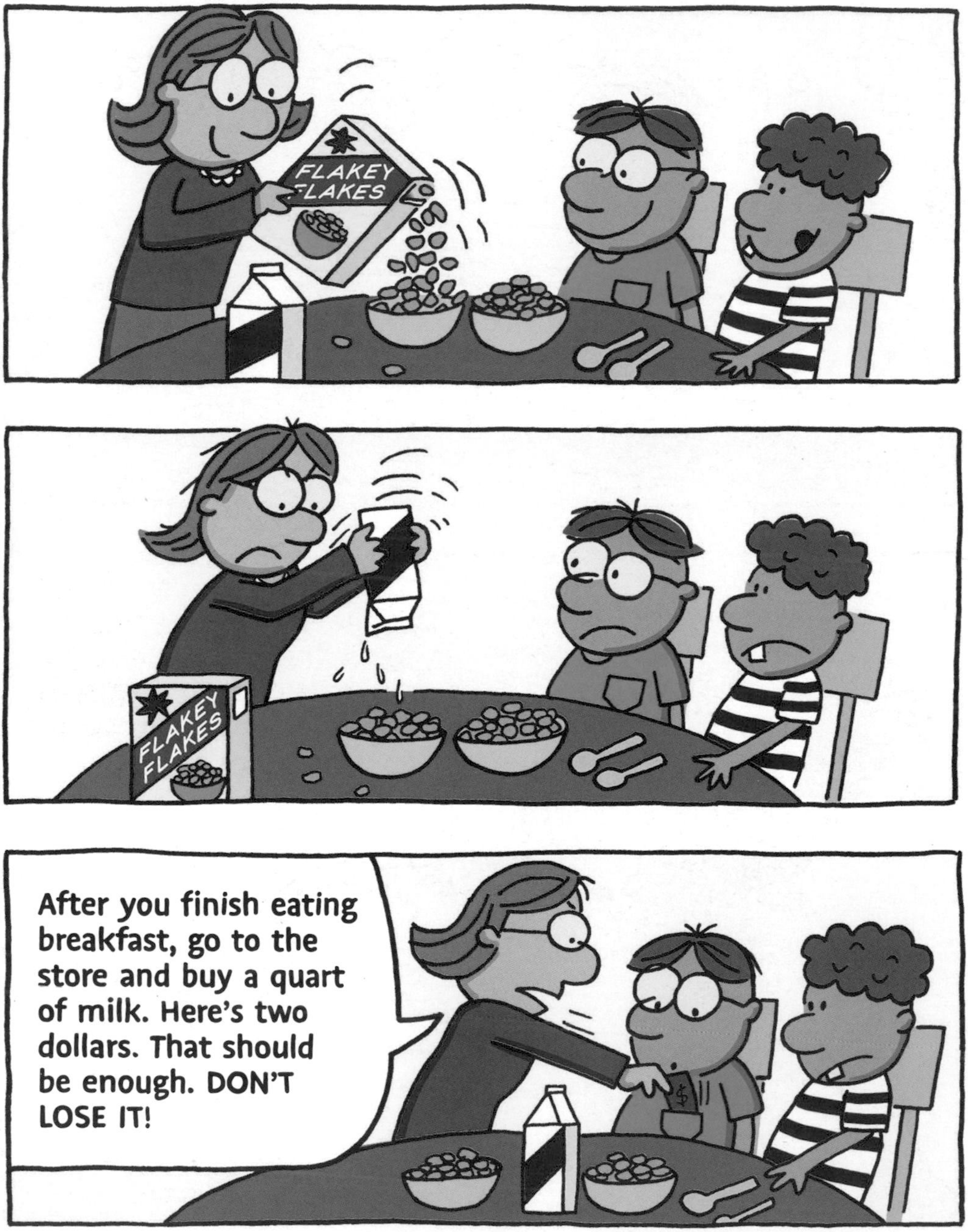
FLAKEY
FLAKEY FLAKES
After you finish eating breakfast, go to the store and buy a quart of milk. Here's two dollars. That should be enough. DON'T LOSE IT!

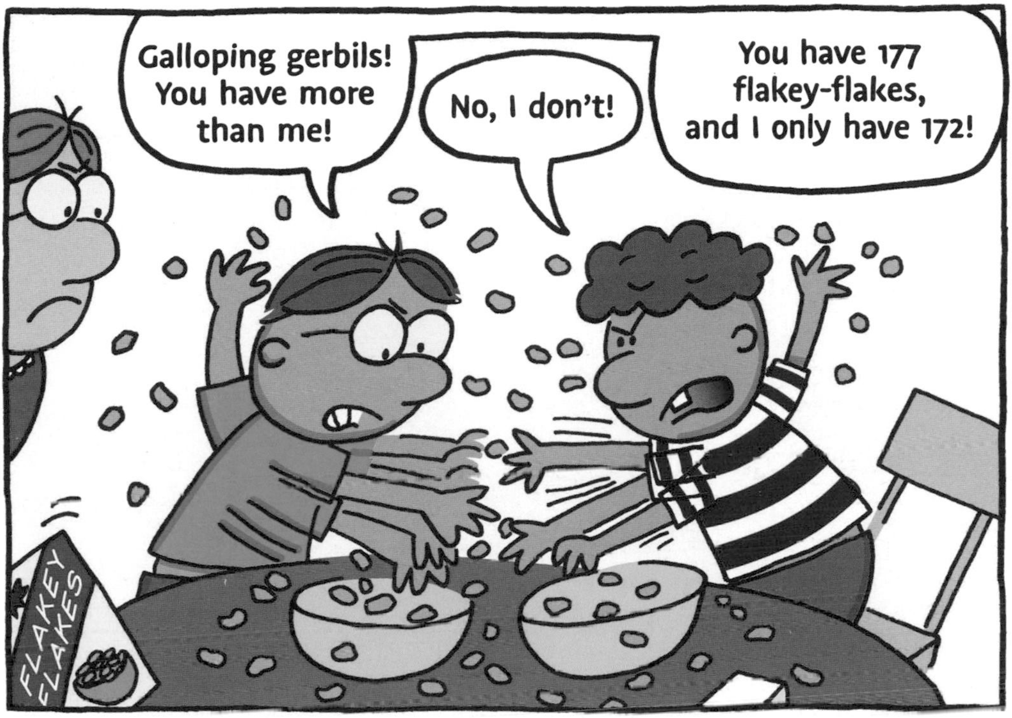
Galloping gerbils! You have more than me!
No, I don't!
You have 177 flakey-flakes, and I only have 172!
FLAKEY FLAKES

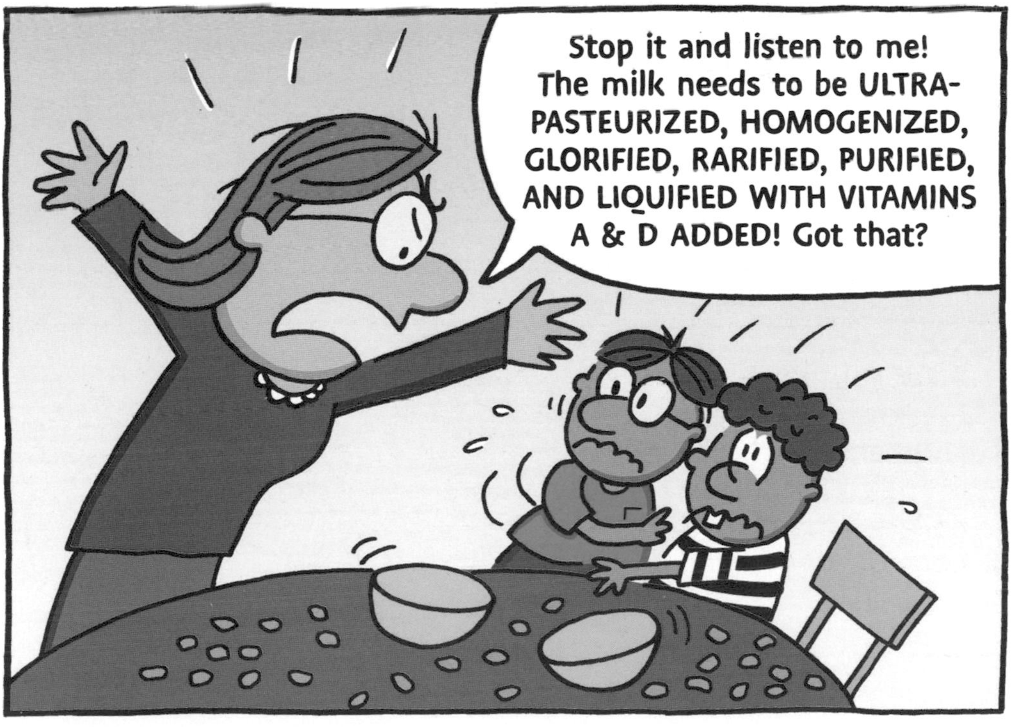
Stop it and listen to me! The milk needs to be ULTRA-PASTEURIZED, HOMOGENIZED, GLORIFIED, RARIFIED, PURIFIED, AND LIQUIFIED WITH VITAMINS A & D ADDED! Got that?

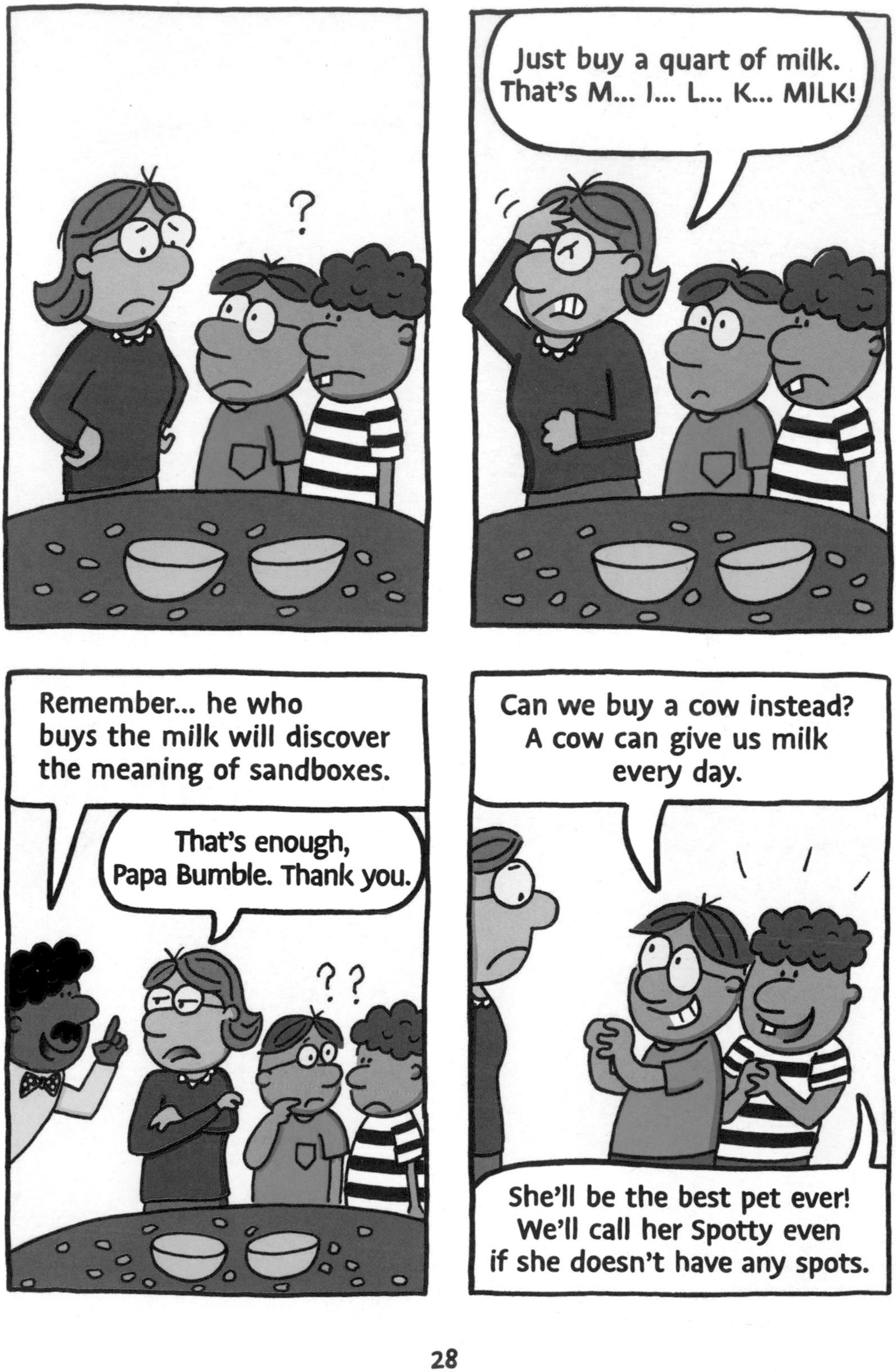
?
Just buy a quart of milk. That's M... I... L... K... MILK!
Remember... he who buys the milk will discover the meaning of sandboxes.
That's enough, Papa Bumble. Thank you.
? ?
Can we buy a cow instead? A cow can give us milk every day.
She'll be the best pet ever! We'll call her Spotty even if she doesn't have any spots.

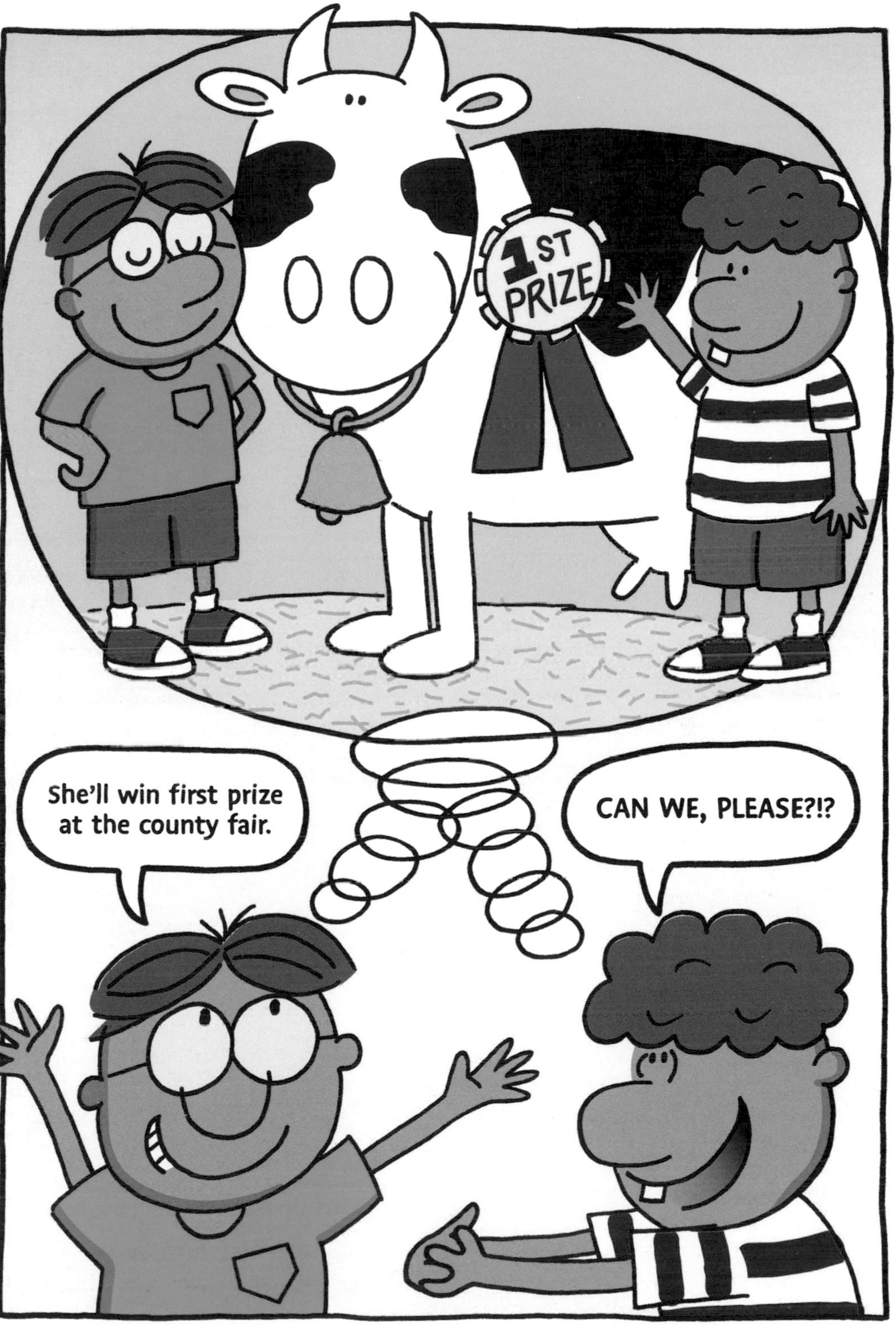
1ST PRIZE
She'll win first prize at the county fair.
CAN WE, PLEASE?!?

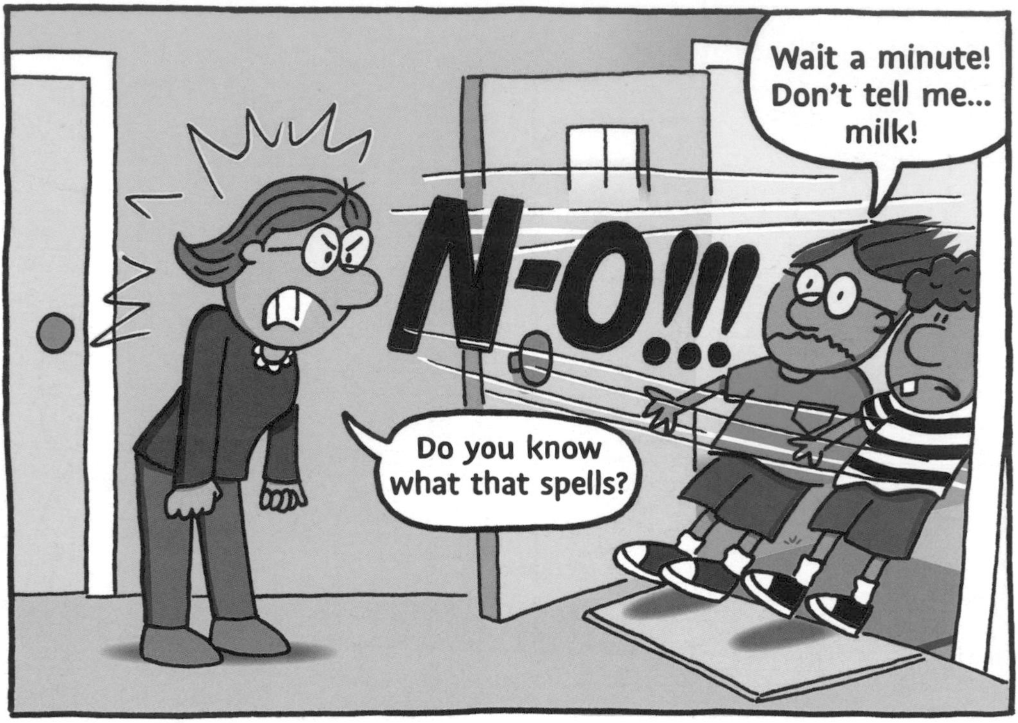
Wait a minute!
Don't tell me...
milk!
N-O!!!
Do you know
what that spells?

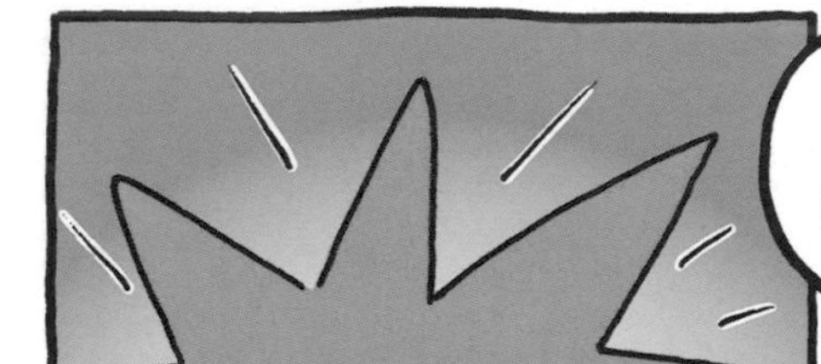
SLAM!!!

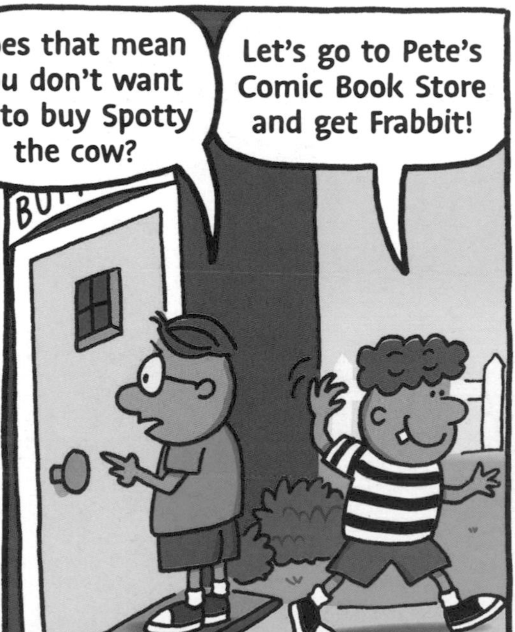
Does that mean
you don't want
us to buy Spotty
the cow?
Let's go to Pete's
Comic Book Store
and get Frabbit!

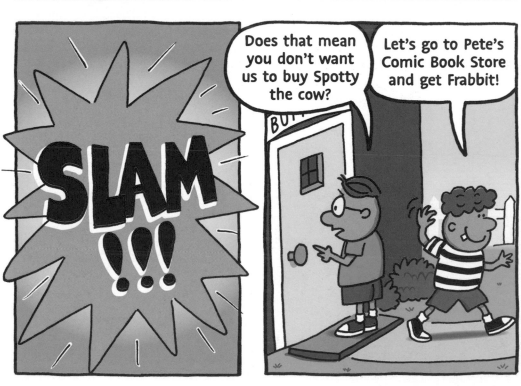

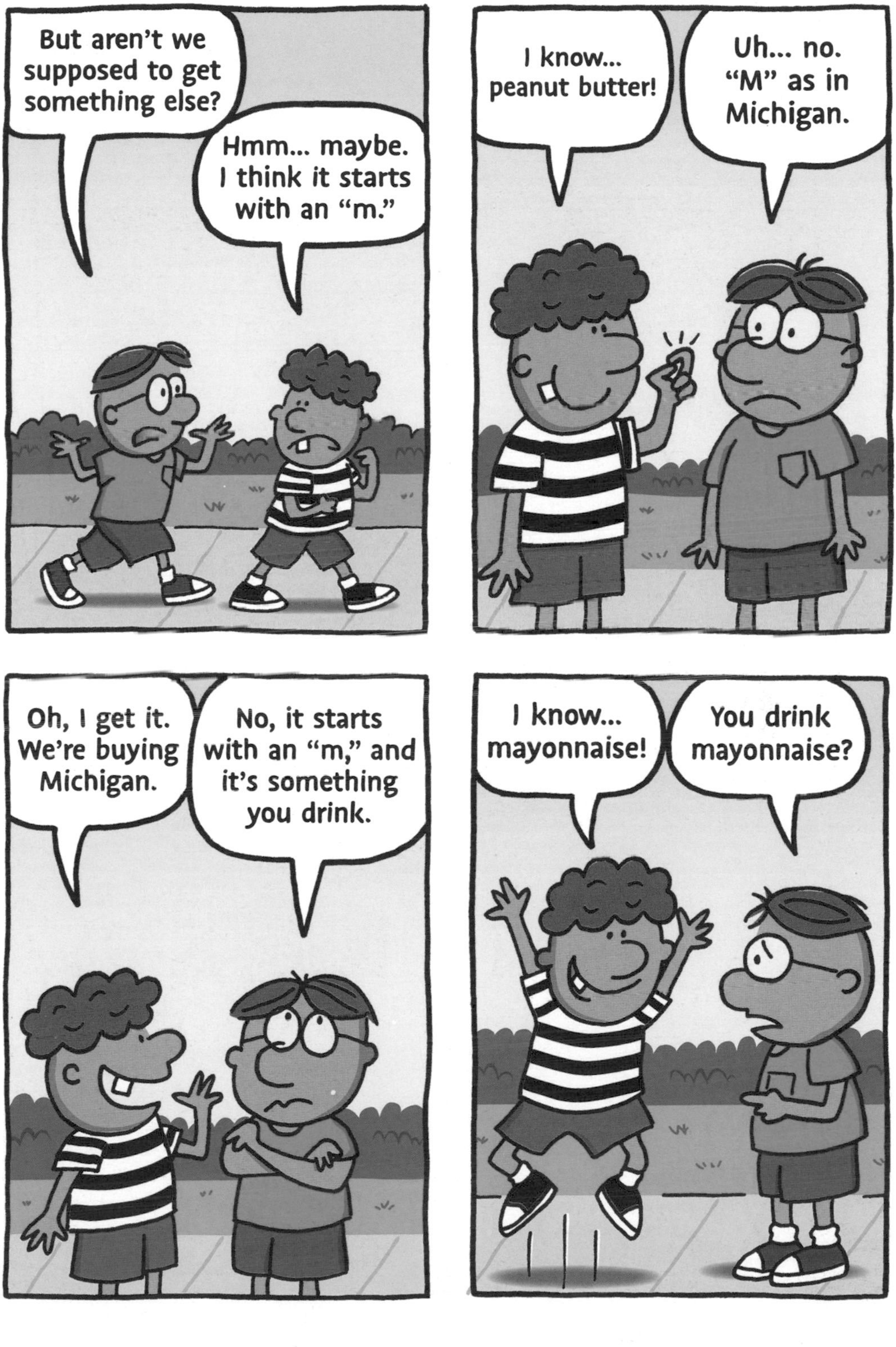
But aren't we supposed to get something else?
Hmm... maybe. I think it starts with an "m."
I know... peanut butter!
Uh... no. "M" as in Michigan.
Oh, I get it. We're buying Michigan.
No, it starts with an "m," and it's something you drink.
I know... mayonnaise!
You drink mayonnaise?

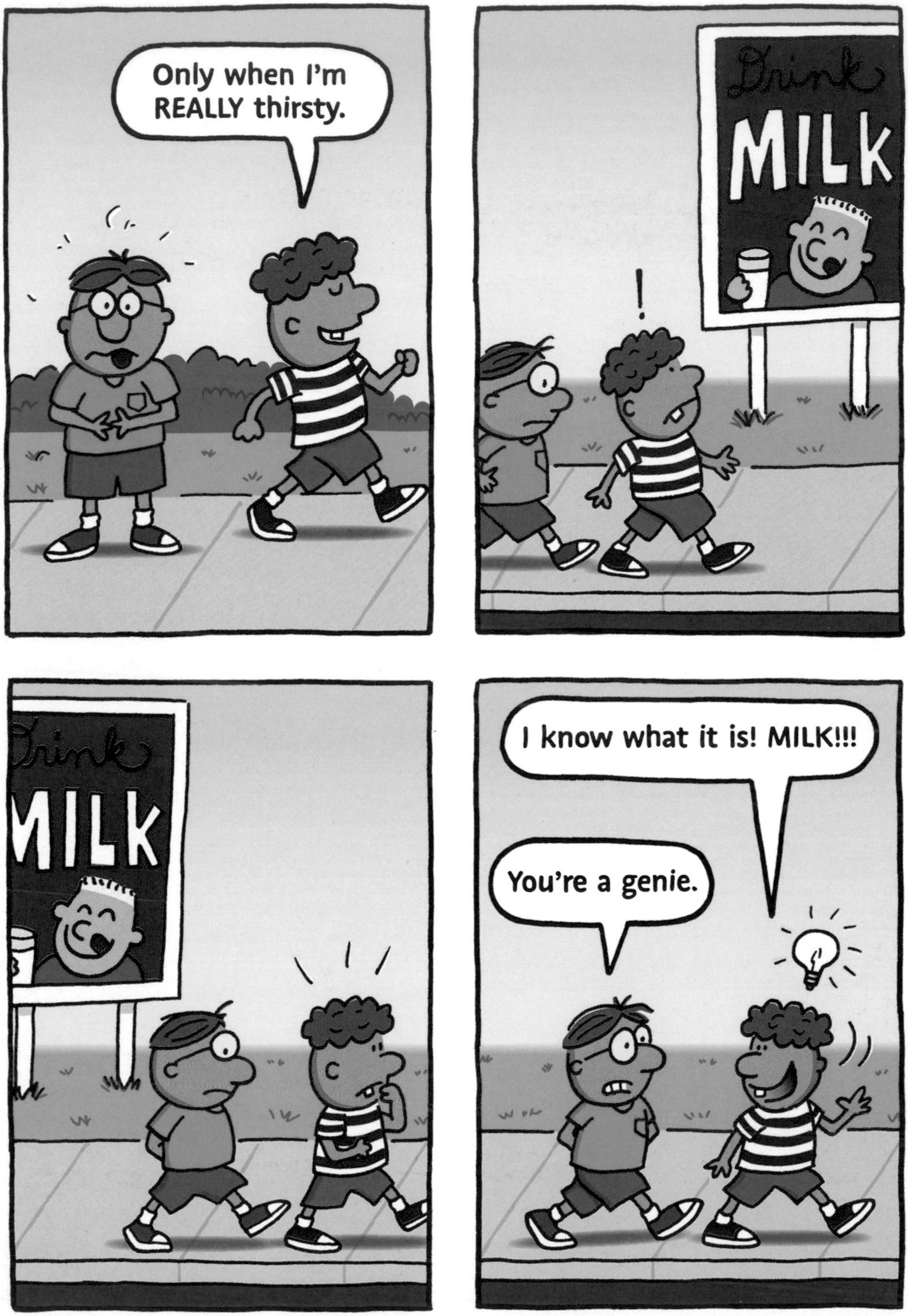
Only when I'm REALLY thirsty.
!
Drink
MILK
Drink
MILK
I know what it is! MILK!!!
You're a genie.

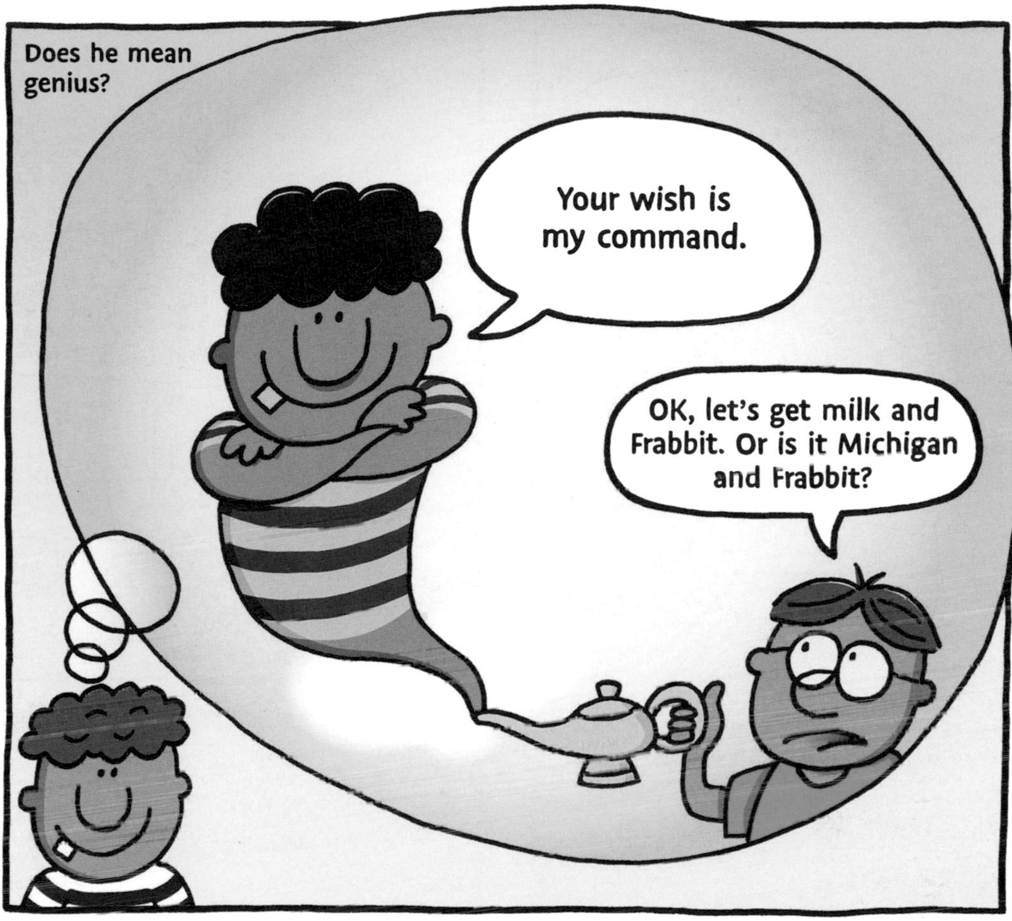
Does he mean genius?
Your wish is my command.
OK, let's get milk and Frabbit. Or is it Michigan and Frabbit?

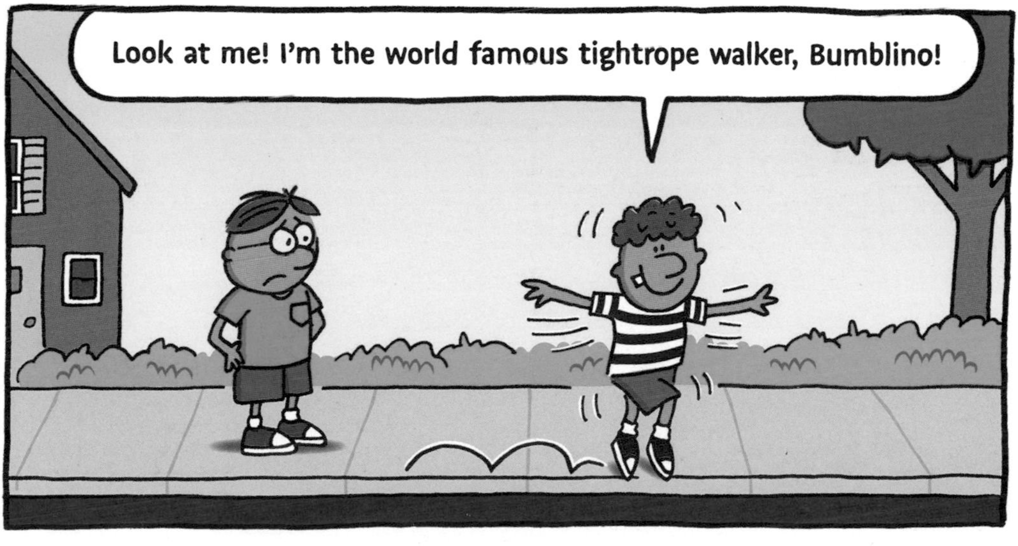
Look at me! I'm the world famous tightrope walker, Bumblino!

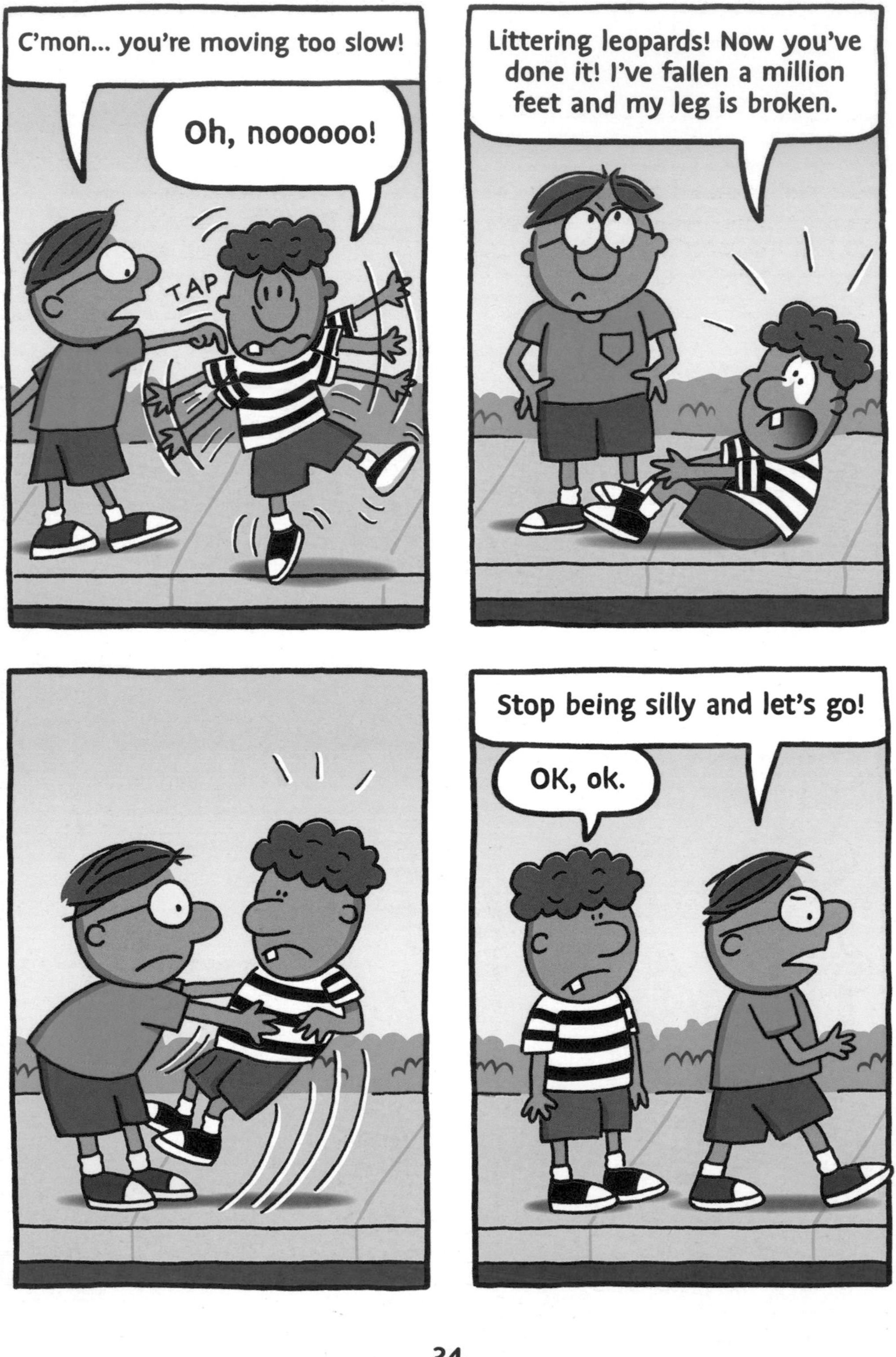
C'mon… you're moving too slow!
Oh, noooooo!
TAP
Littering leopards! Now you've done it! I've fallen a million feet and my leg is broken.
Stop being silly and let's go!
OK, ok.

# CHAPTER 5 - SOMEONE'S COMING!

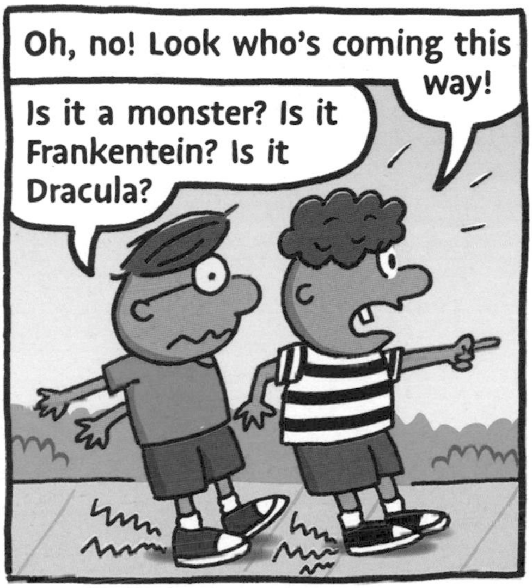
Oh, no! Look who's coming this way!
Is it a monster? Is it Frankentein? Is it Dracula?

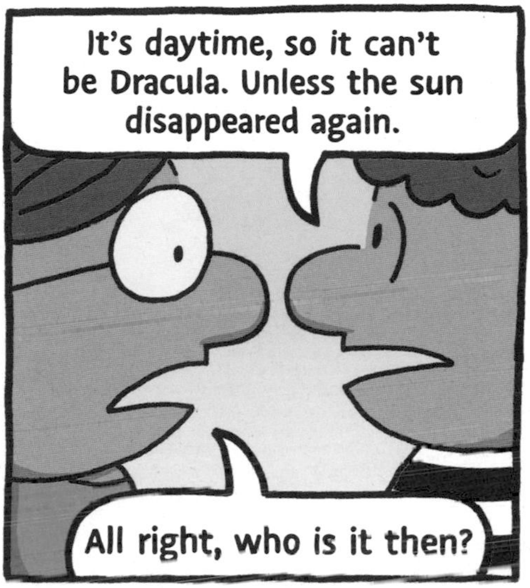
It's daytime, so it can't be Dracula. Unless the sun disappeared again.
All right, who is it then?

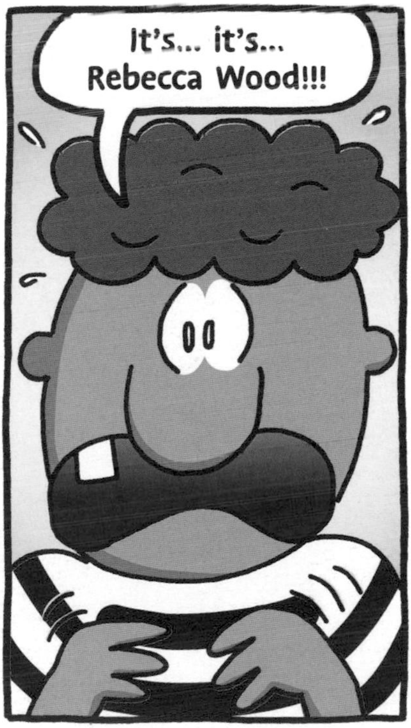
It's... it's... Rebecca Wood!!!

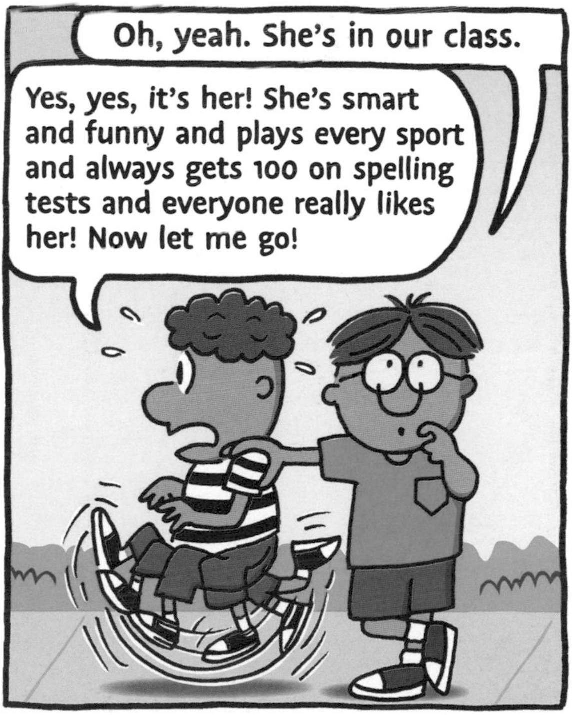
Oh, yeah. She's in our class.
Yes, yes, it's her! She's smart and funny and plays every sport and always gets 100 on spelling tests and everyone really likes her! Now let me go!

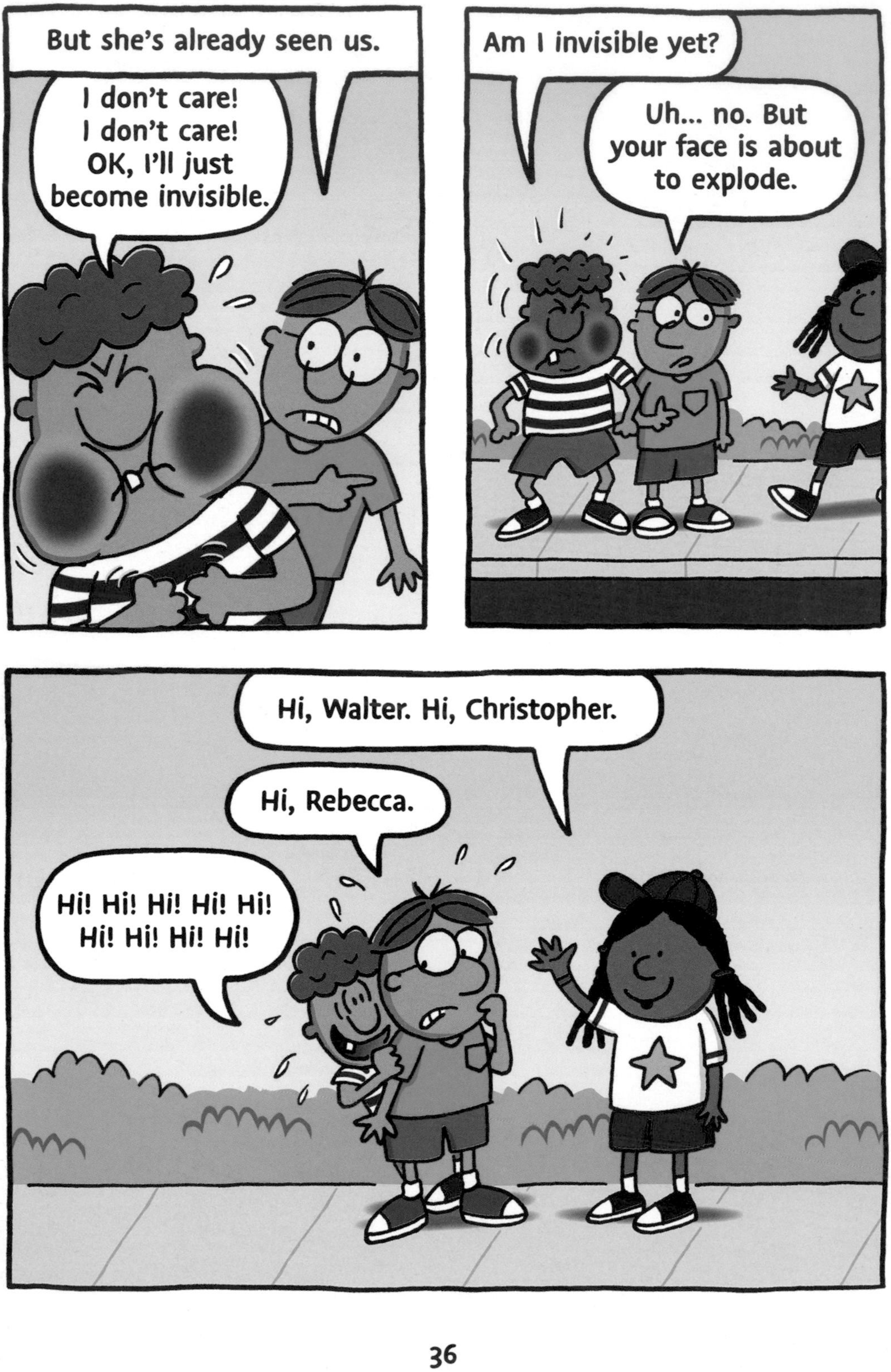
But she's already seen us.
I don't care! I don't care! OK, I'll just become invisible.
Am I invisible yet?
Uh... no. But your face is about to explode.
Hi, Walter. Hi, Christopher.
Hi, Rebecca.
Hi! Hi! Hi! Hi! Hi! Hi! Hi! Hi! Hi!

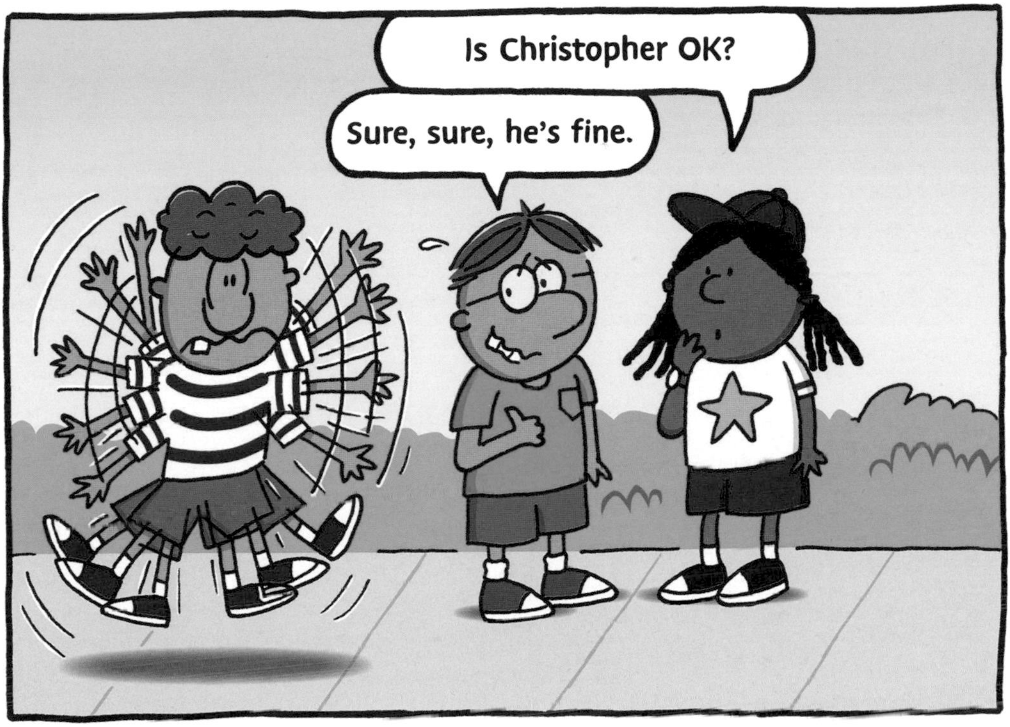
Is Christopher OK?
Sure, sure, he's fine.

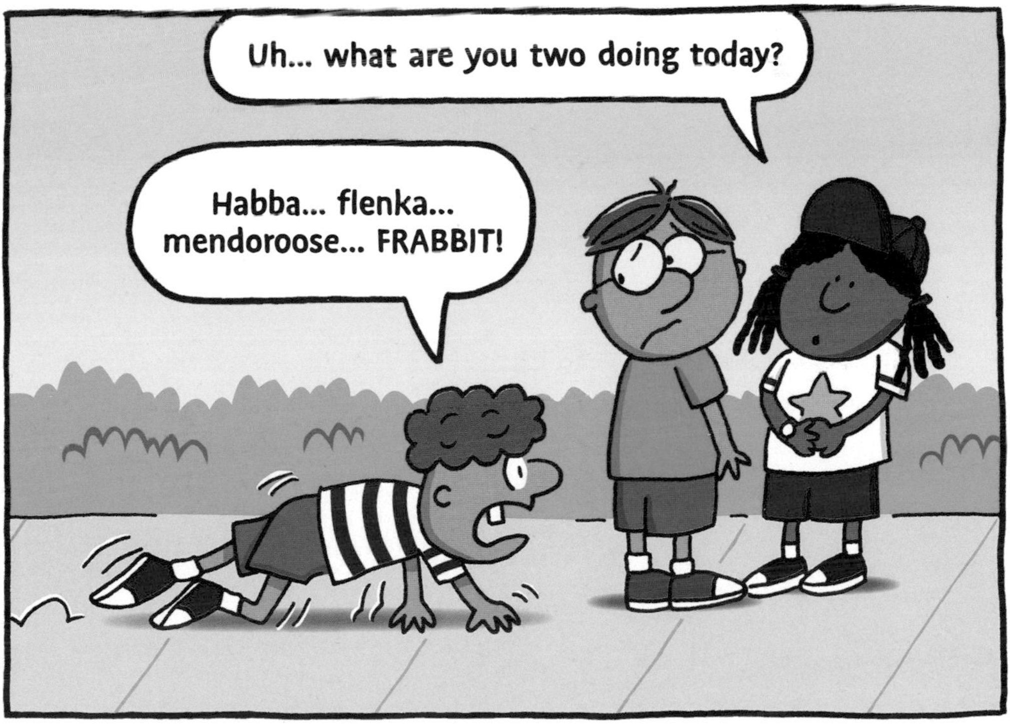
Uh... what are you two doing today?
Habba... flenka... mendoroose... FRABBIT!

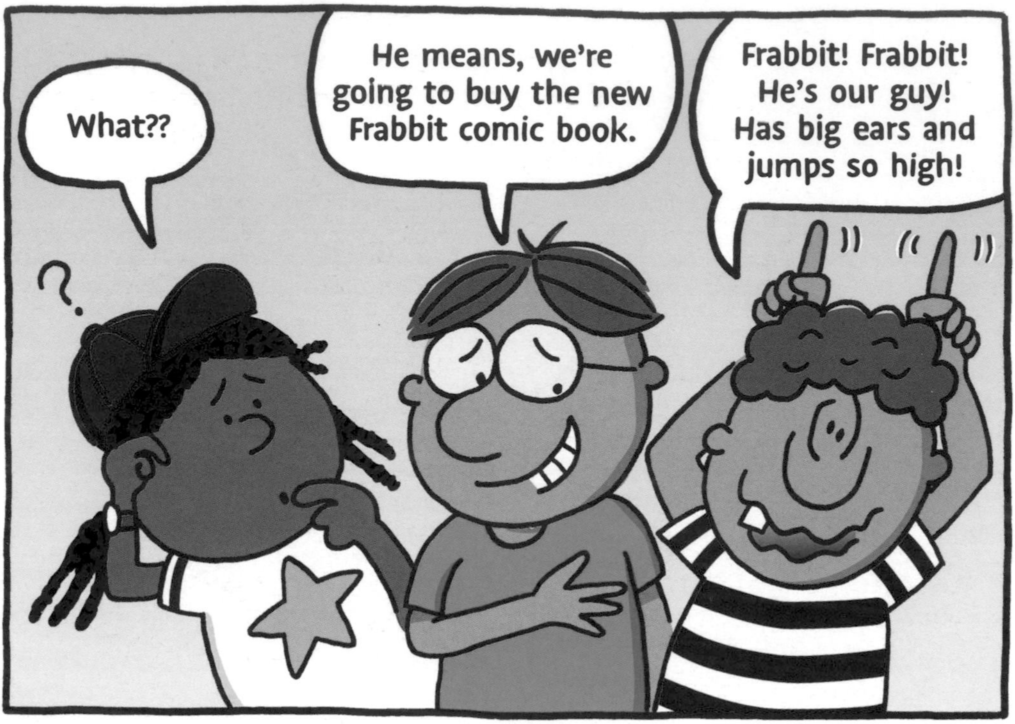
What??
He means, we're going to buy the new Frabbit comic book.
Frabbit! Frabbit! He's our guy! Has big ears and jumps so high!

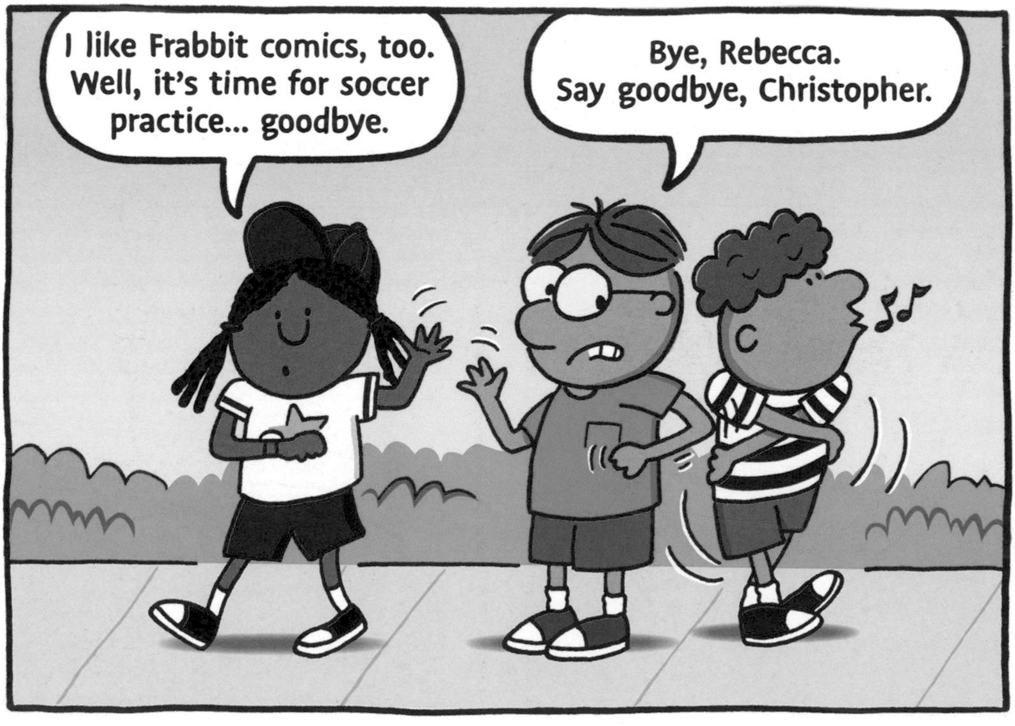
I like Frabbit comics, too. Well, it's time for soccer practice... goodbye.
Bye, Rebecca. Say goodbye, Christopher.

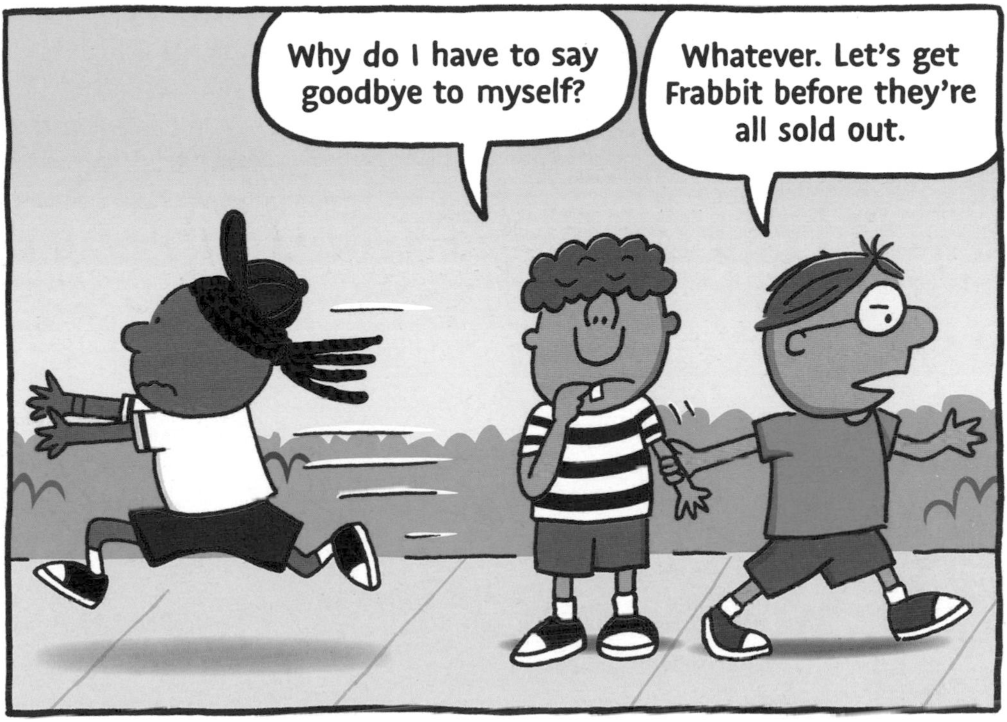
Why do I have to say goodbye to myself?
Whatever. Let's get Frabbit before they're all sold out.

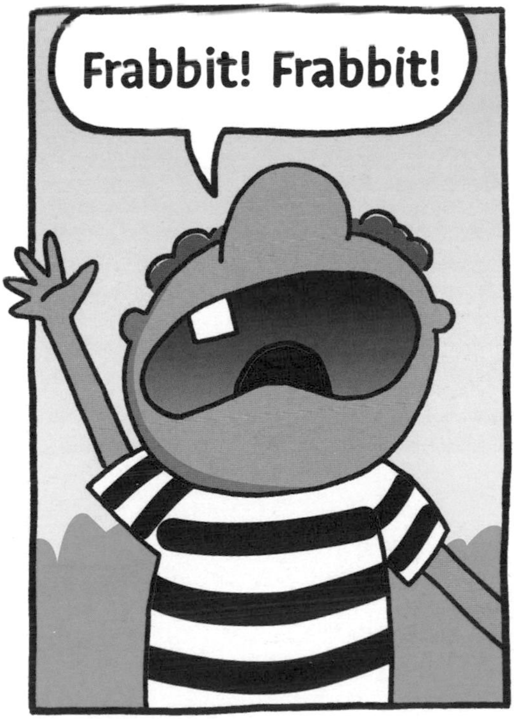
Frabbit! Frabbit!

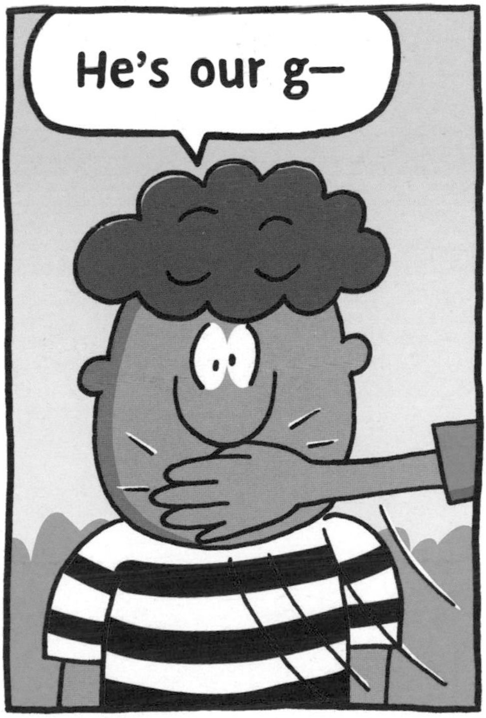
He's our g—

# CHAPTER 6 - PETE'S COMIC BOOK STORE!

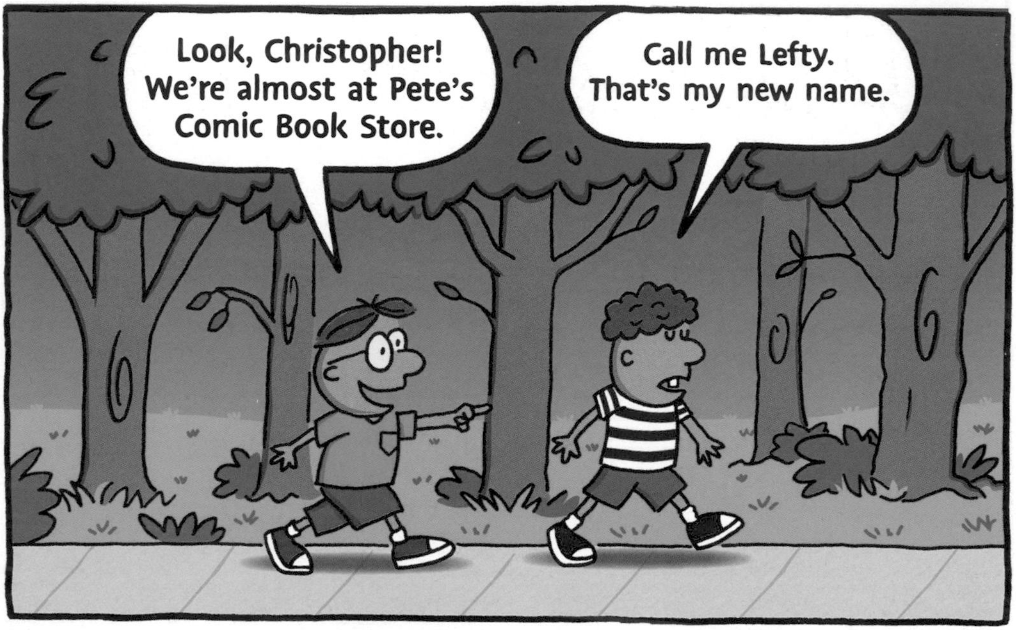
Look, Christopher! We're almost at Pete's Comic Book Store.
Call me Lefty. That's my new name.

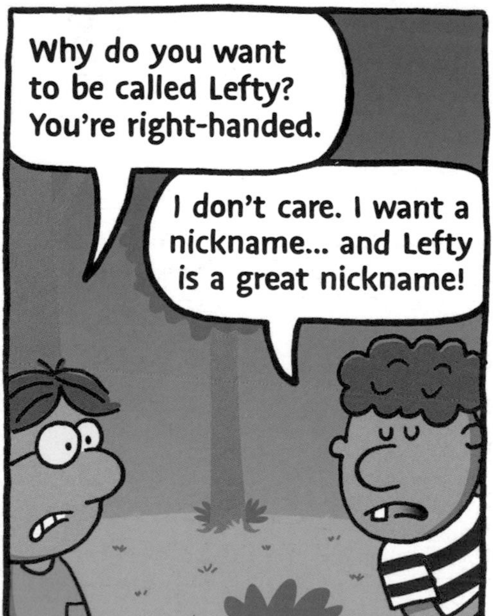
Why do you want to be called Lefty? You're right-handed.
I don't care. I want a nickname... and Lefty is a great nickname!

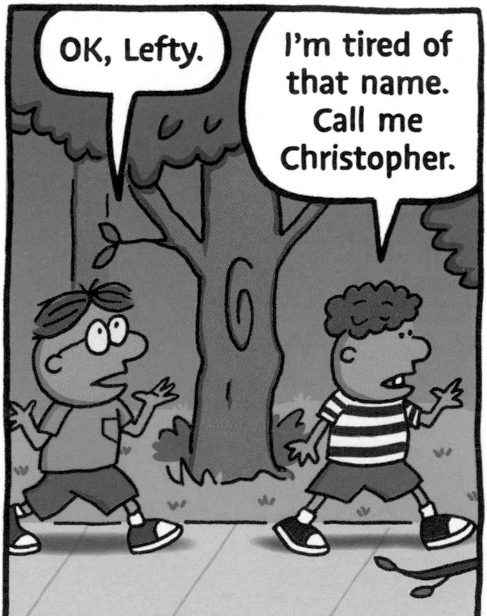
OK, Lefty.
I'm tired of that name. Call me Christopher.

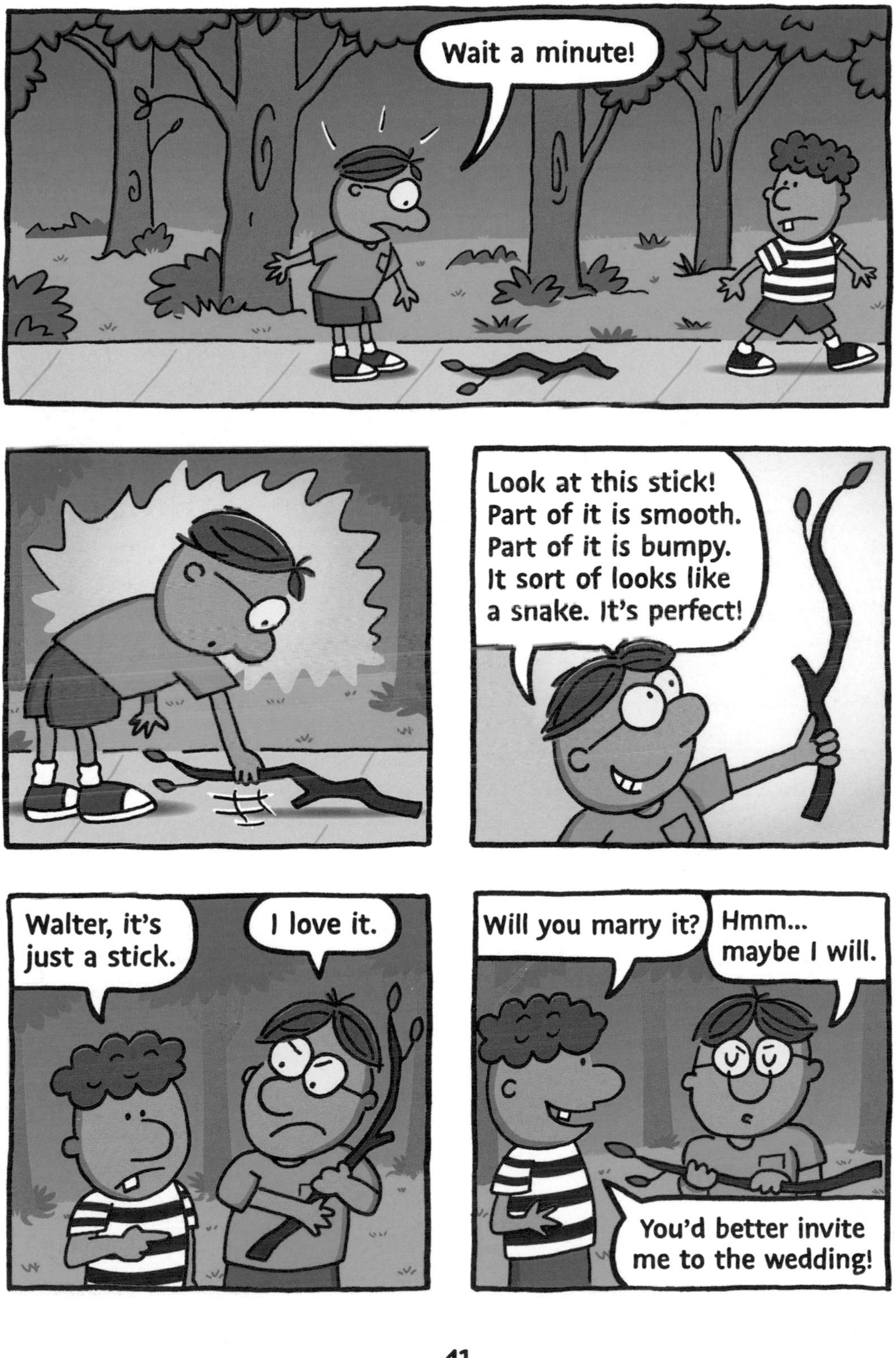
Wait a minute!
Look at this stick! Part of it is smooth. Part of it is bumpy. It sort of looks like a snake. It's perfect!
Walter, it's just a stick.
I love it.
Will you marry it?
Hmm... maybe I will.
You'd better invite me to the wedding!

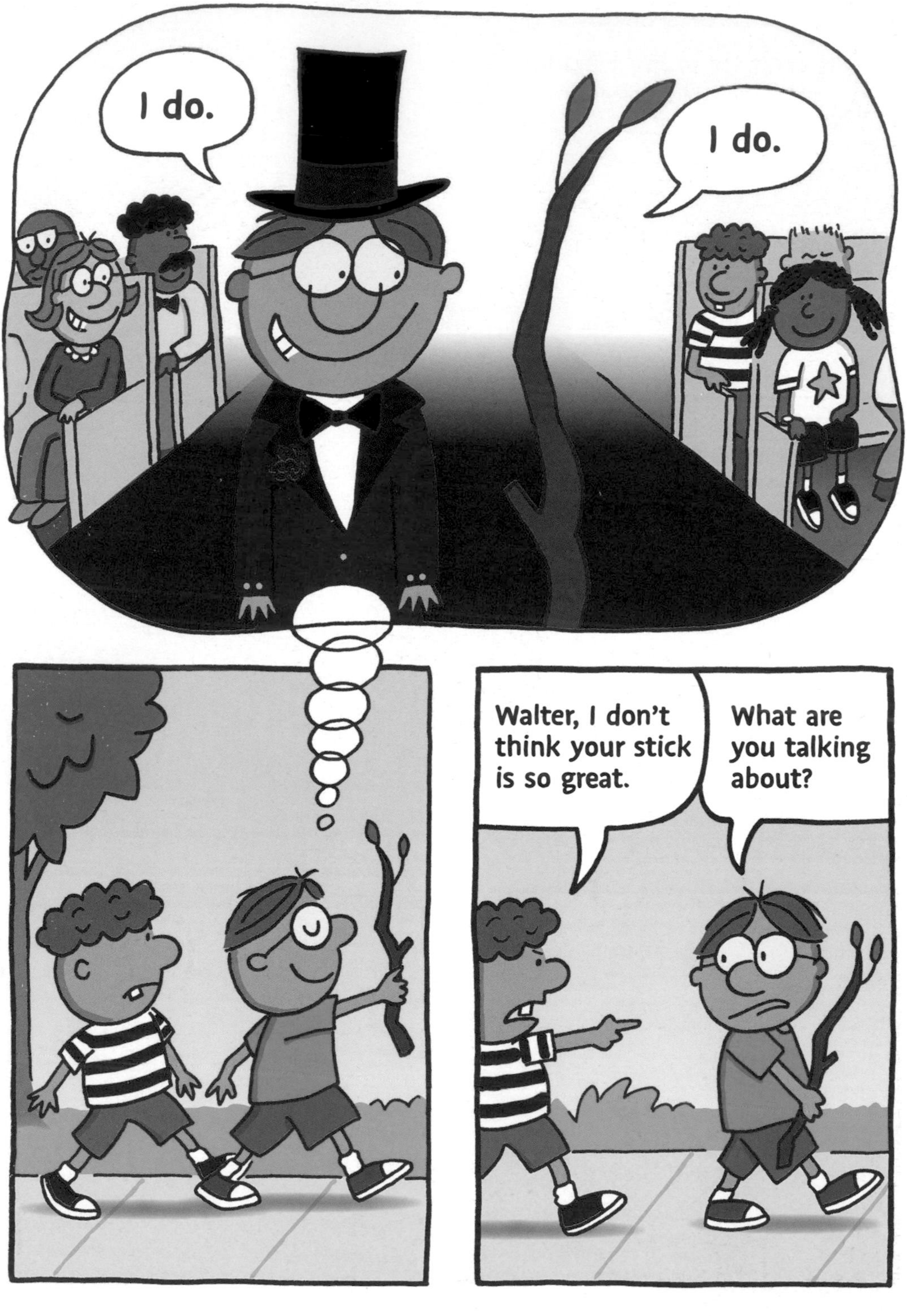
I do.
I do.
Walter, I don't think your stick is so great.
What are you talking about?

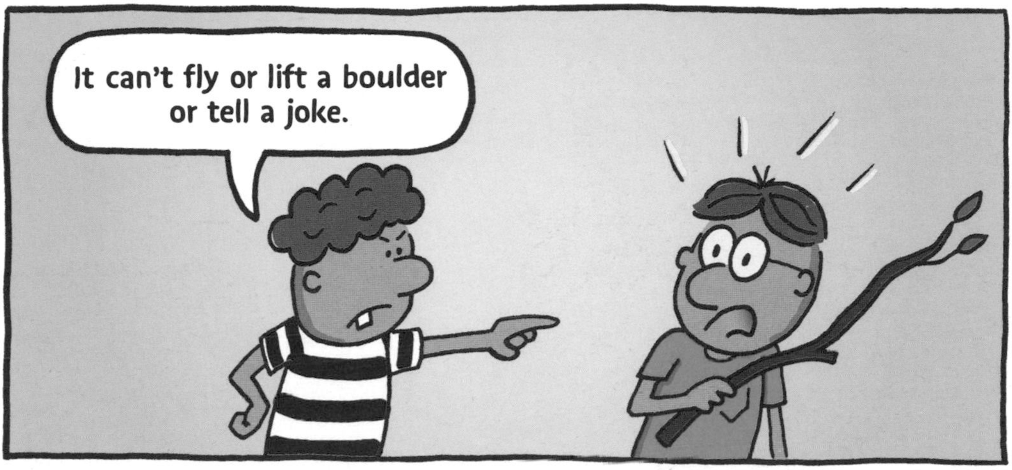
It can't fly or lift a boulder or tell a joke.

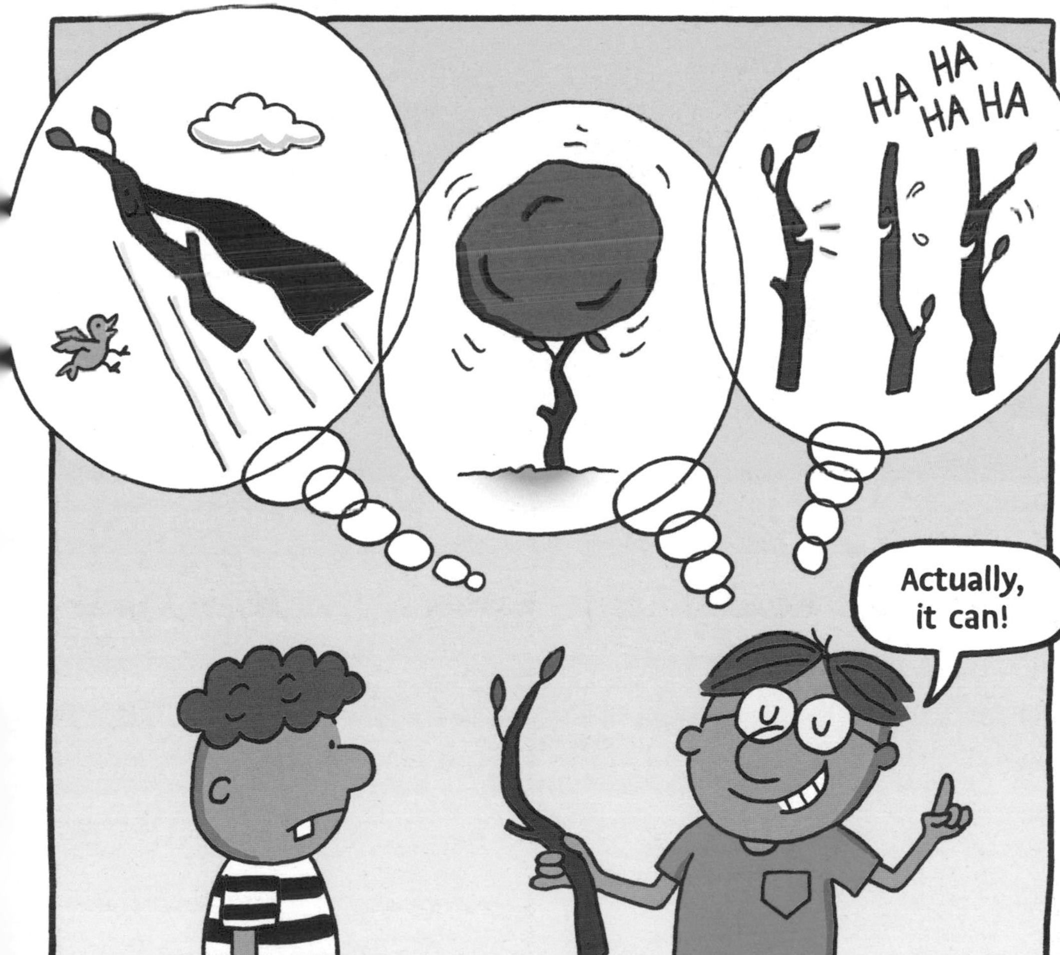
HA HA
HA HA
Actually, it can!

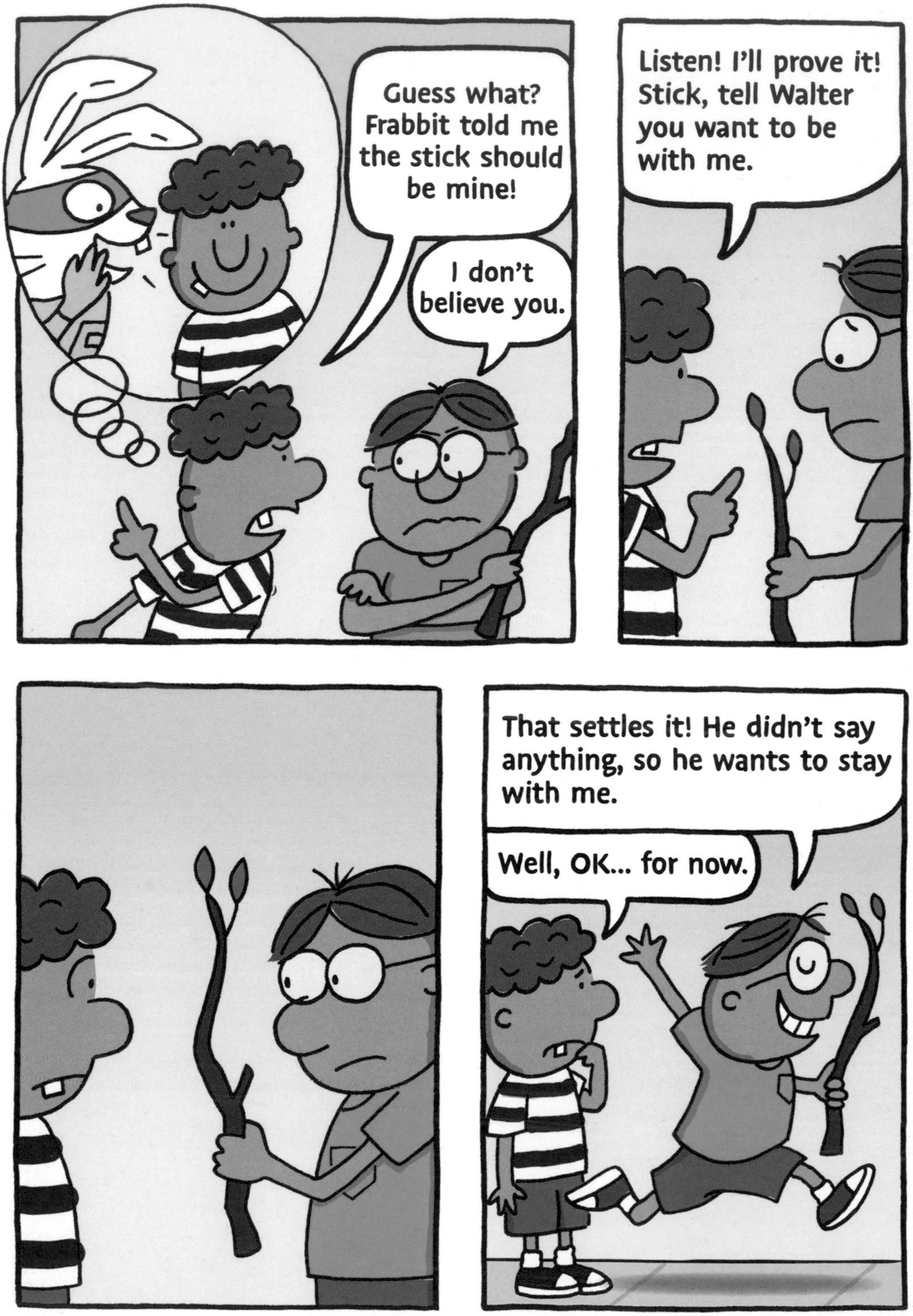
Guess what? Frabbit told me the stick should be mine!
I don't believe you.
Listen! I'll prove it! Stick, tell Walter you want to be with me.
That settles it! He didn't say anything, so he wants to stay with me.
Well, OK... for now.

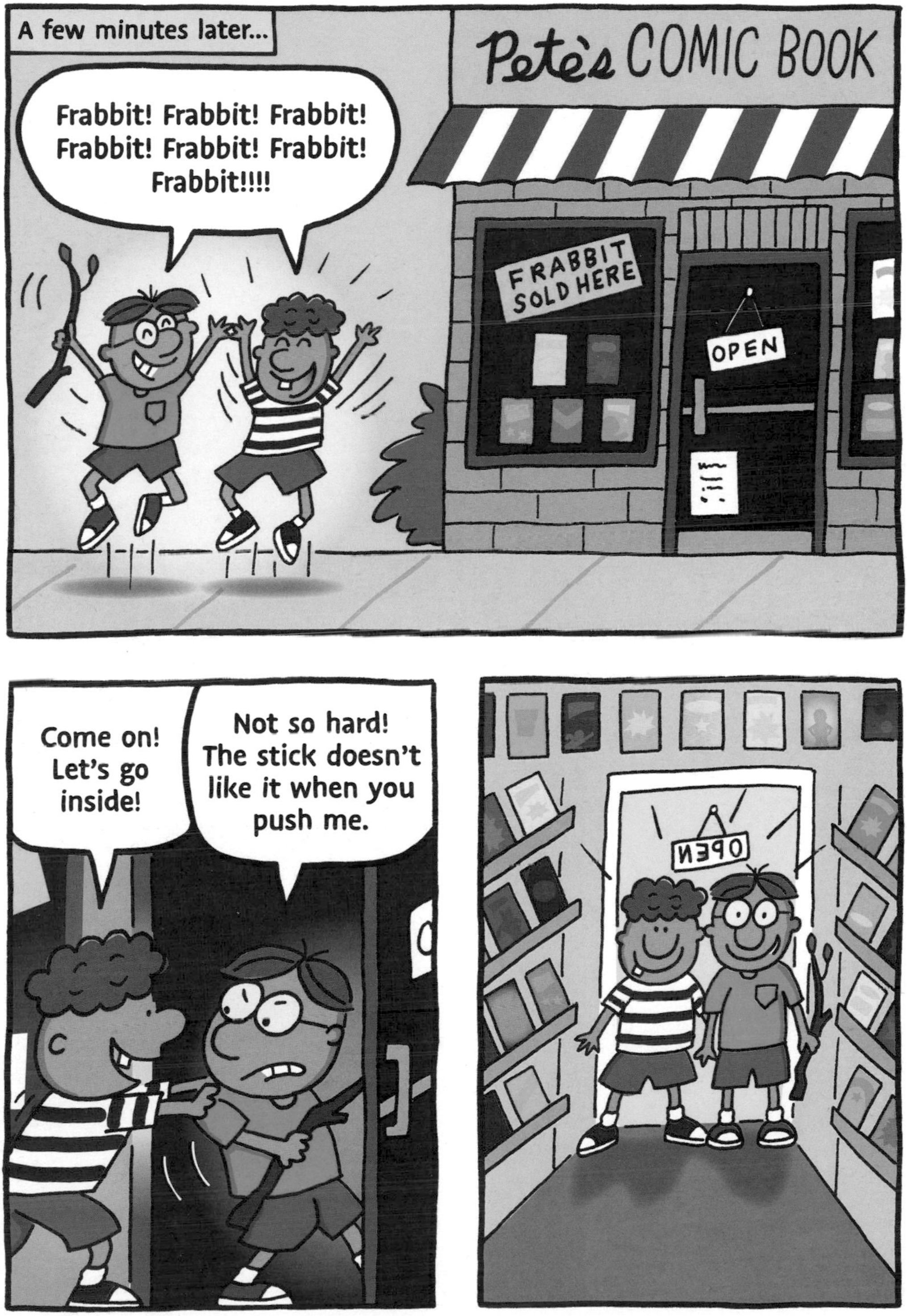
A few minutes later...
Pete's COMIC BOOK
Frabbit! Frabbit! Frabbit! Frabbit! Frabbit! Frabbit! Frabbit!!!!
FRABBIT SOLD HERE
OPEN
Come on! Let's go inside!
Not so hard! The stick doesn't like it when you push me.
OPEN

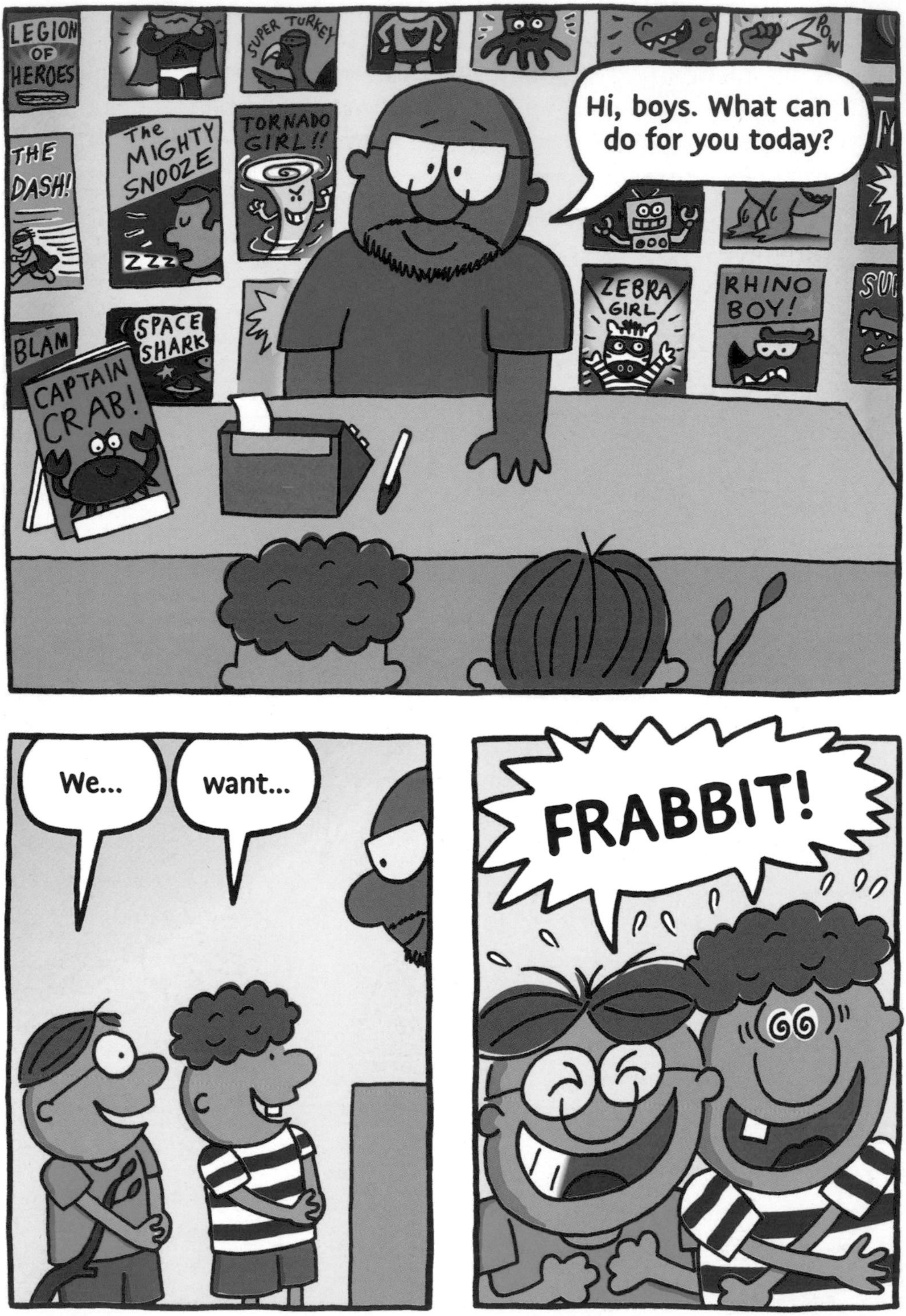
LEGION OF HEROES
SUPER TURKEY
POW
THE DASH!
The MIGHTY SNOOZE
ZZZ
TORNADO GIRL!!
SPACE SHARK
BLAM
CAPTAIN CRAB!
ZEBRA GIRL
RHINO BOY!
Hi, boys. What can I do for you today?
We...
want...
FRABBIT!

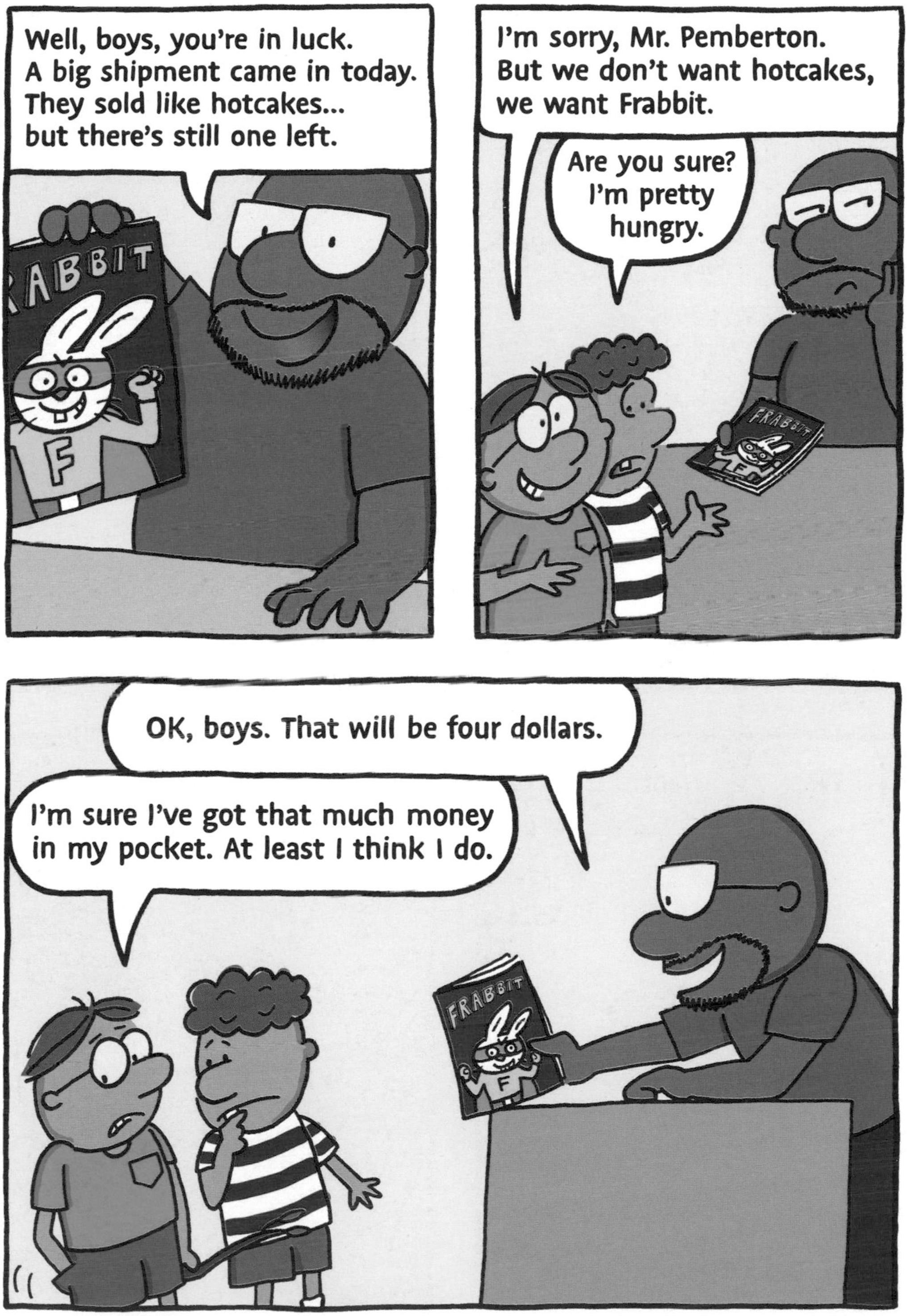
Well, boys, you're in luck. A big shipment came in today. They sold like hotcakes... but there's still one left.
FRABBIT
I'm sorry, Mr. Pemberton. But we don't want hotcakes, we want Frabbit.
Are you sure? I'm pretty hungry.
OK, boys. That will be four dollars.
I'm sure I've got that much money in my pocket. At least I think I do.
FRABBIT

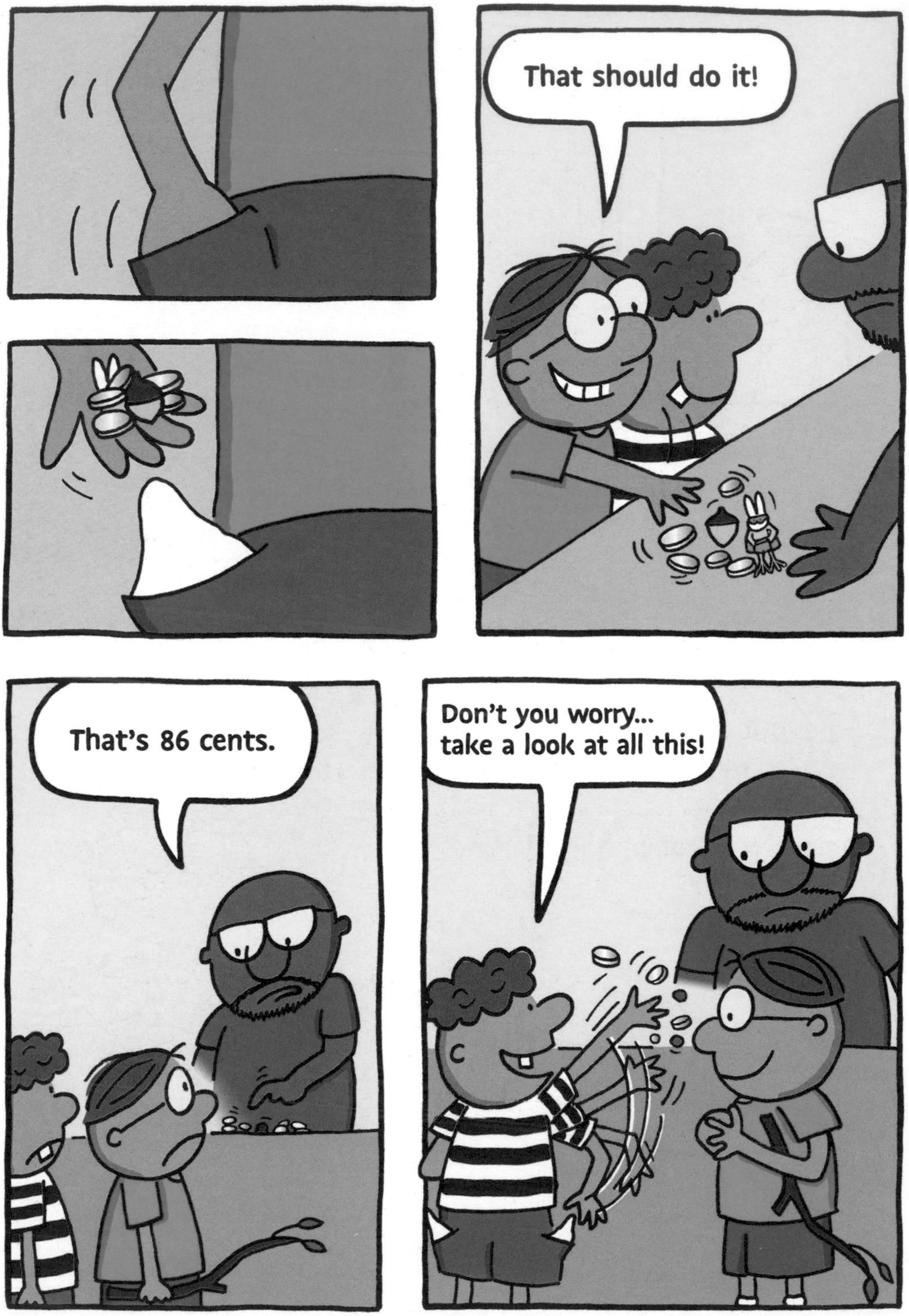
That should do it!
That's 86 cents.
Don't you worry...
take a look at all this!

Sorry, boys. All you have is $2.12. Come back with two more dollars and this comic book is yours.
THE DASH!
MIGHTY SNOOZE
TORNADO GIRL
SPACE SHARK
FRABBIT
But we really, really, really, really want it. That's five 'reallys'.
Actually, it's only four 'reallys'!
FRABBIT

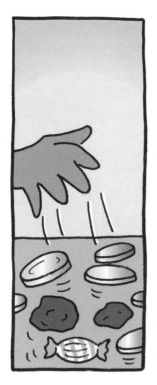

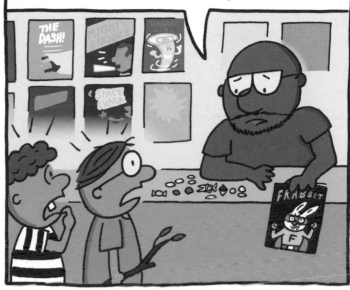

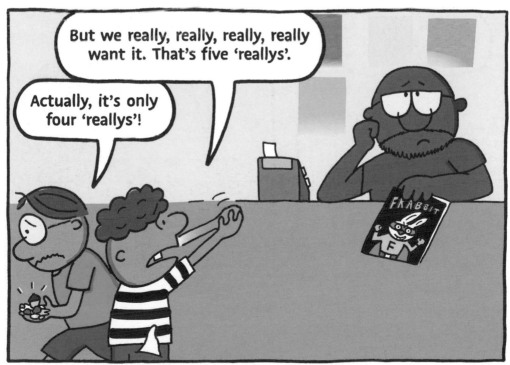

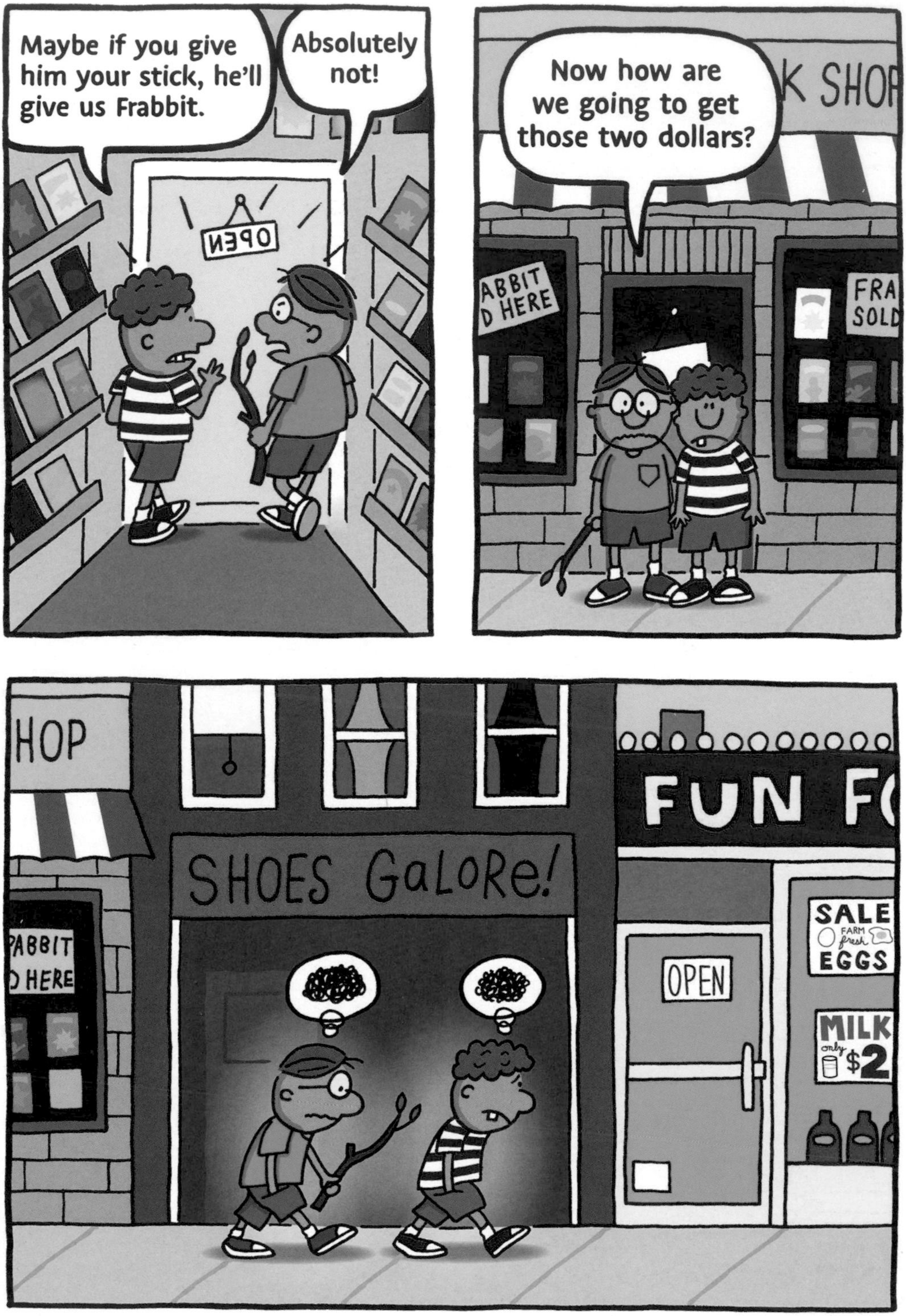
Maybe if you give him your stick, he'll give us Frabbit.
Absolutely not!
OPEN
Now how are we going to get those two dollars?
K SHOP
ABBIT
D HERE
FRA
SOLD
HOP
SHOES GaLoRe!
FUN F
PABBIT
D HERE
OPEN
SALE
FARM fresh
EGGS
MILK
only $2

# CHAPTER 7 - THE WORLD'S WORST MAGIC SHOW!

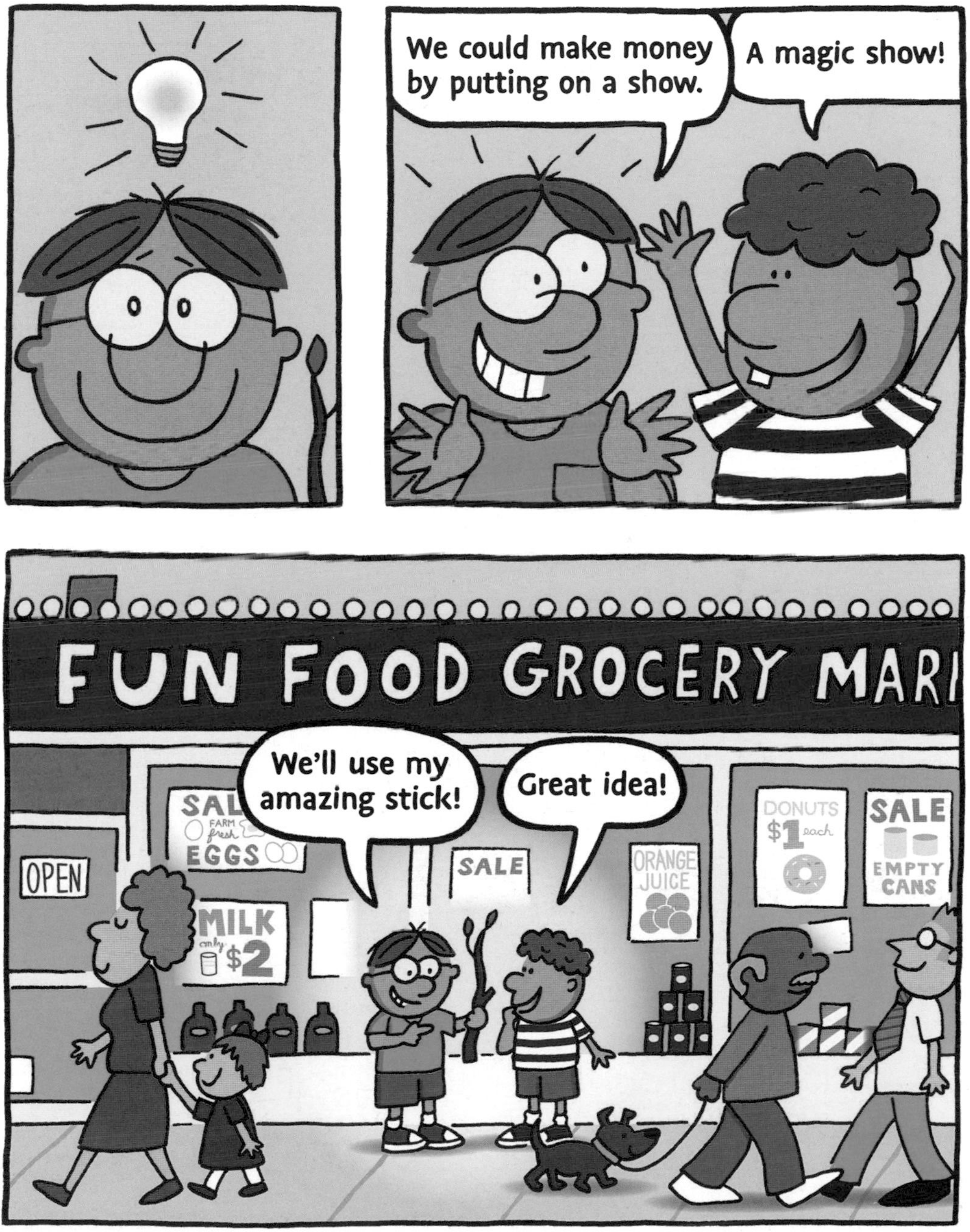
We could make money by putting on a show.
A magic show!
FUN FOOD GROCERY MAR
We'll use my amazing stick!
Great idea!
SAL FARM fresh EGGS
OPEN
MILK only $2
SALE
ORANGE JUICE
DONUTS $1 each
SALE EMPTY CANS

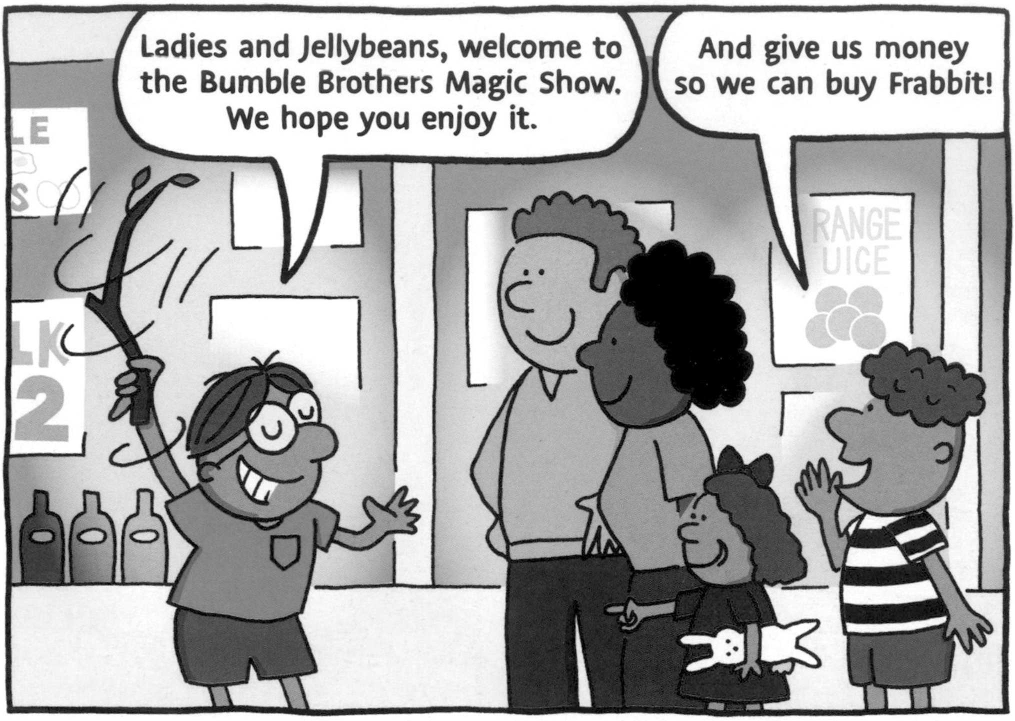
Ladies and Jellybeans, welcome to the Bumble Brothers Magic Show. We hope you enjoy it.
And give us money so we can buy Frabbit!

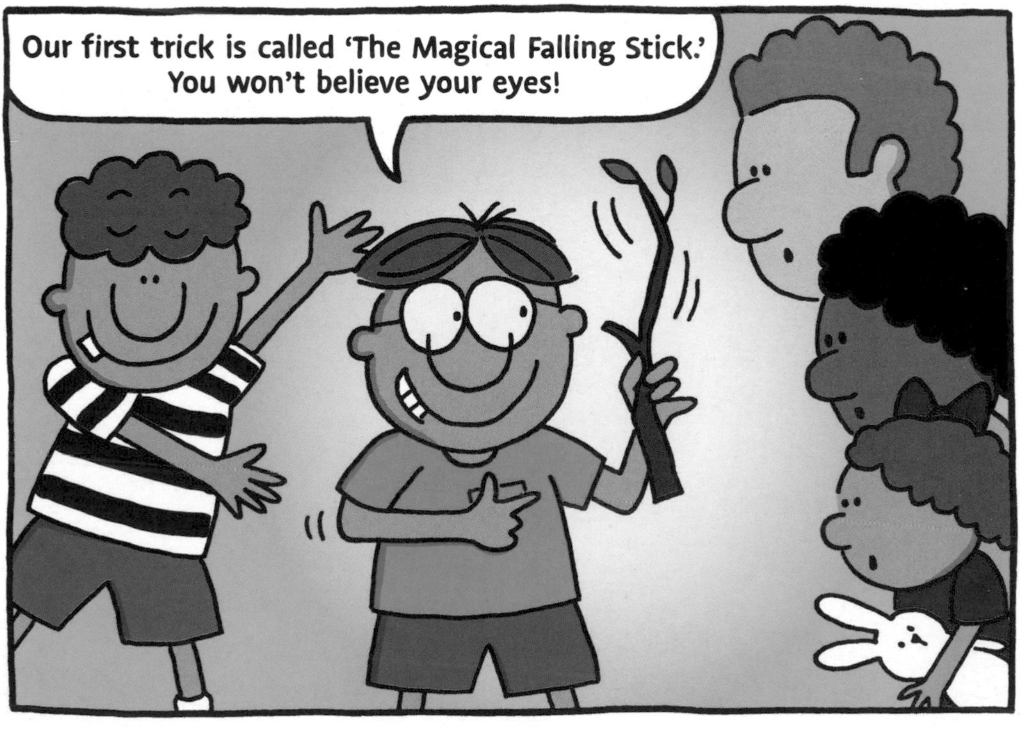
Our first trick is called 'The Magical Falling Stick.' You won't believe your eyes!

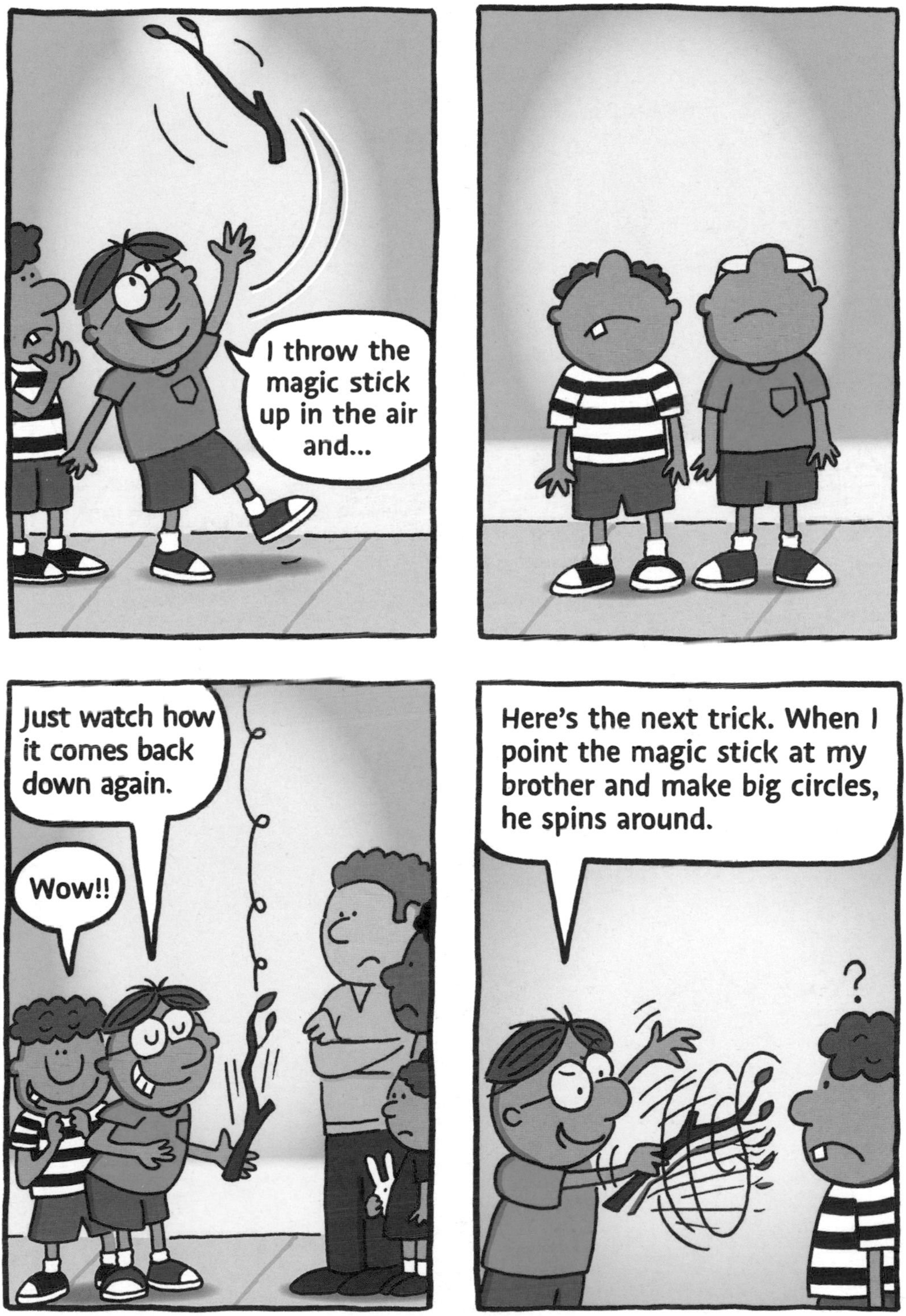
I throw the magic stick up in the air and...
Just watch how it comes back down again.
Wow!!
Here's the next trick. When I point the magic stick at my brother and make big circles, he spins around.
?

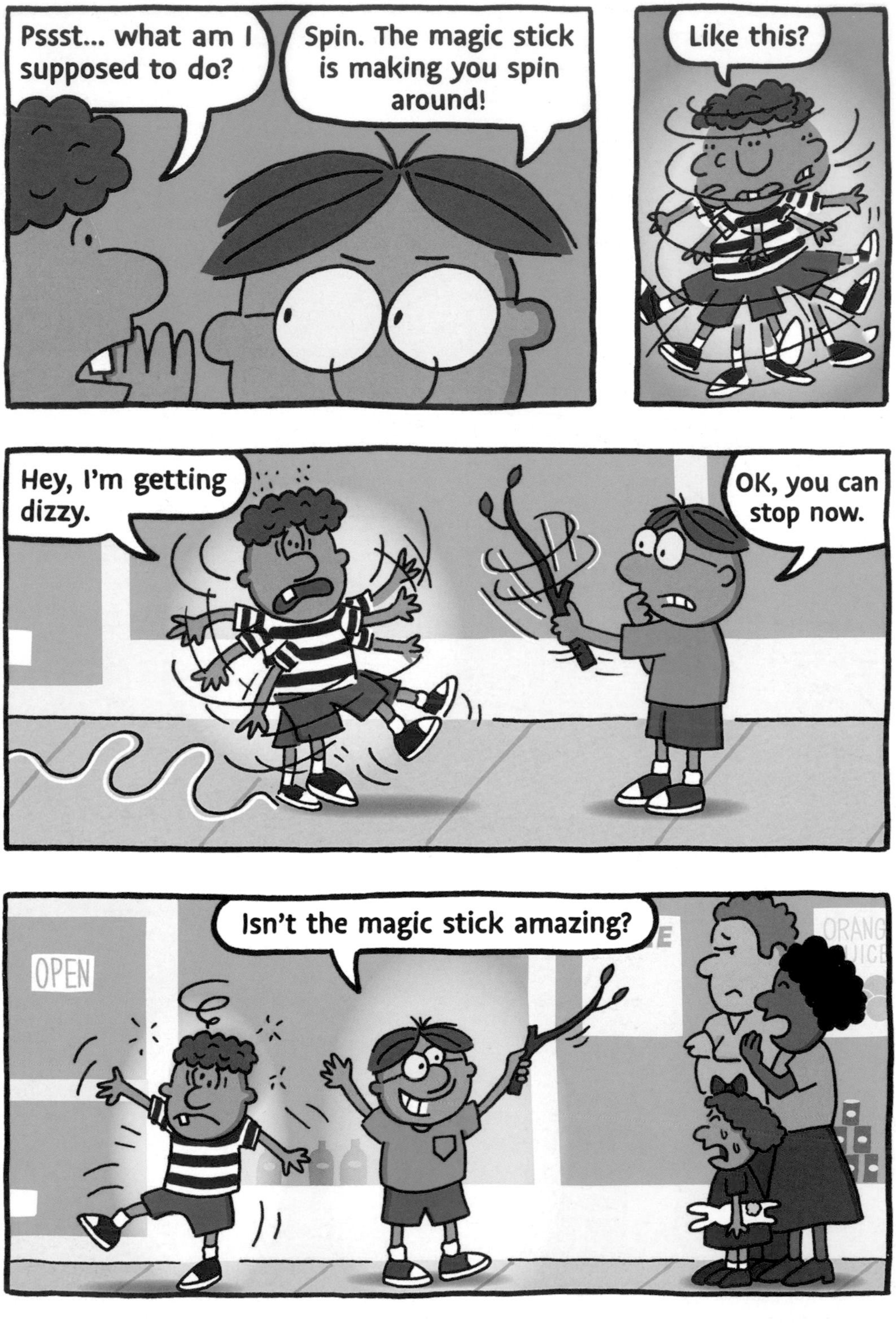
Pssst... what am I supposed to do?
Spin. The magic stick is making you spin around!
Like this?
Hey, I'm getting dizzy.
OK, you can stop now.
OPEN
Isn't the magic stick amazing?
ORANGE JUICE

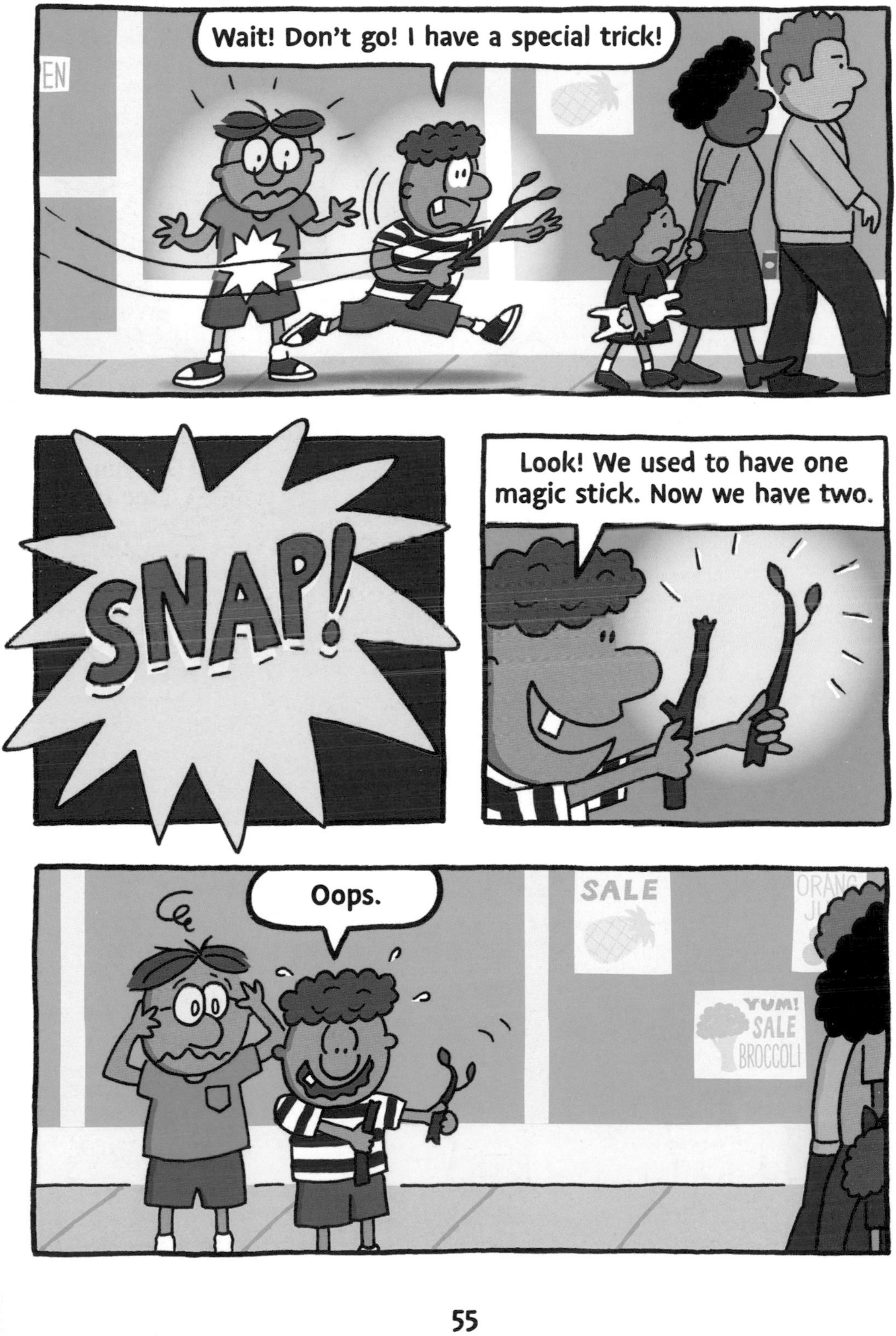
Wait! Don't go! I have a special trick!
SNAP!
Look! We used to have one magic stick. Now we have two.
Oops.
SALE
YUM! SALE BROCCOLI

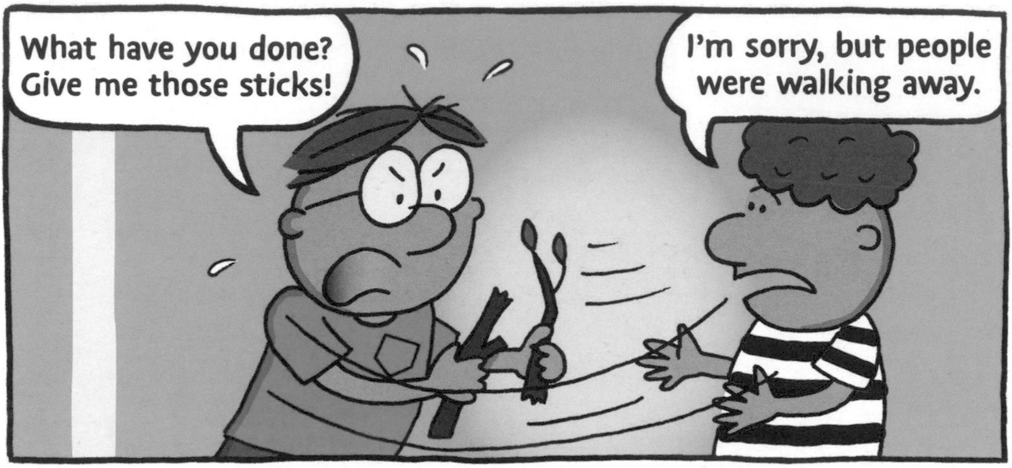
What have you done? Give me those sticks!
I'm sorry, but people were walking away.

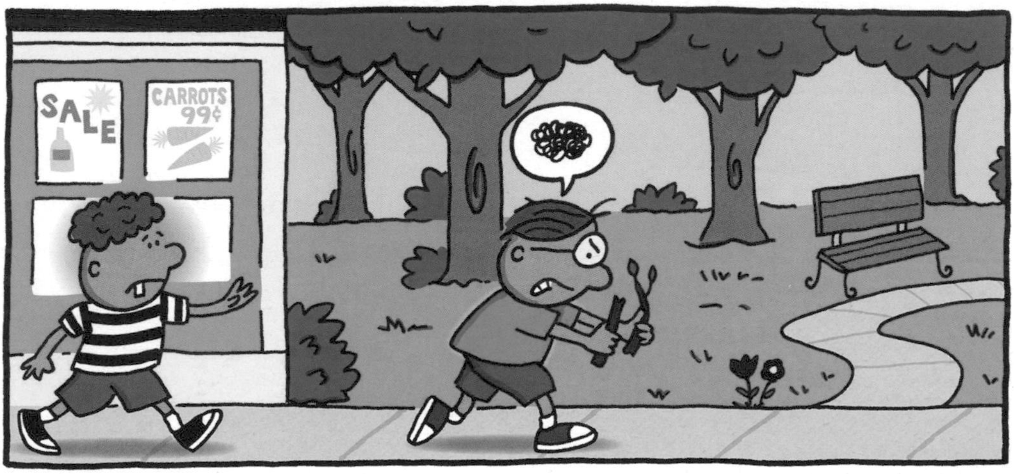
SALE
CARROTS 99¢

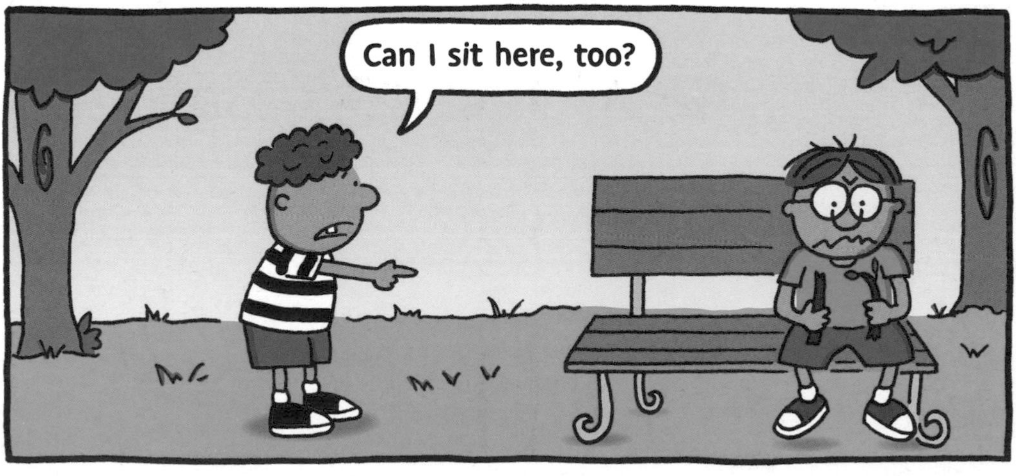
Can I sit here, too?

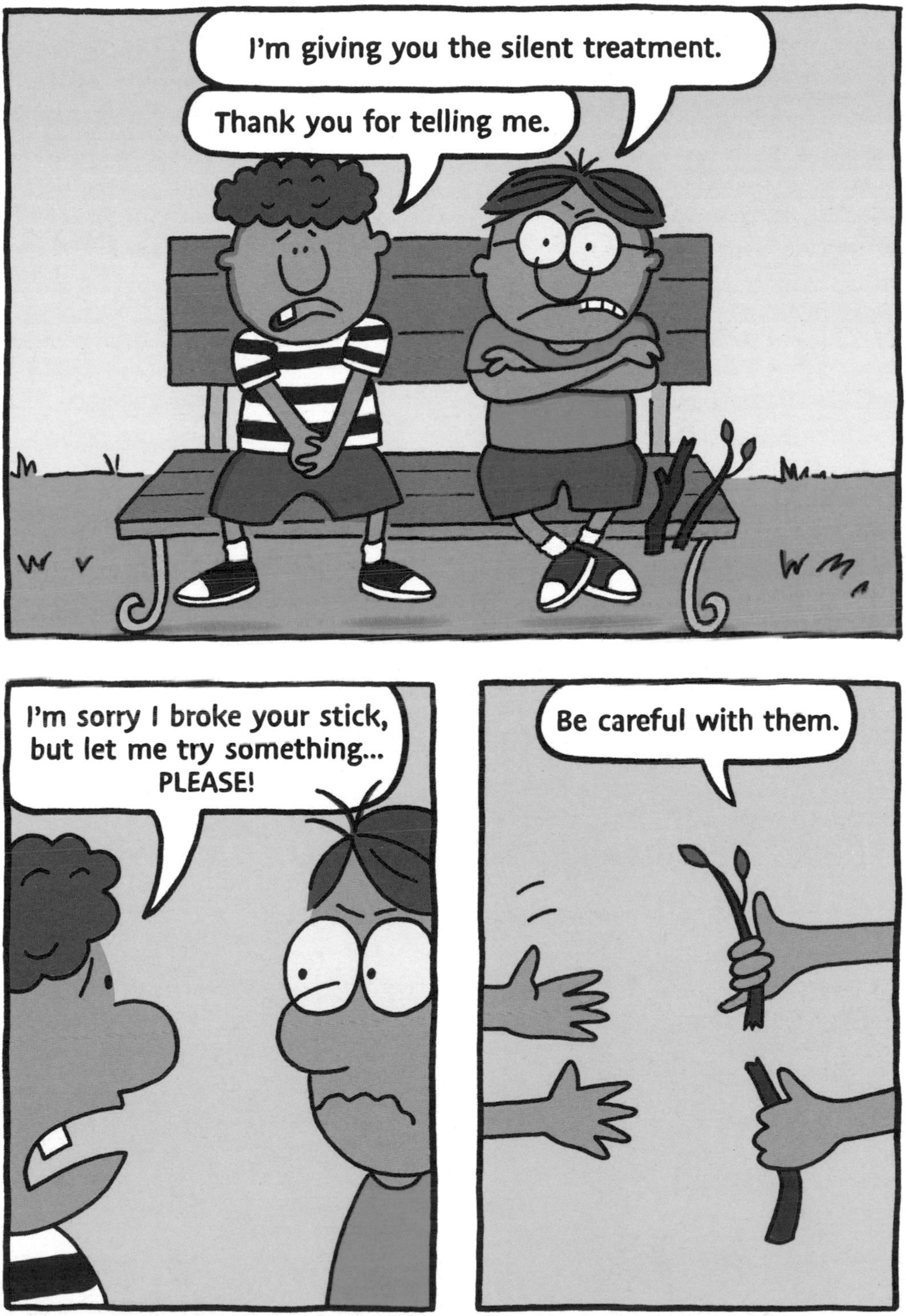
I'm giving you the silent treatment.
Thank you for telling me.
I'm sorry I broke your stick, but let me try something... PLEASE!
Be careful with them.

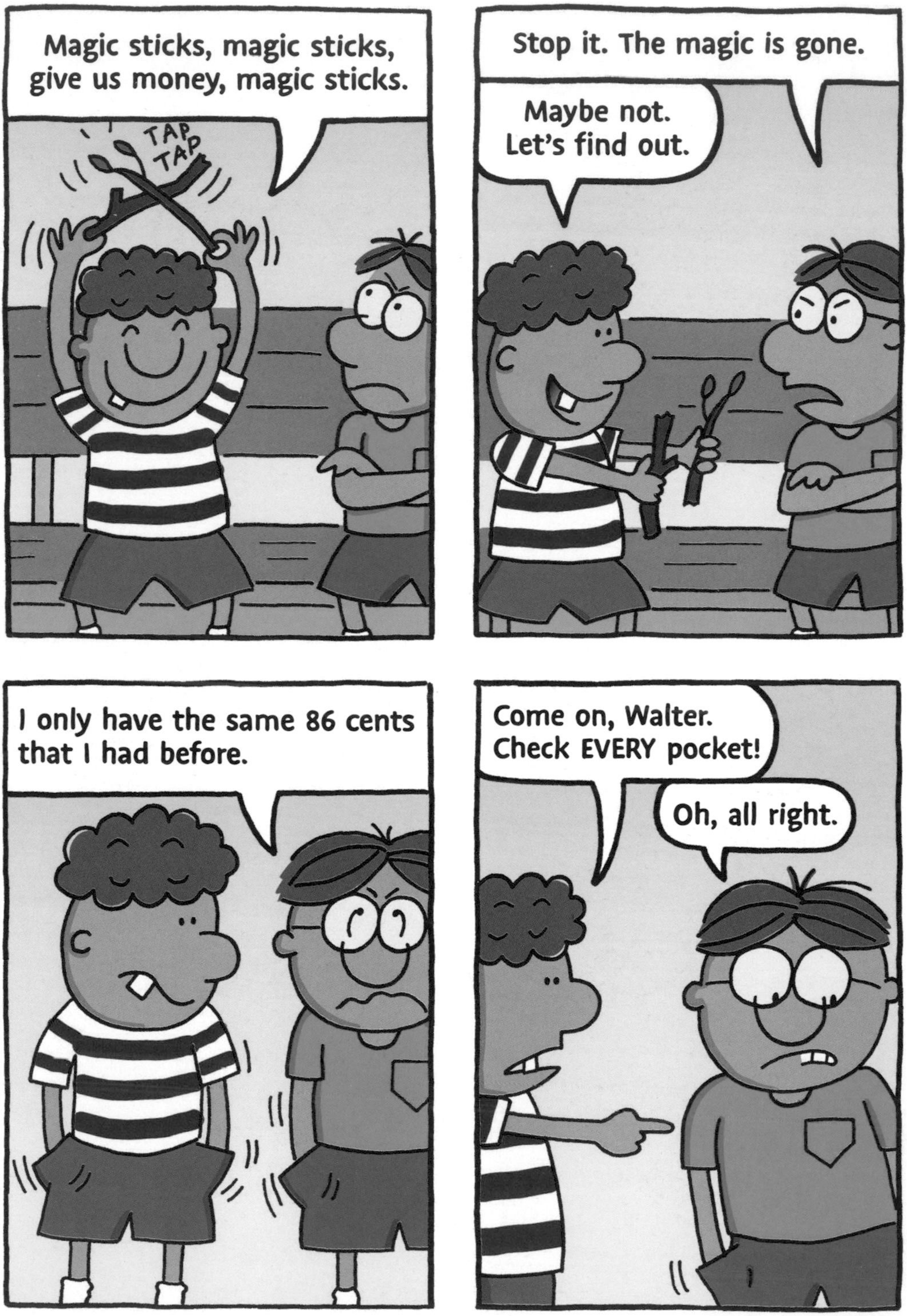
Magic sticks, magic sticks, give us money, magic sticks.
TAP TAP
Stop it. The magic is gone.
Maybe not. Let's find out.
I only have the same 86 cents that I had before.
Come on, Walter. Check EVERY pocket!
Oh, all right.

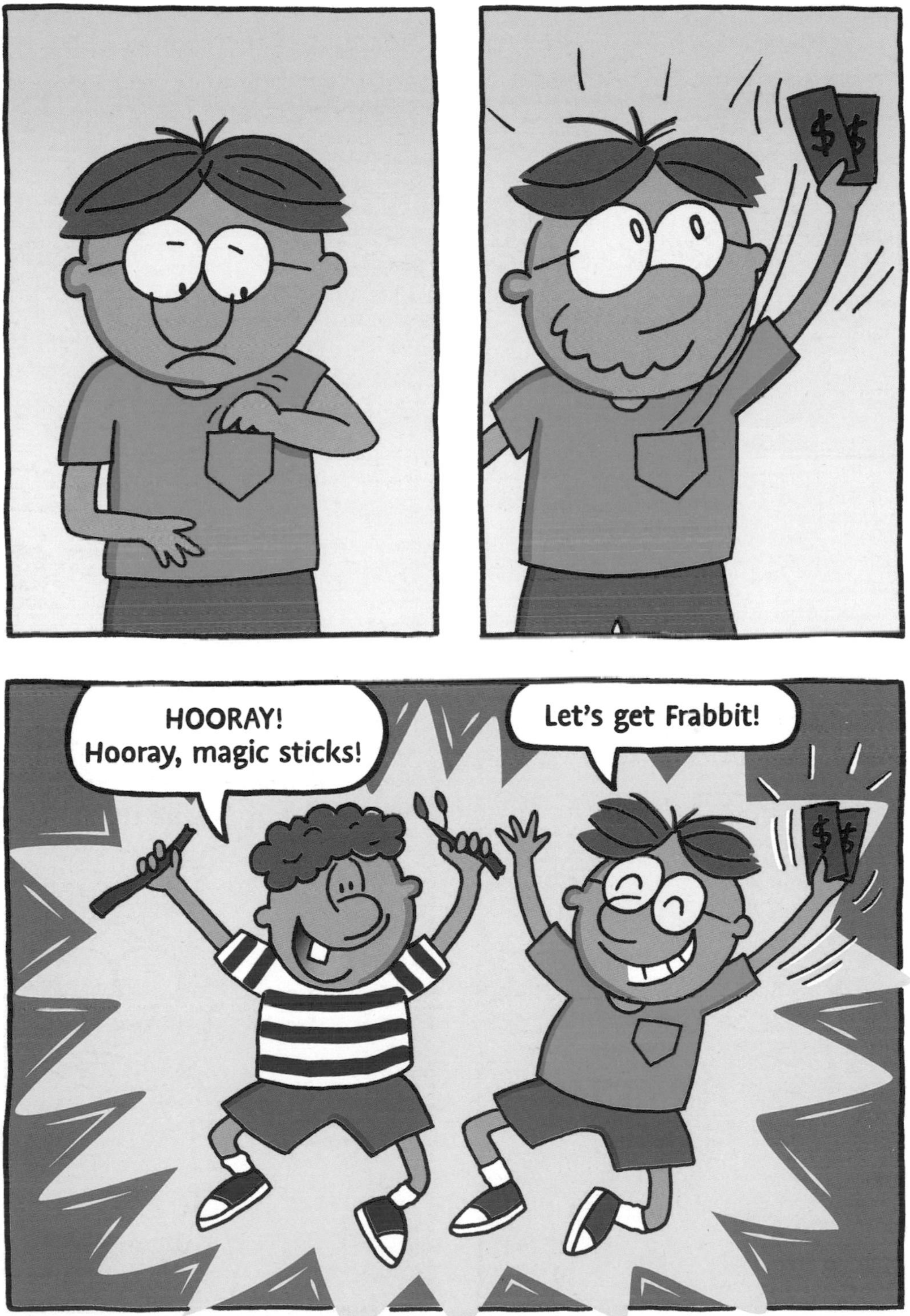
HOORAY!
Hooray, magic sticks!
Let's get Frabbit!

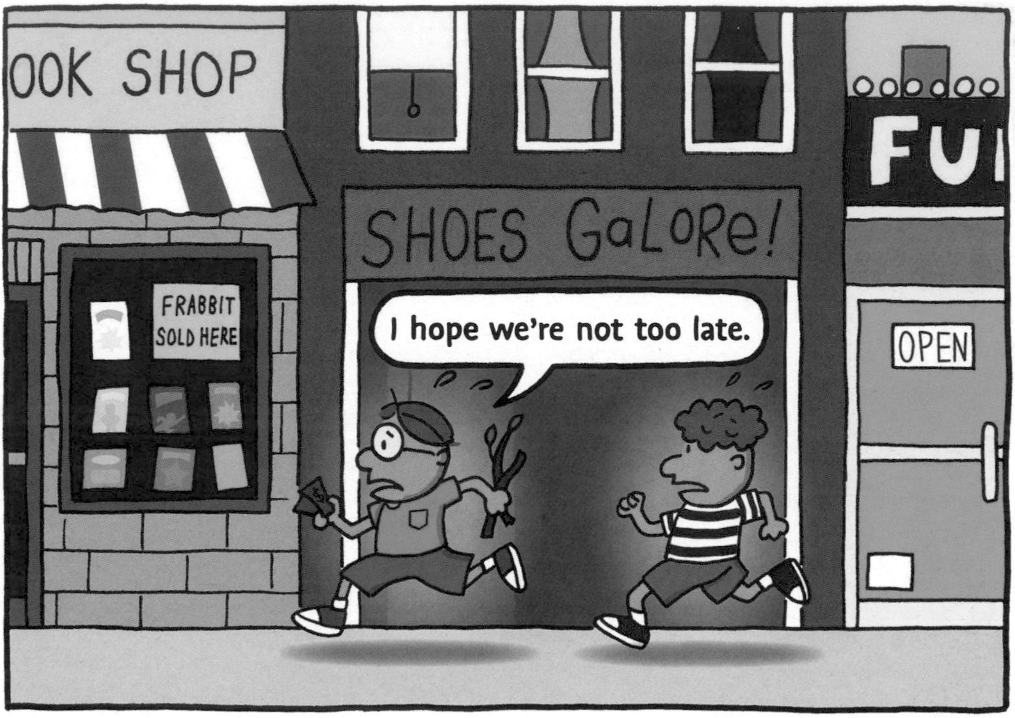
OOK SHOP
SHOES GaLORe!
FRABBIT SOLD HERE
I hope we're not too late.
OPEN
FU

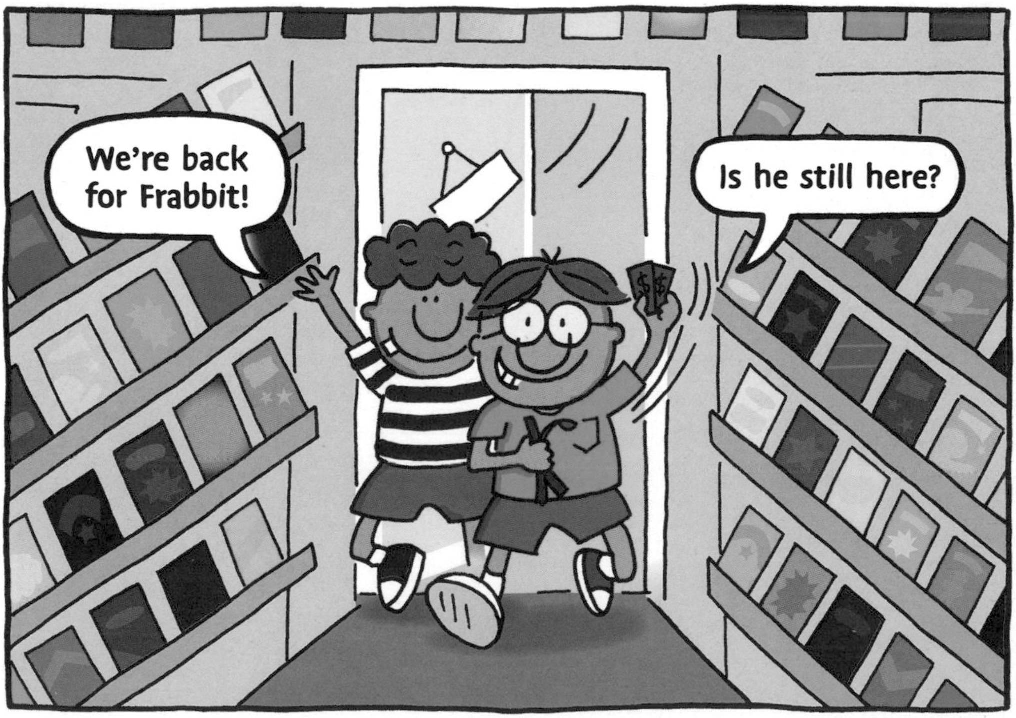
We're back for Frabbit!
Is he still here?

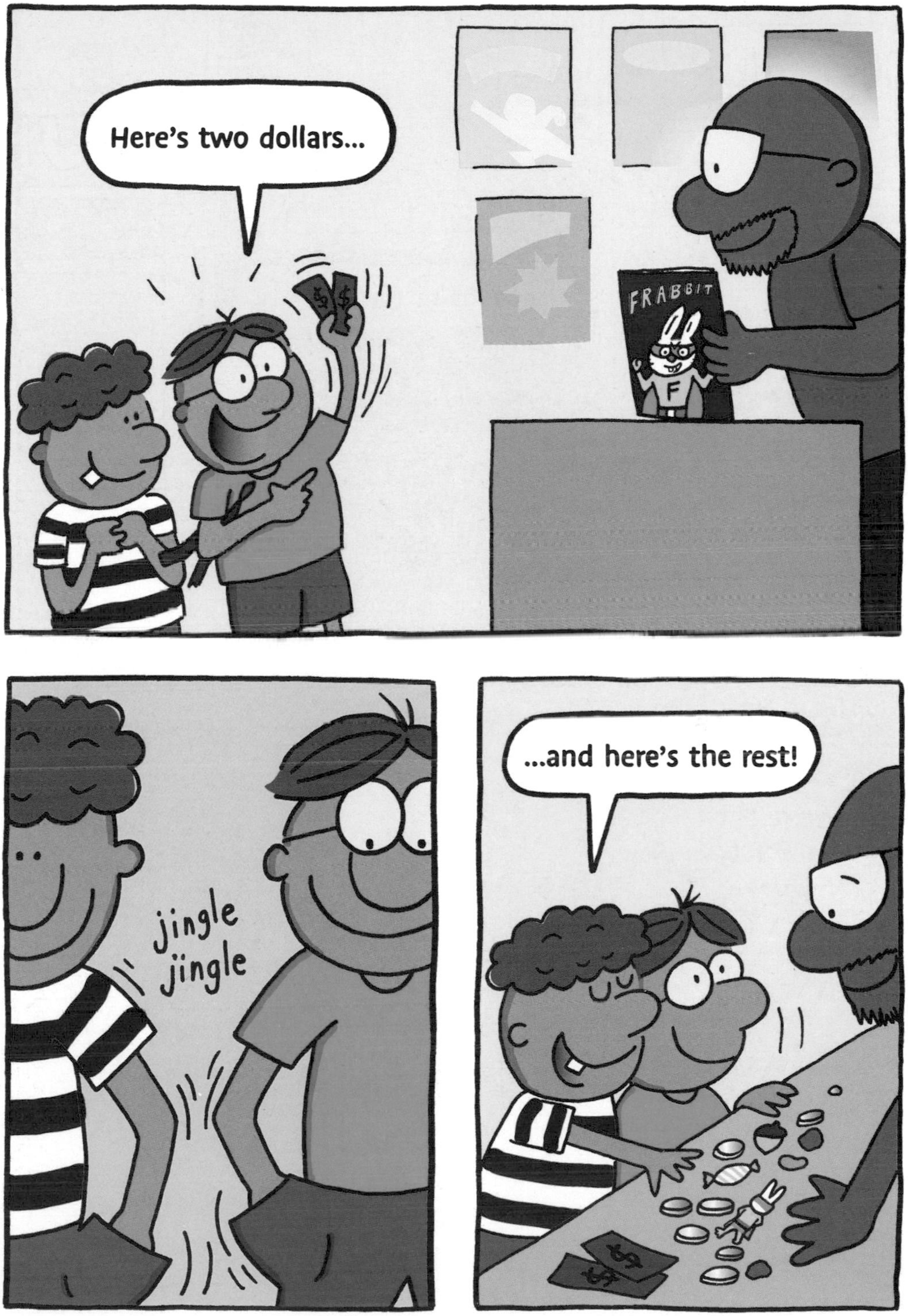
Here's two dollars...
FRABBIT
F
jingle
jingle
...and here's the rest!

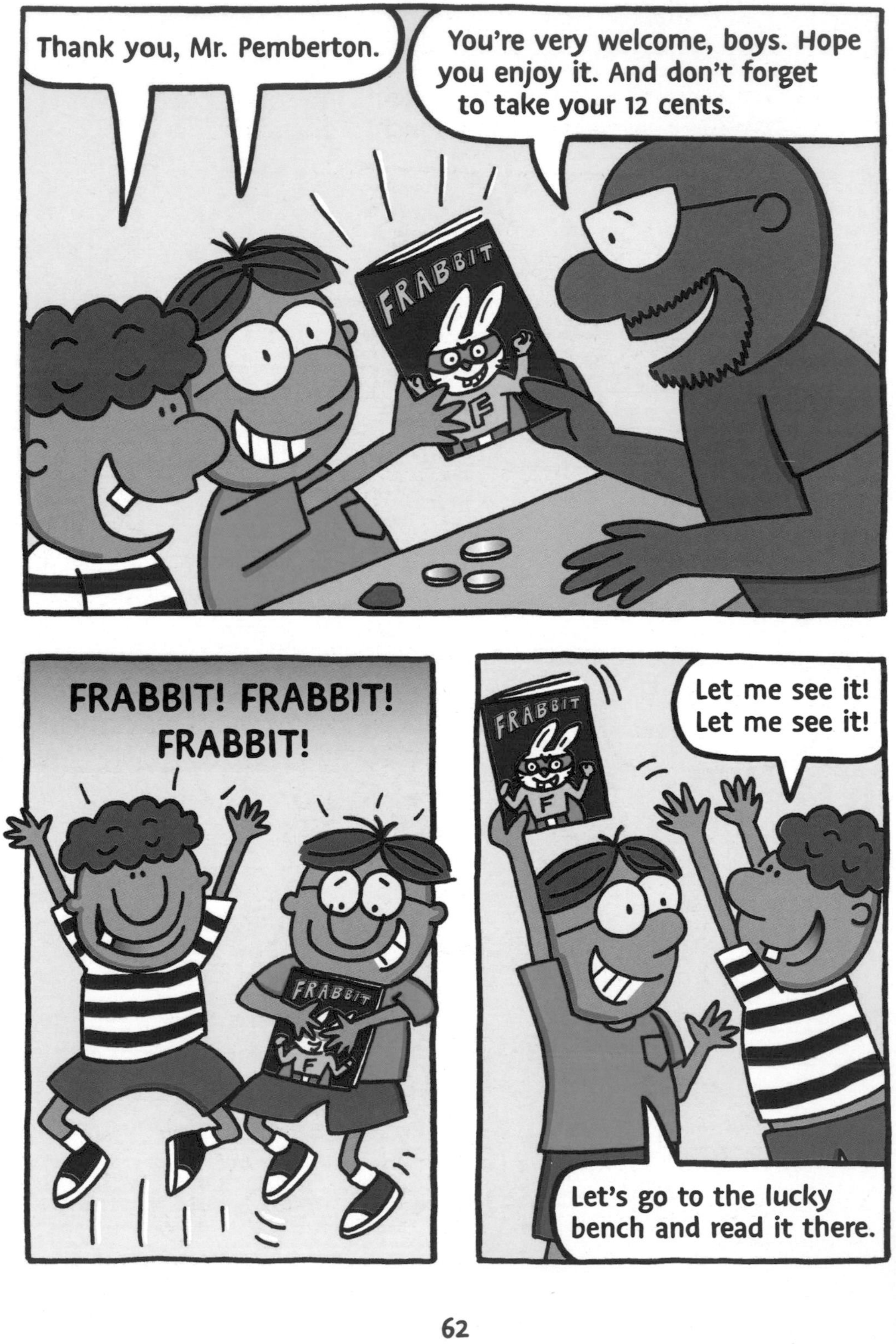
Thank you, Mr. Pemberton.
You're very welcome, boys. Hope you enjoy it. And don't forget to take your 12 cents.
FRABBIT
FRABBIT! FRABBIT! FRABBIT!
Let me see it! Let me see it!
Let's go to the lucky bench and read it there.

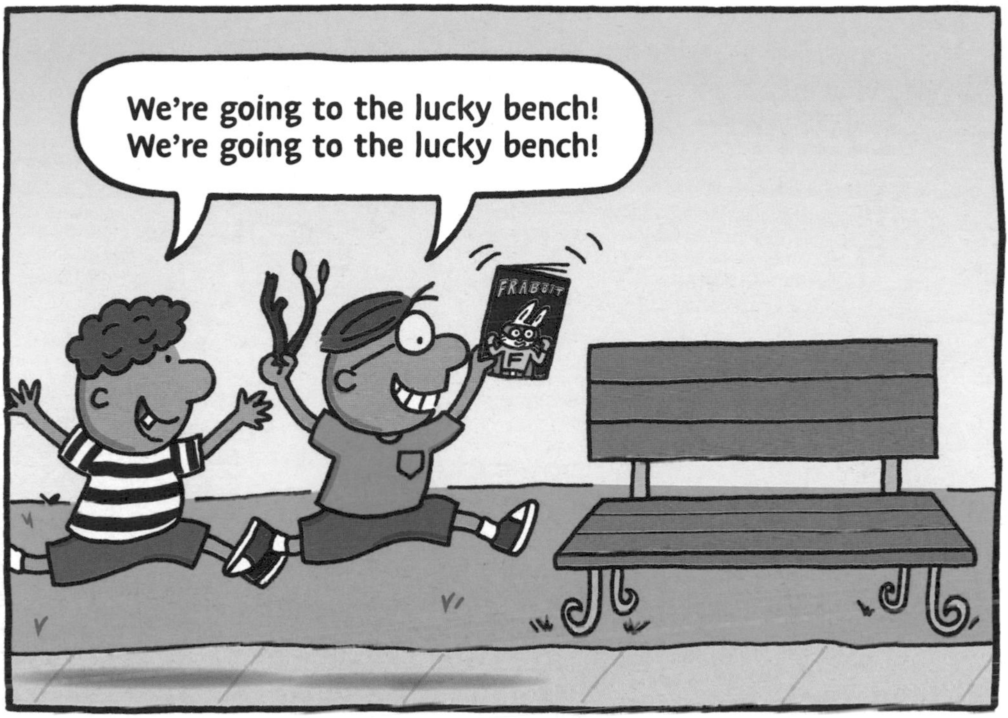
We're going to the lucky bench!
We're going to the lucky bench!
FRABBIT

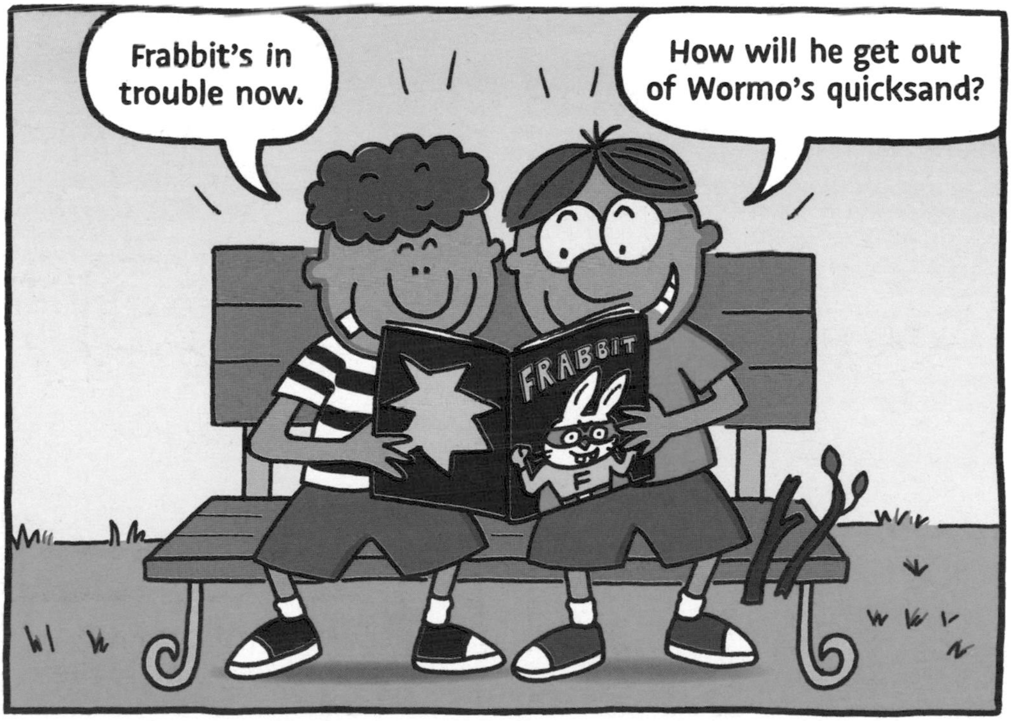
Frabbit's in trouble now.
How will he get out of Wormo's quicksand?
FRABBIT

# CHAPTER 8 - HAROLD THE BULLY!

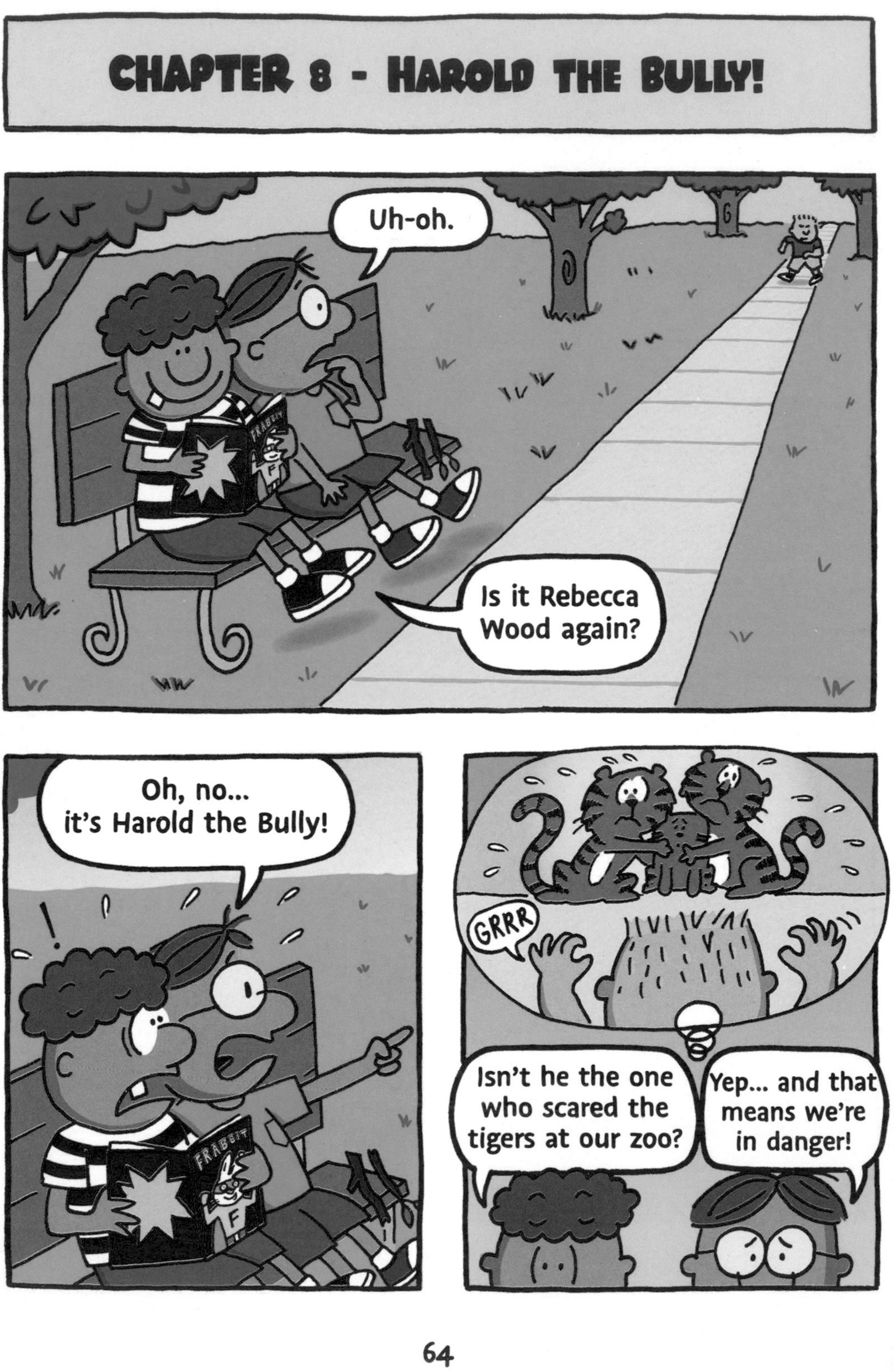
Uh-oh.
Is it Rebecca Wood again?
Oh, no... it's Harold the Bully!
GRRR
Isn't he the one who scared the tigers at our zoo?
Yep... and that means we're in danger!

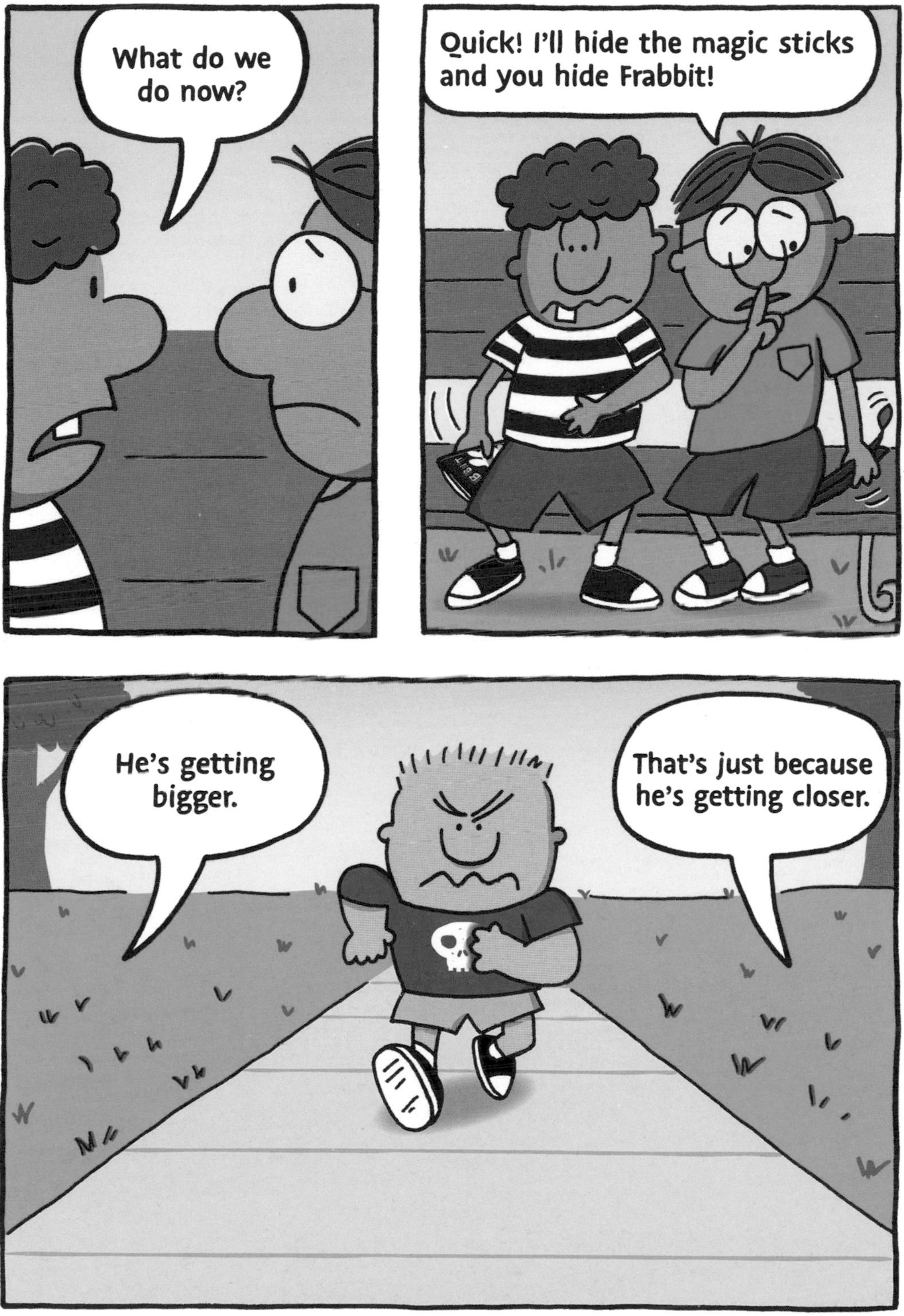
What do we do now?
Quick! I'll hide the magic sticks and you hide Frabbit!
He's getting bigger.
That's just because he's getting closer.

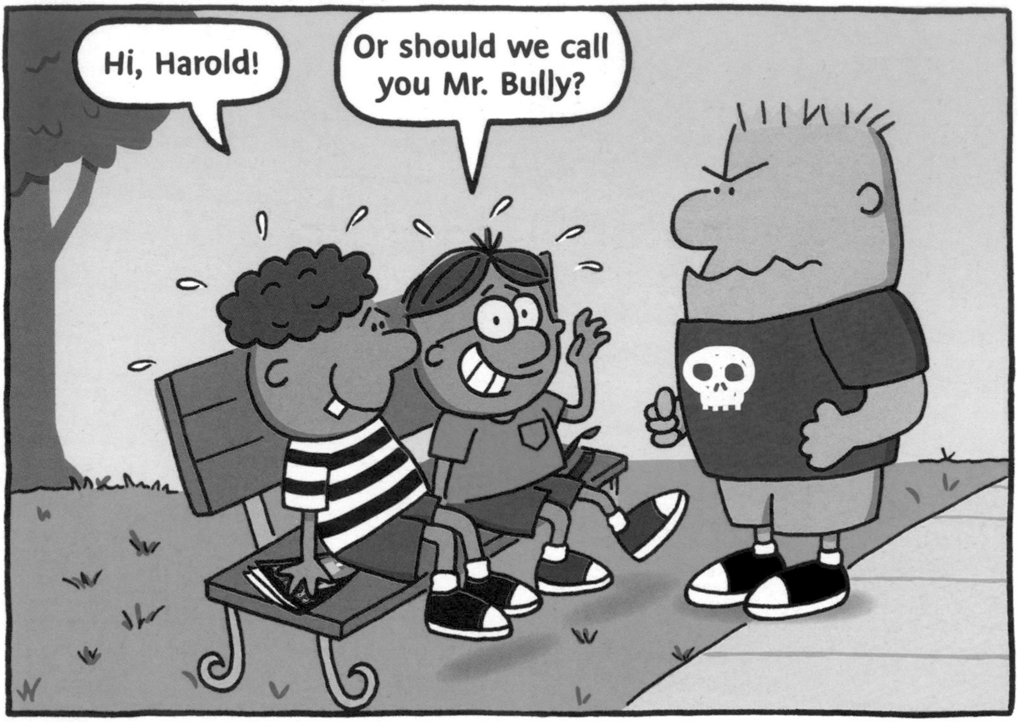
Hi, Harold!
Or should we call you Mr. Bully?

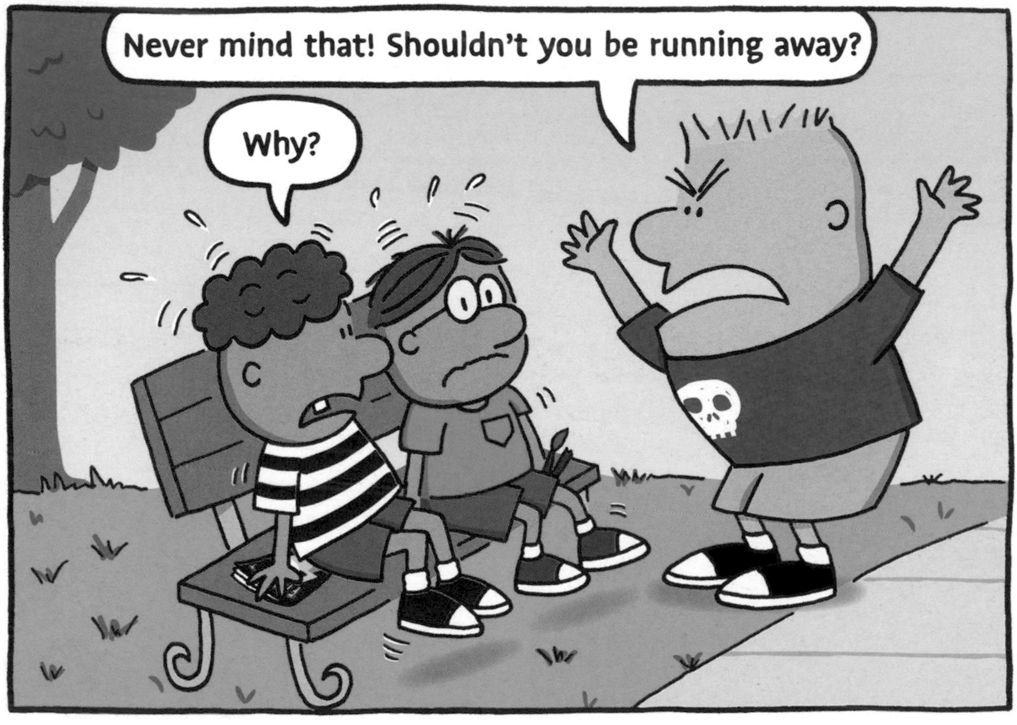
Never mind that! Shouldn't you be running away?
Why?

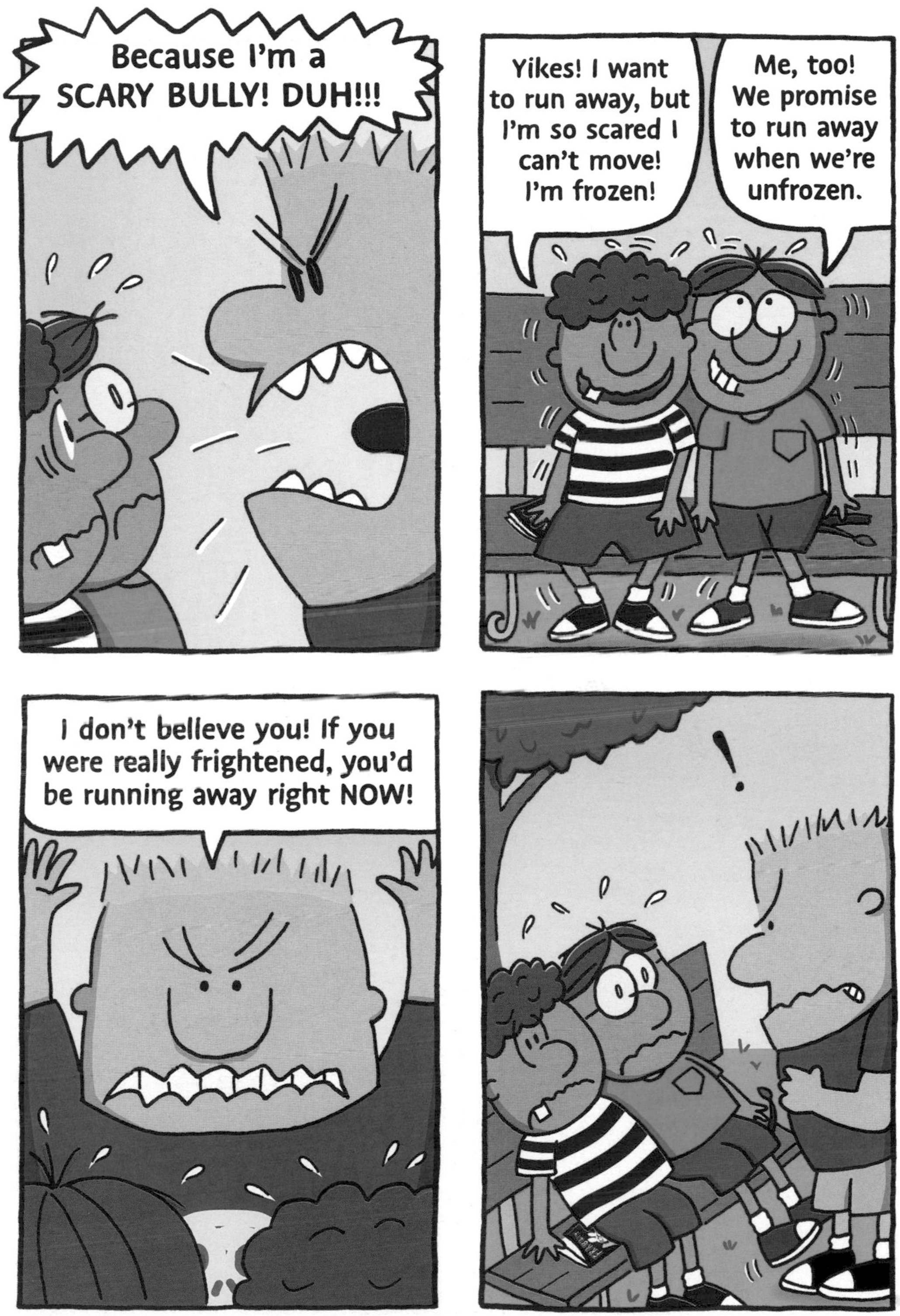
Because I'm a SCARY BULLY! DUH!!!
Yikes! I want to run away, but I'm so scared I can't move! I'm frozen!
Me, too! We promise to run away when we're unfrozen.
I don't believe you! If you were really frightened, you'd be running away right NOW!
!

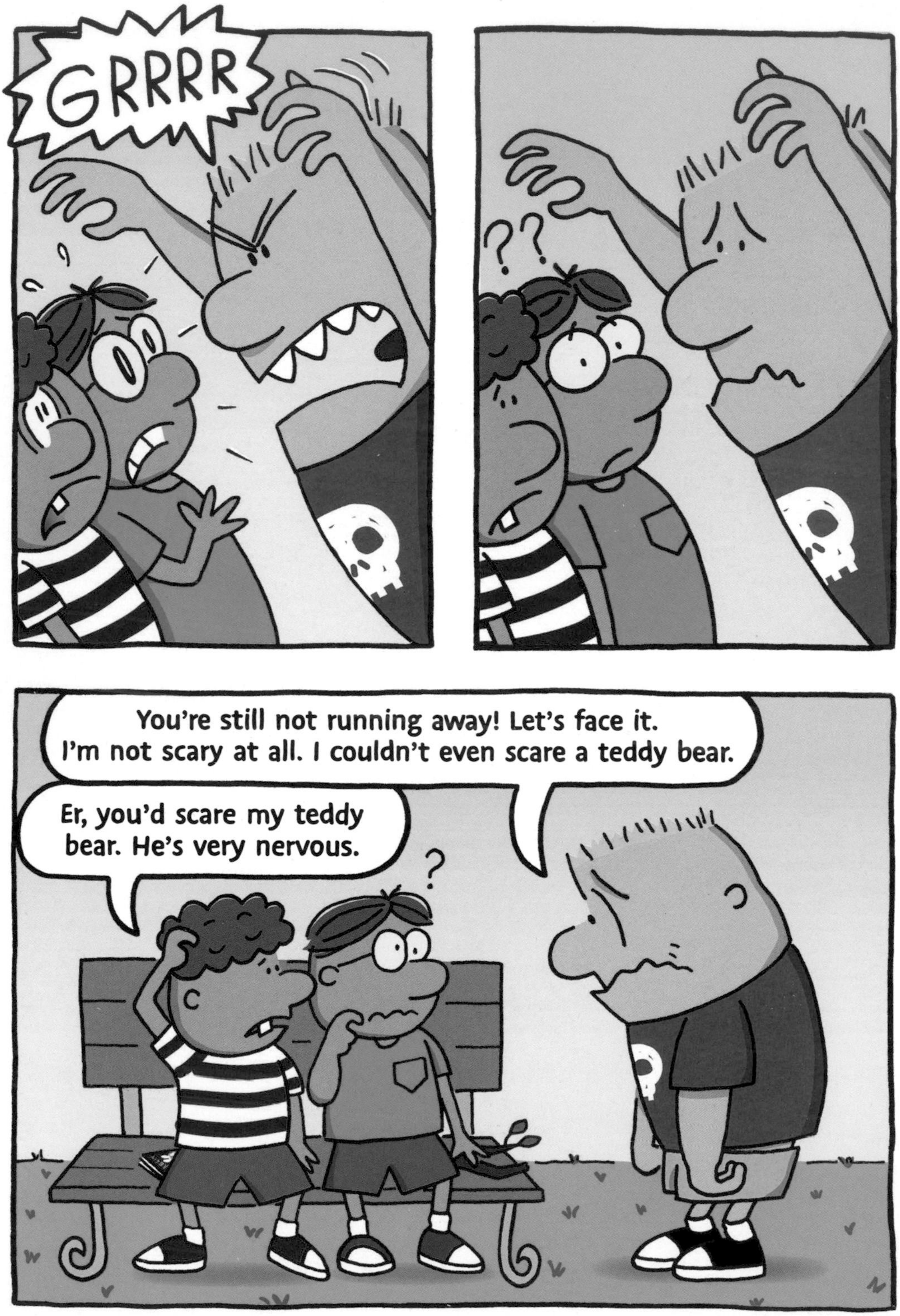
GRRRR
??
?
You're still not running away! Let's face it.
I'm not scary at all. I couldn't even scare a teddy bear.
Er, you'd scare my teddy
bear. He's very nervous.

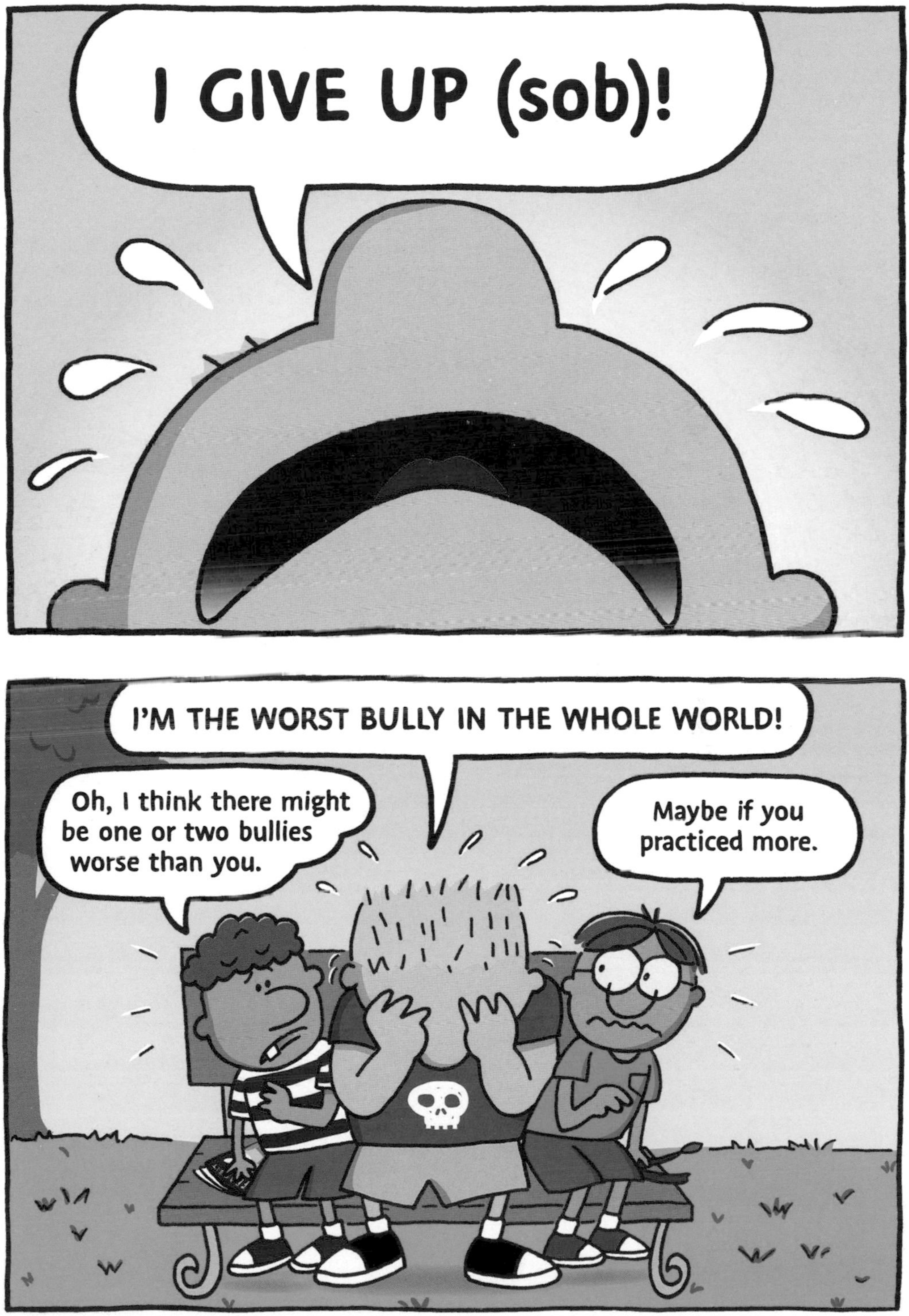
I GIVE UP (sob)!
I'M THE WORST BULLY IN THE WHOLE WORLD!
Oh, I think there might be one or two bullies worse than you.
Maybe if you practiced more.

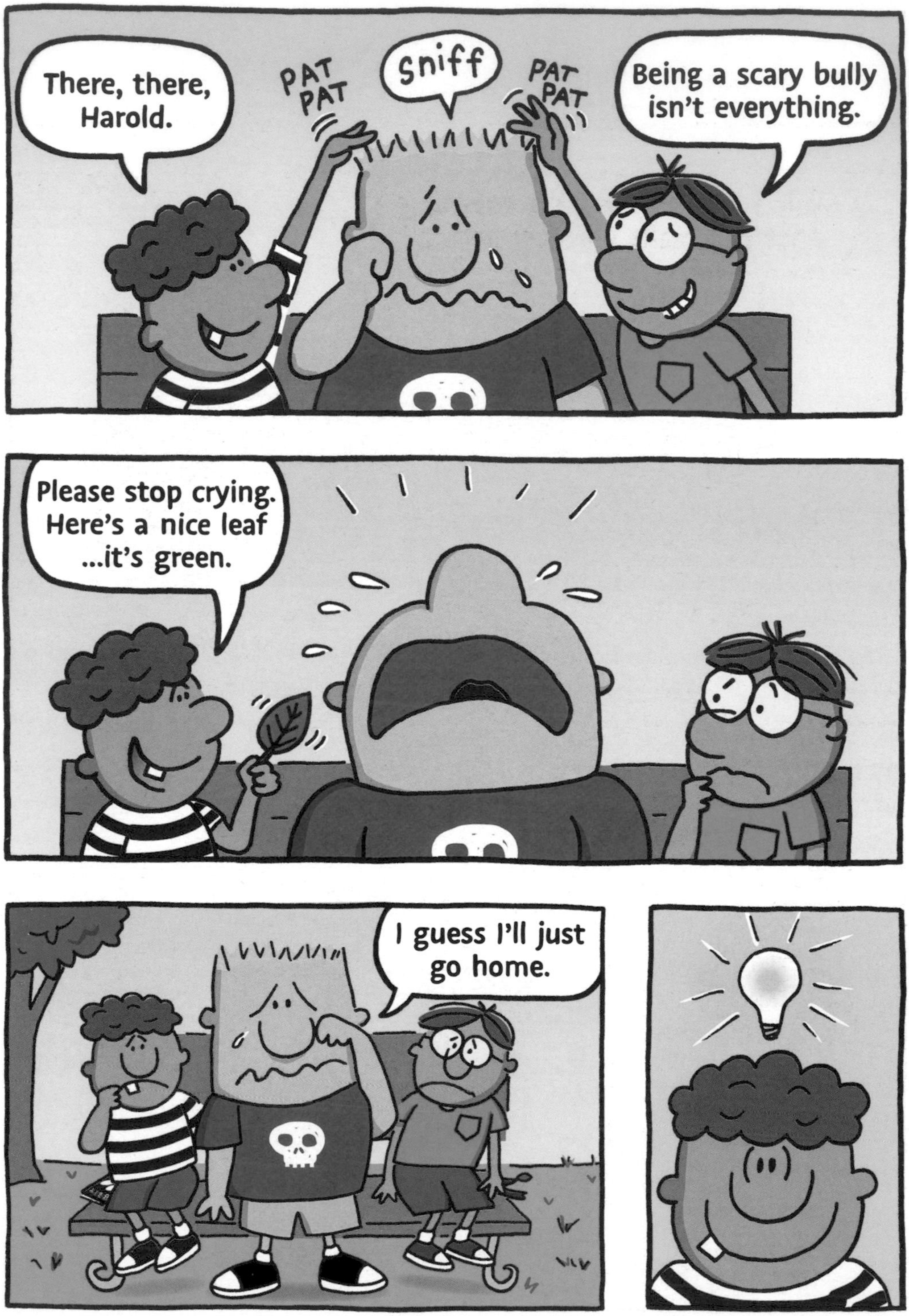
There, there, Harold.
PAT PAT
Sniff
PAT PAT
Being a scary bully isn't everything.
Please stop crying. Here's a nice leaf ...it's green.
I guess I'll just go home.

# CHAPTER 9 - GOODBYE FRABBIT!

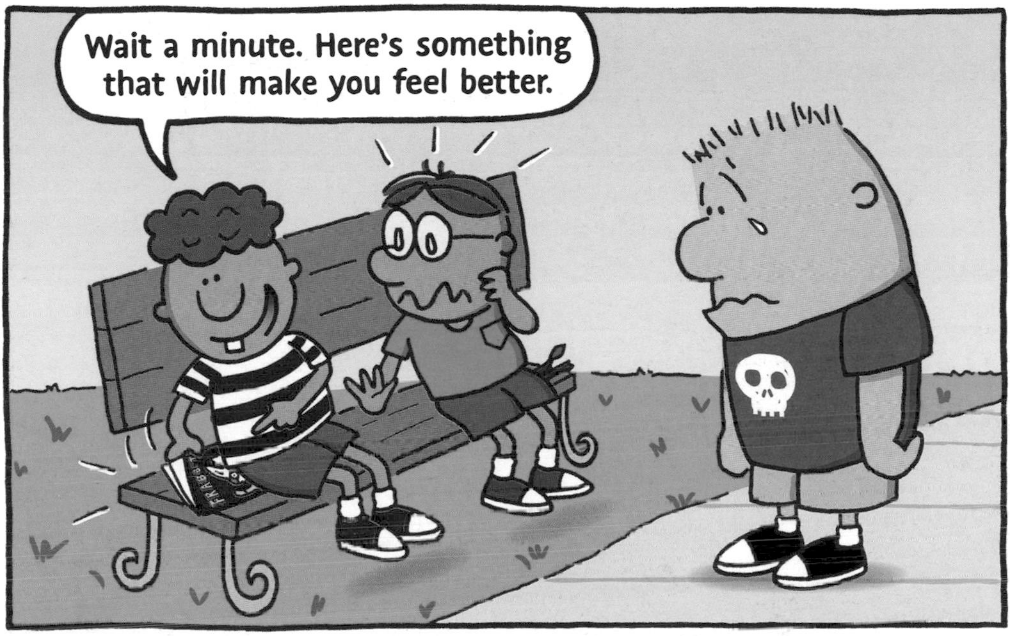
Wait a minute. Here's something that will make you feel better.
FRABBIT

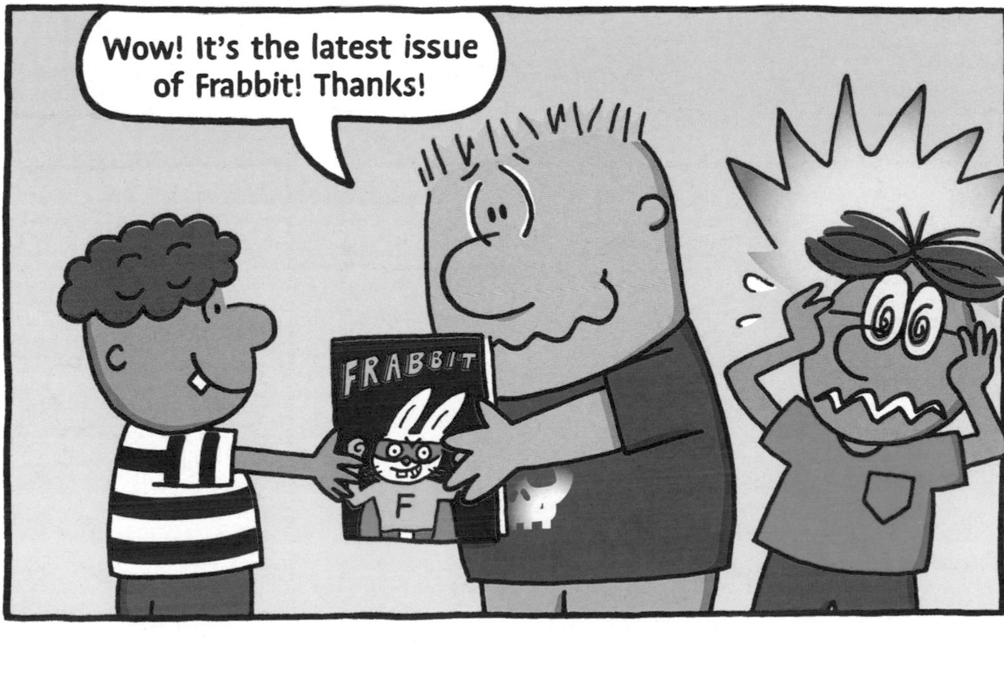
Wow! It's the latest issue of Frabbit! Thanks!
FRABBIT

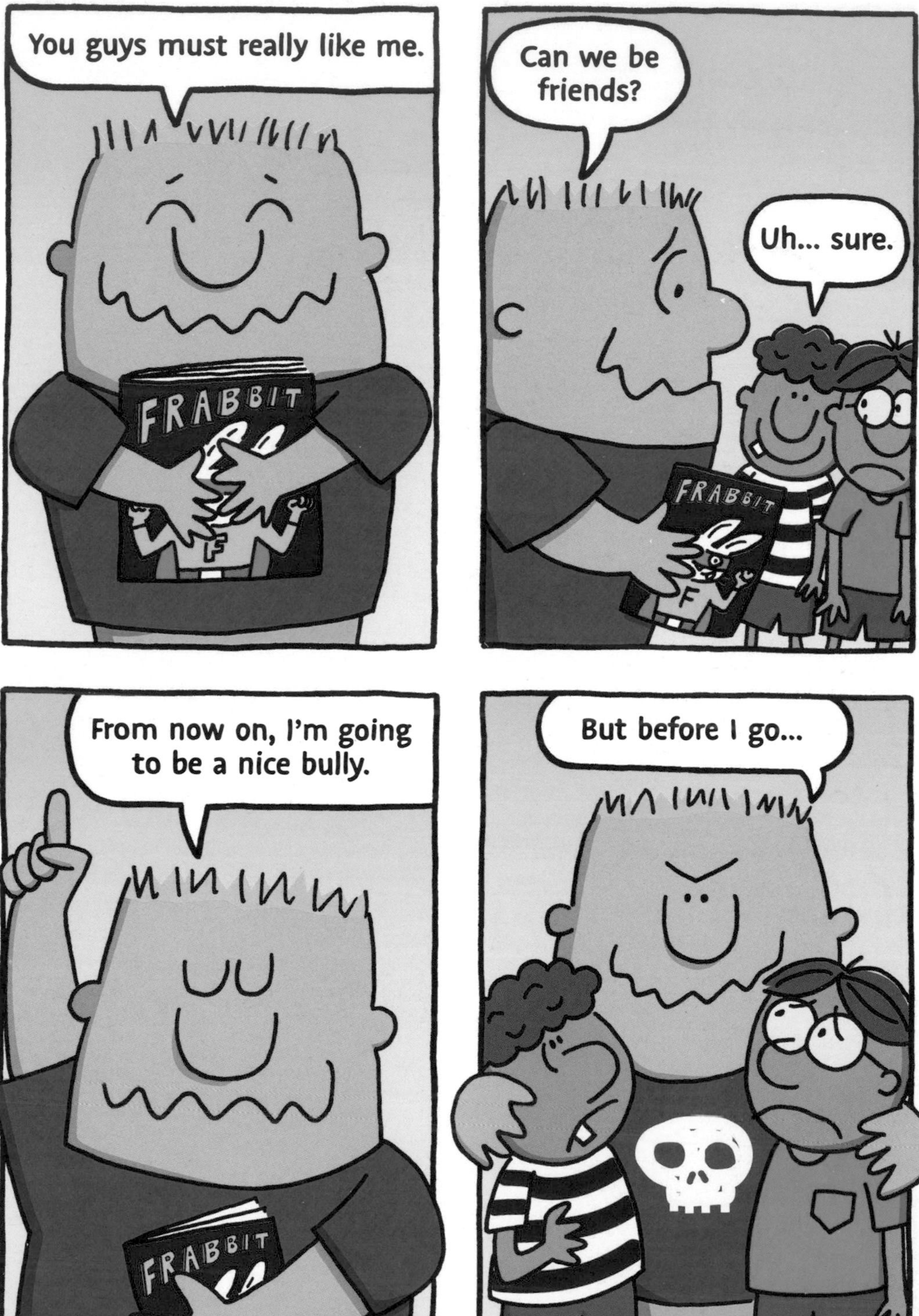
You guys must really like me.
FRABBIT
Can we be friends?
Uh... sure.
FRABBIT
From now on, I'm going to be a nice bully.
FRABBIT
But before I go...

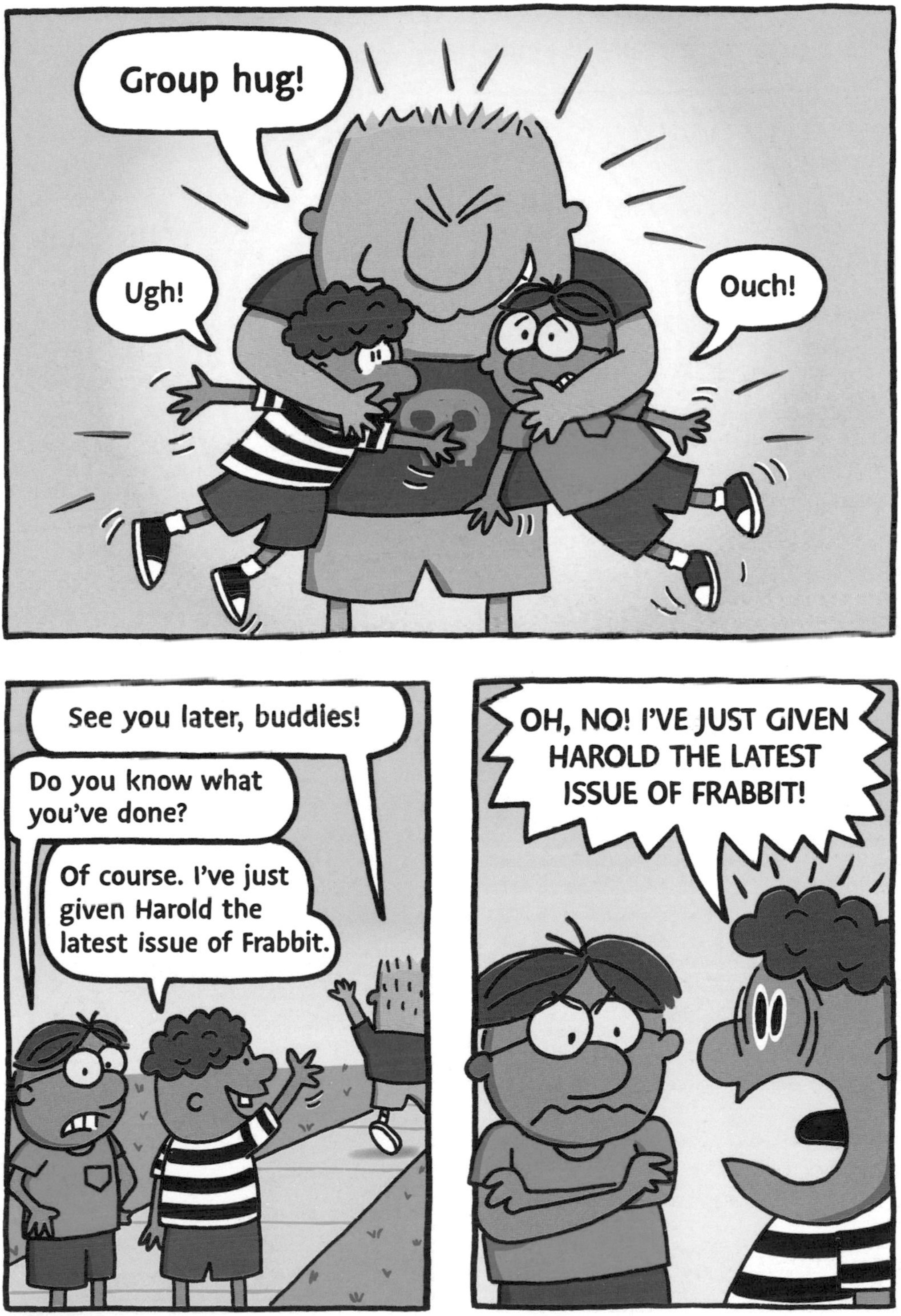
Group hug!
Ugh!
Ouch!
See you later, buddies!
Do you know what you've done?
Of course. I've just given Harold the latest issue of Frabbit.
OH, NO! I'VE JUST GIVEN HAROLD THE LATEST ISSUE OF FRABBIT!

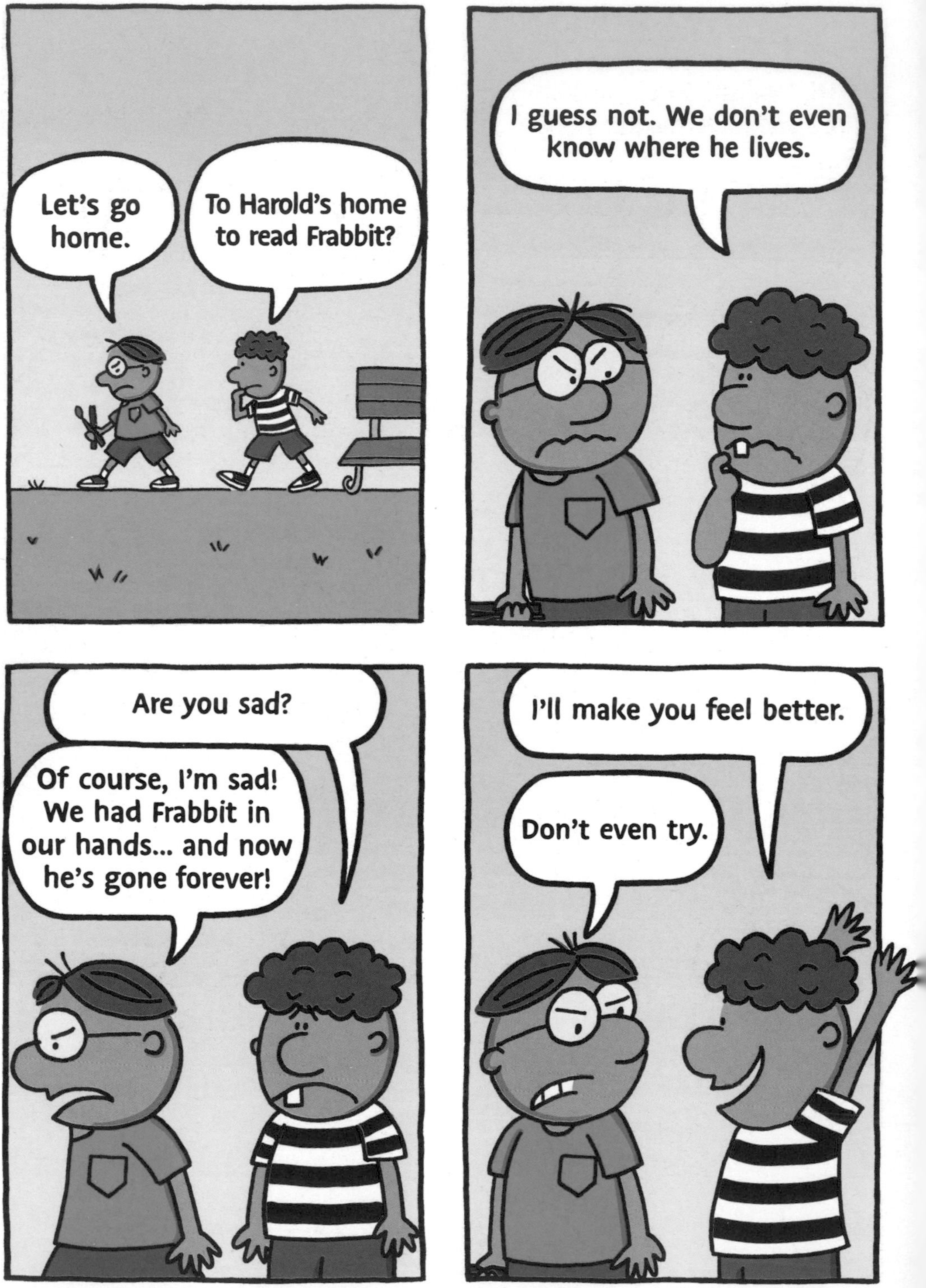
Let's go home.
To Harold's home to read Frabbit?
I guess not. We don't even know where he lives.
Are you sad?
Of course, I'm sad! We had Frabbit in our hands... and now he's gone forever!
I'll make you feel better.
Don't even try.

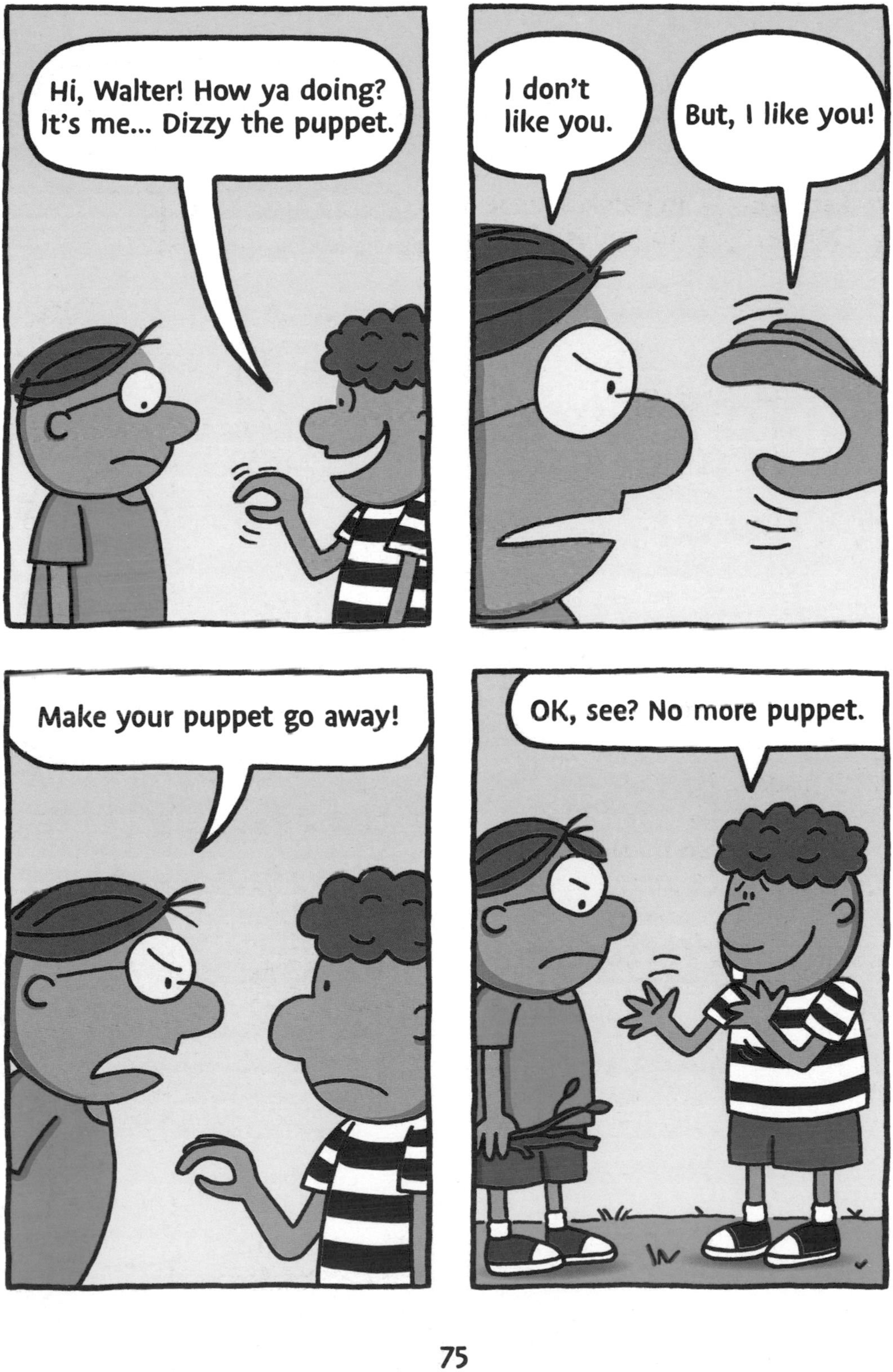
Hi, Walter! How ya doing? It's me... Dizzy the puppet.
I don't like you.
But, I like you!
Make your puppet go away!
OK, see? No more puppet.

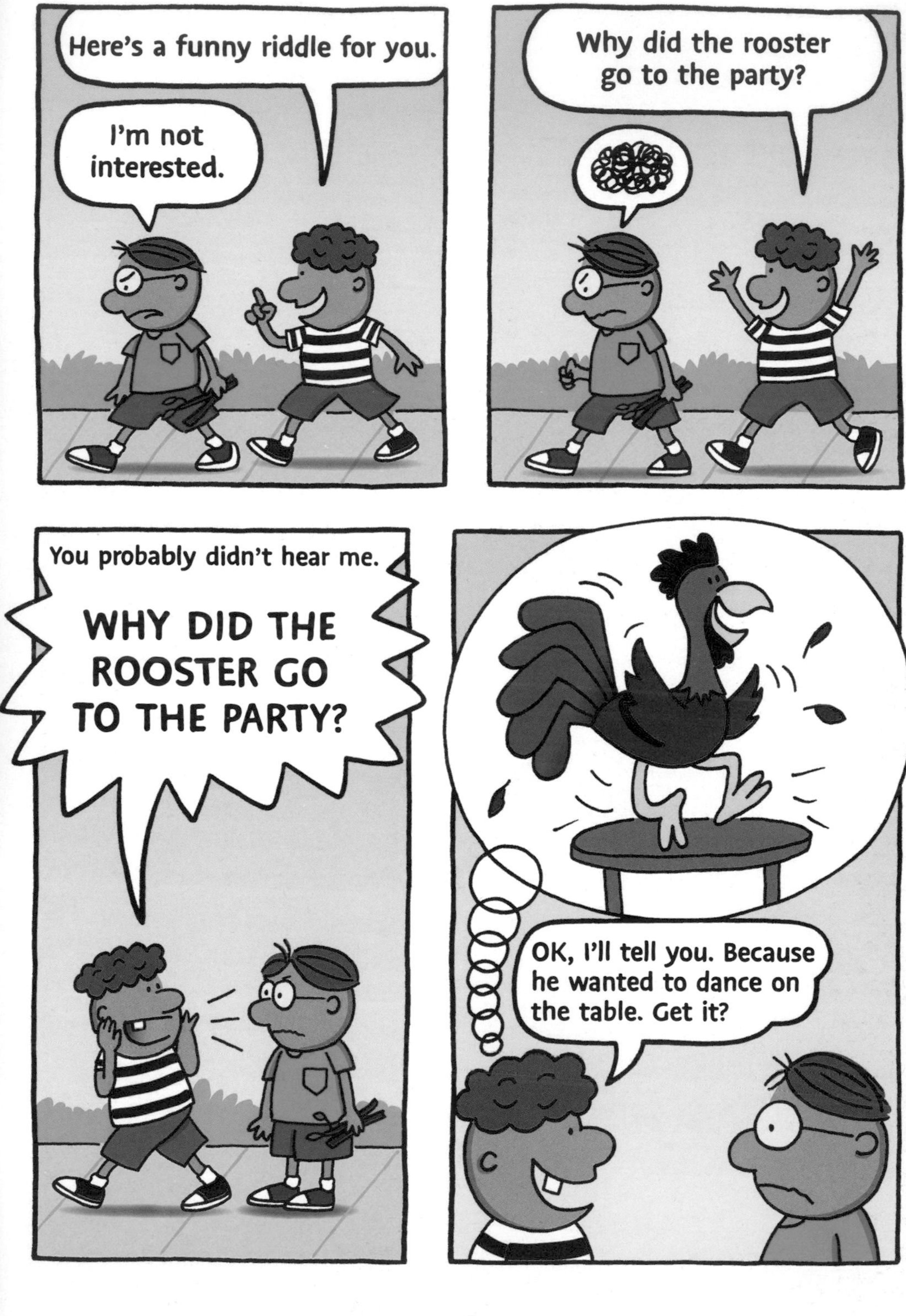
Here's a funny riddle for you.
I'm not interested.
Why did the rooster go to the party?
You probably didn't hear me.
WHY DID THE ROOSTER GO TO THE PARTY?
OK, I'll tell you. Because he wanted to dance on the table. Get it?

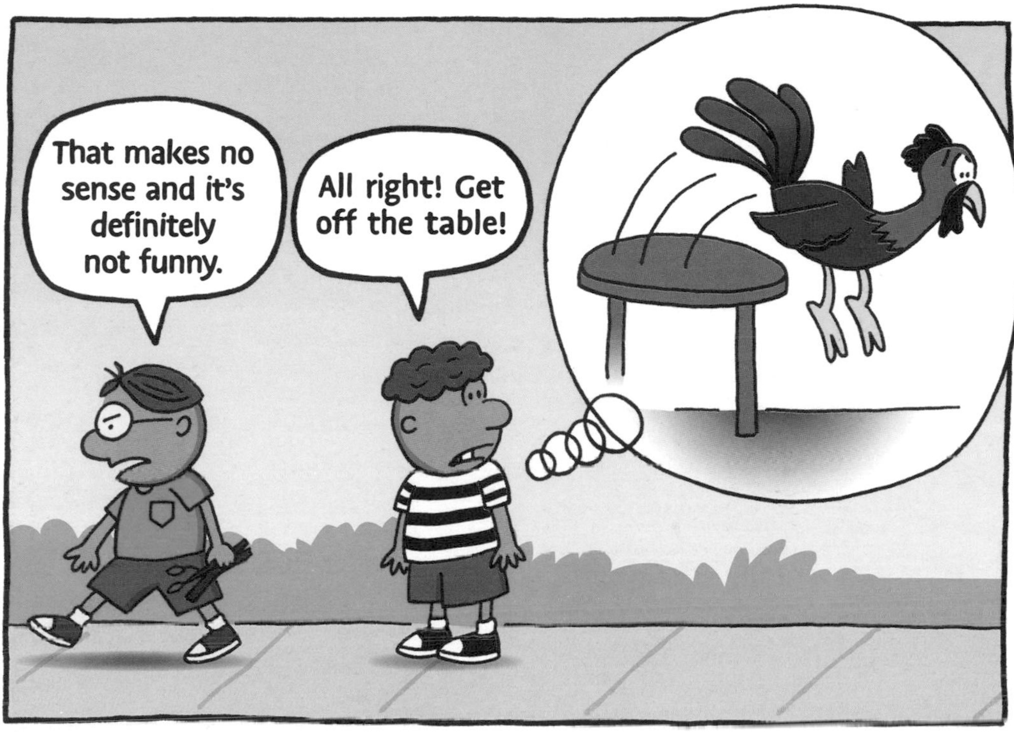
That makes no sense and it's definitely not funny.
All right! Get off the table!

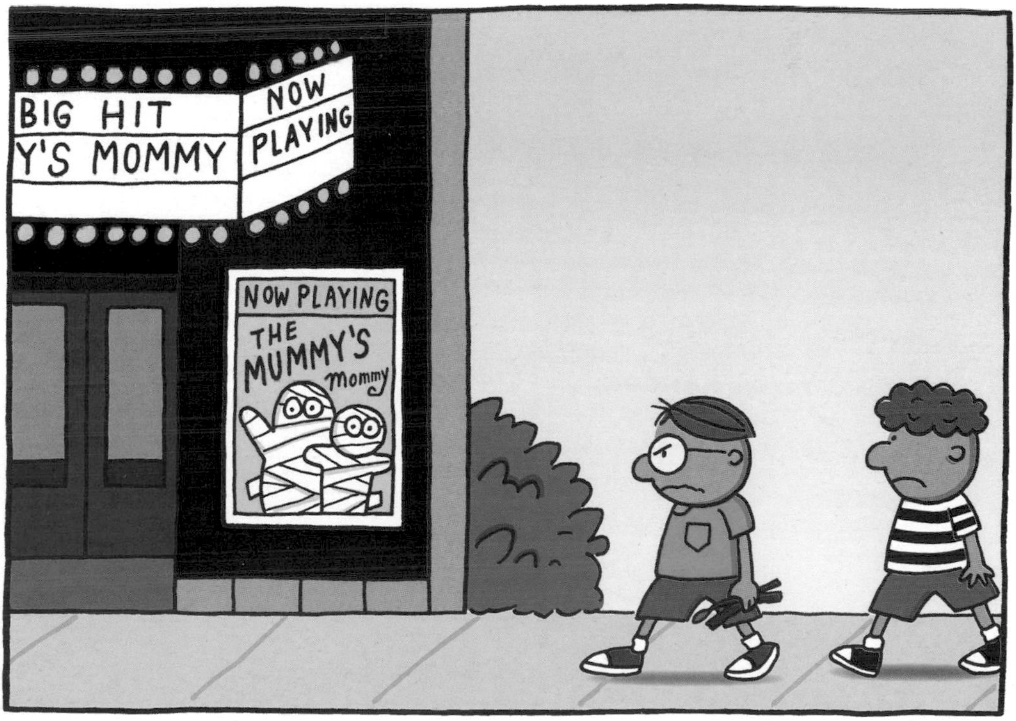
BIG HIT
Y'S MOMMY
NOW PLAYING
NOW PLAYING
THE MUMMY'S mommy

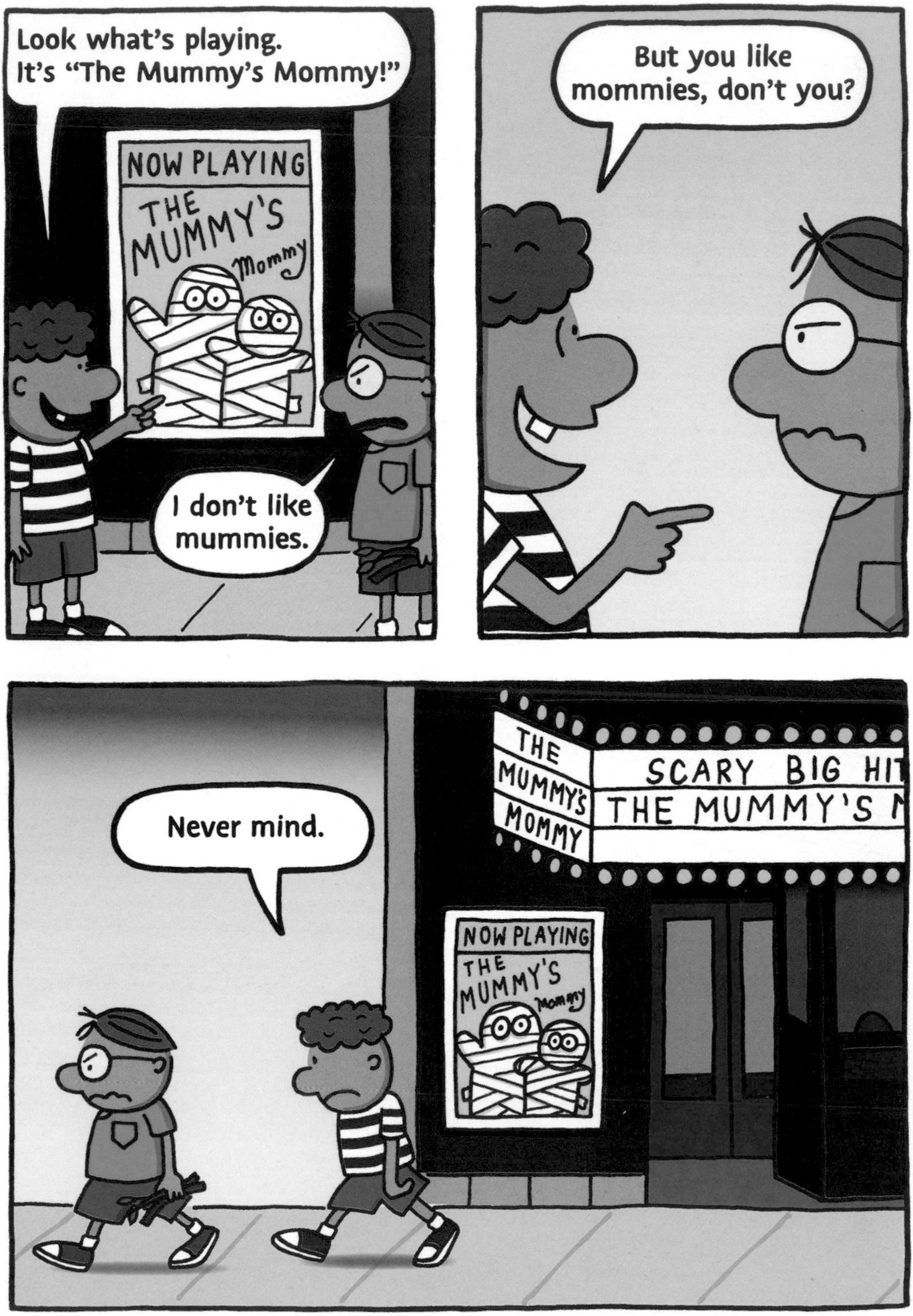
Look what's playing. It's "The Mummy's Mommy!"
NOW PLAYING
THE MUMMY'S Mommy
I don't like mummies.
But you like mommies, don't you?
THE MUMMY'S MOMMY
SCARY BIG HIT
Never mind.
NOW PLAYING
THE MUMMY'S Mommy

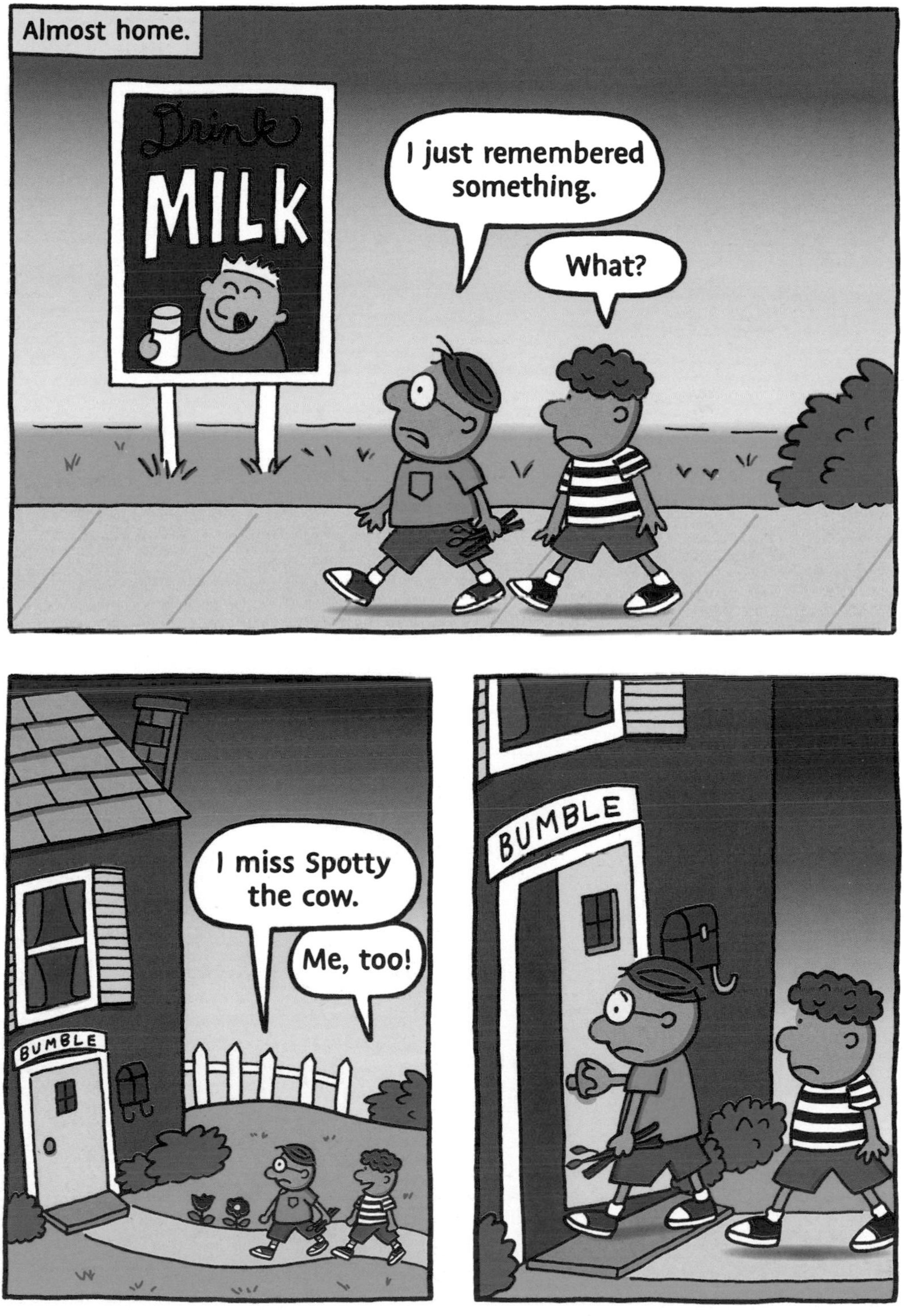
Almost home.
Drink
MILK
I just remembered something.
What?
BUMBLE
I miss Spotty the cow.
Me, too!
BUMBLE

# CHAPTER 10 - HOME AGAIN!

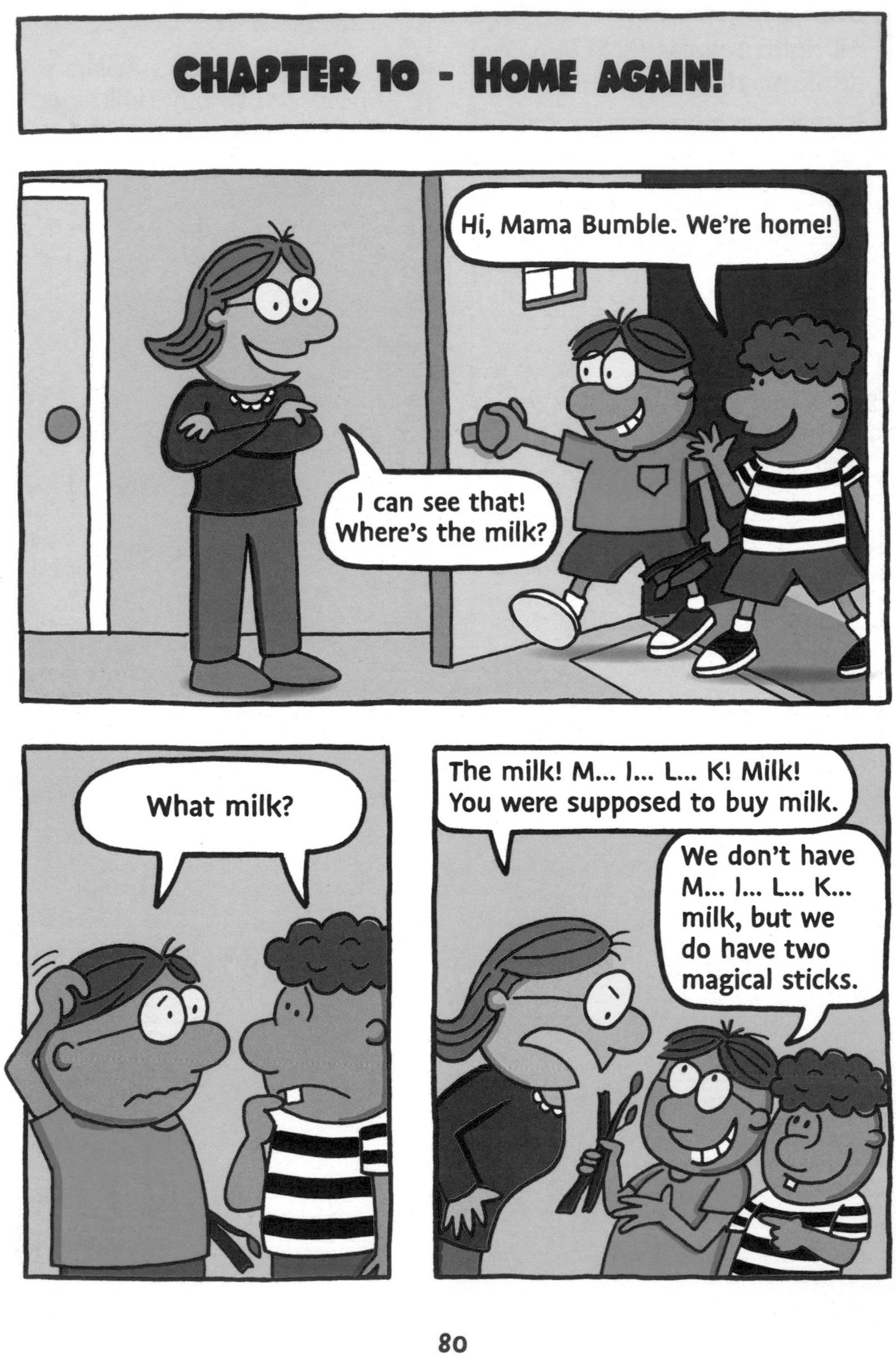

Hi, Mama Bumble. We're home!
I can see that! Where's the milk?
What milk?
The milk! M... I... L... K! Milk! You were supposed to buy milk.
We don't have M... I... L... K... milk, but we do have two magical sticks.

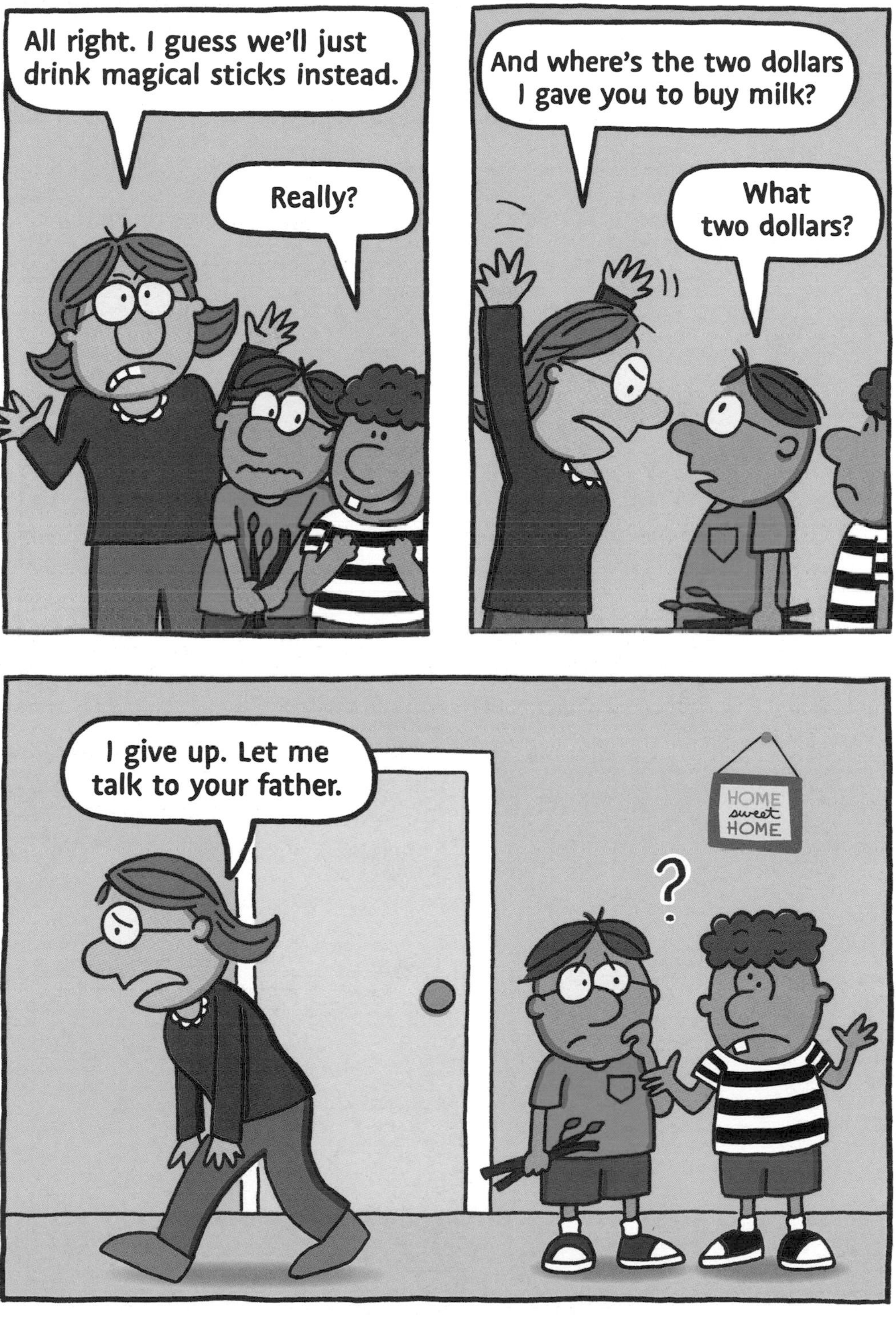
All right. I guess we'll just drink magical sticks instead.
Really?
And where's the two dollars I gave you to buy milk?
What two dollars?
I give up. Let me talk to your father.
HOME sweet HOME
?

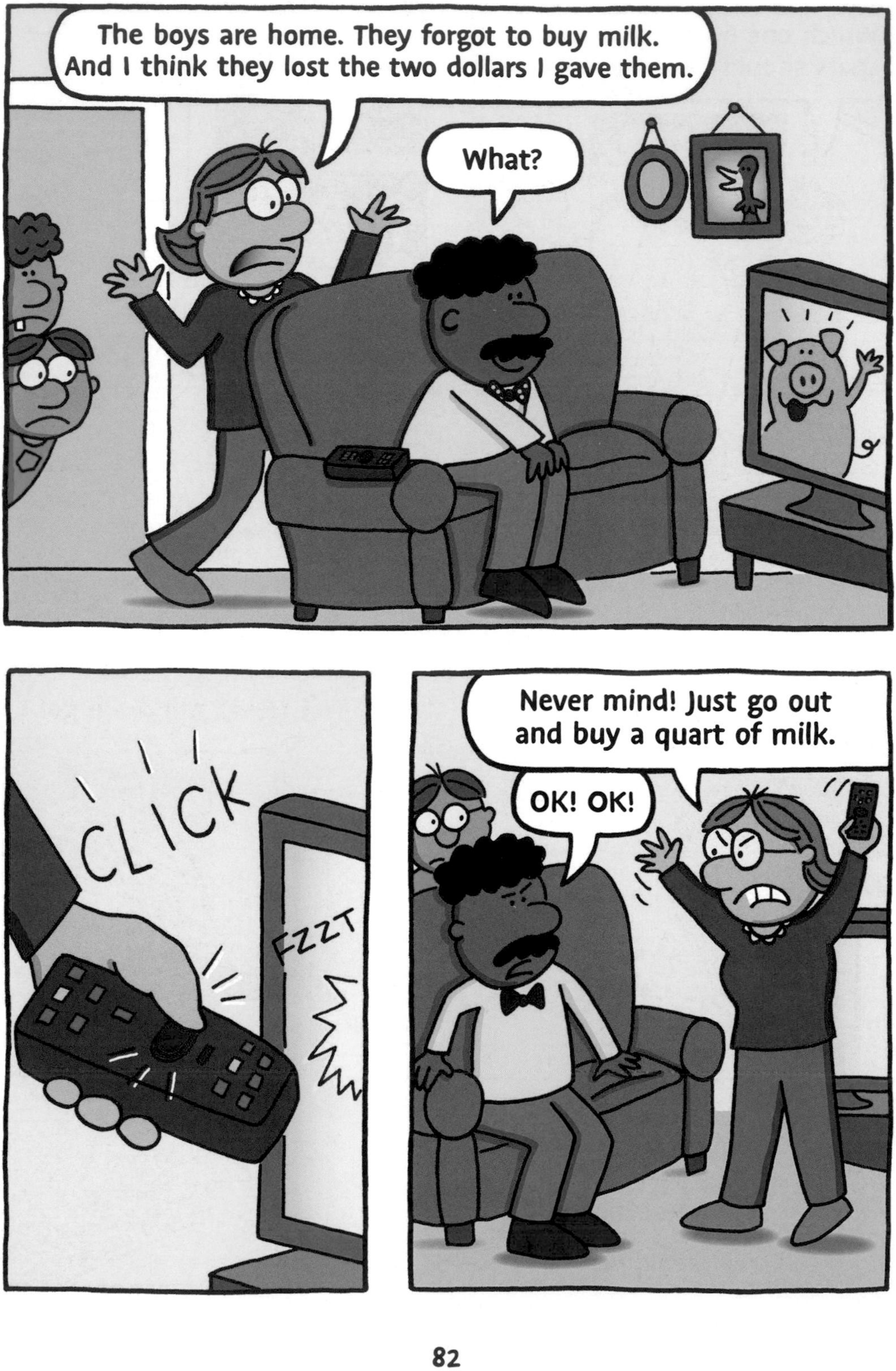
The boys are home. They forgot to buy milk. And I think they lost the two dollars I gave them.
What?
CLICK
FZZT
Never mind! Just go out and buy a quart of milk.
OK! OK!

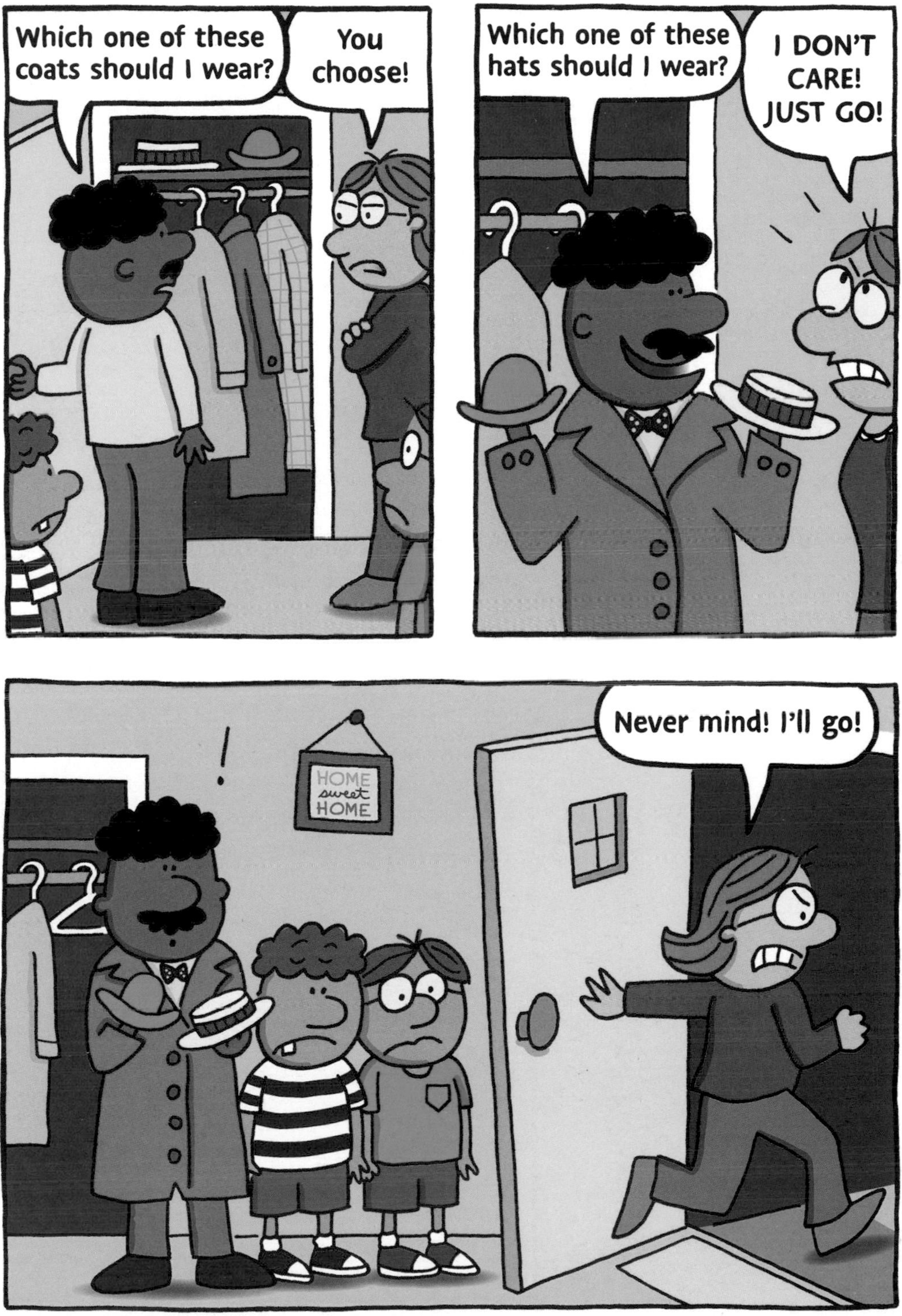
Which one of these coats should I wear?
You choose!
Which one of these hats should I wear?
I DON'T CARE! JUST GO!
!
HOME sweet HOME
Never mind! I'll go!

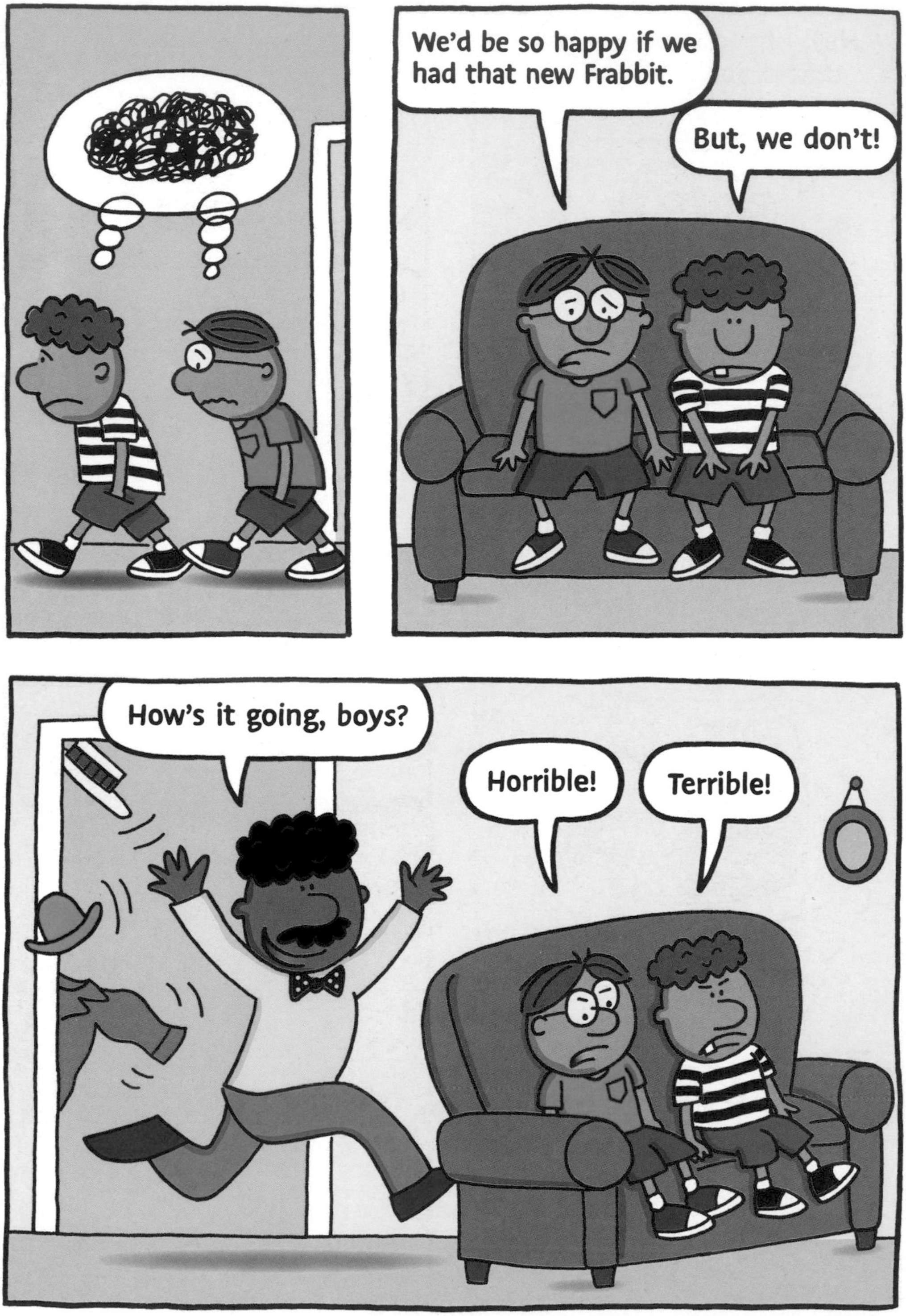

We'd be so happy if we had that new Frabbit.
But, we don't!
How's it going, boys?
Horrible!
Terrible!

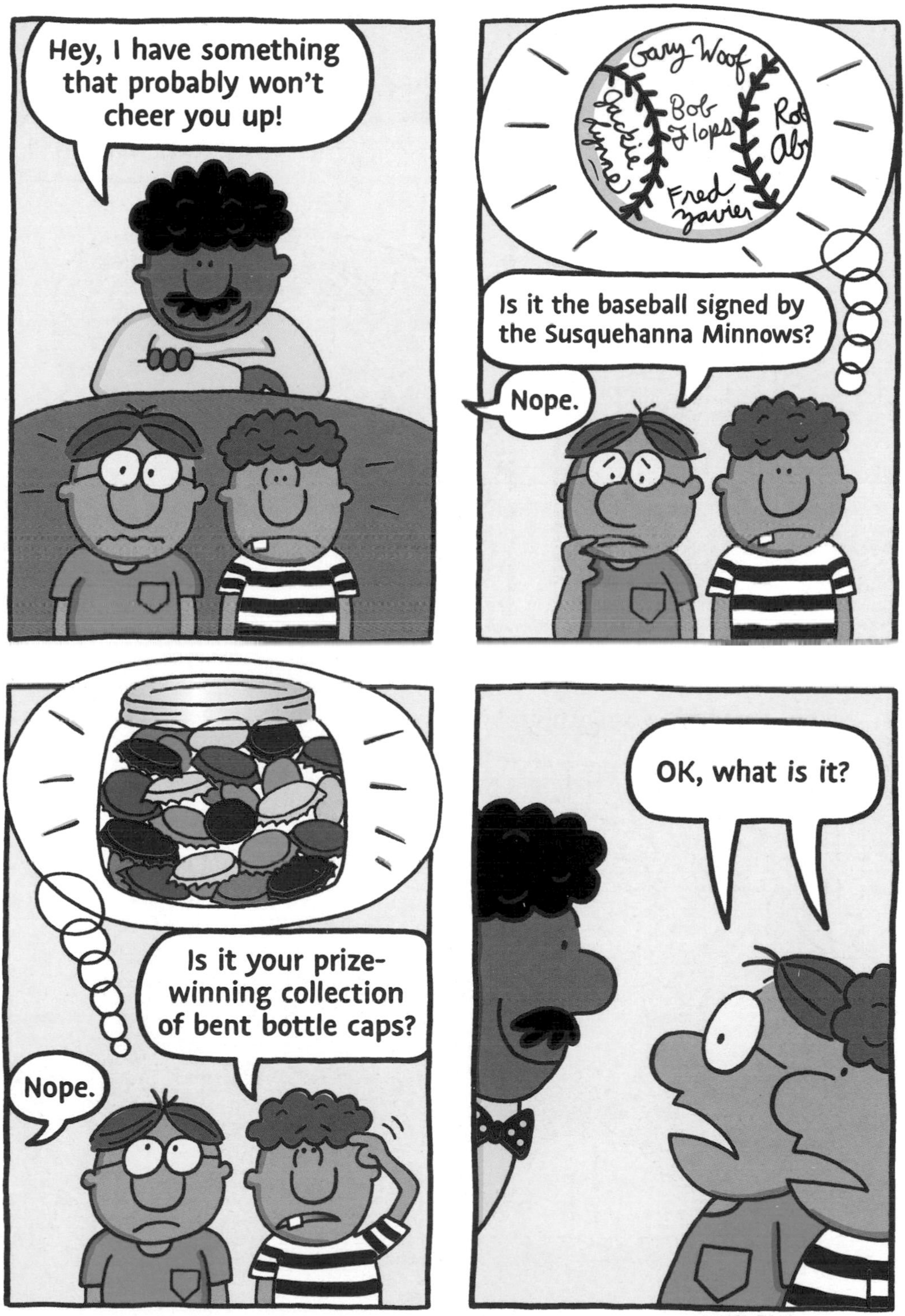
Hey, I have something that probably won't cheer you up!
Gary Woof
Bob Flops
Fred zavier
Is it the baseball signed by the Susquehanna Minnows?
Nope.
Is it your prize-winning collection of bent bottle caps?
Nope.
OK, what is it?

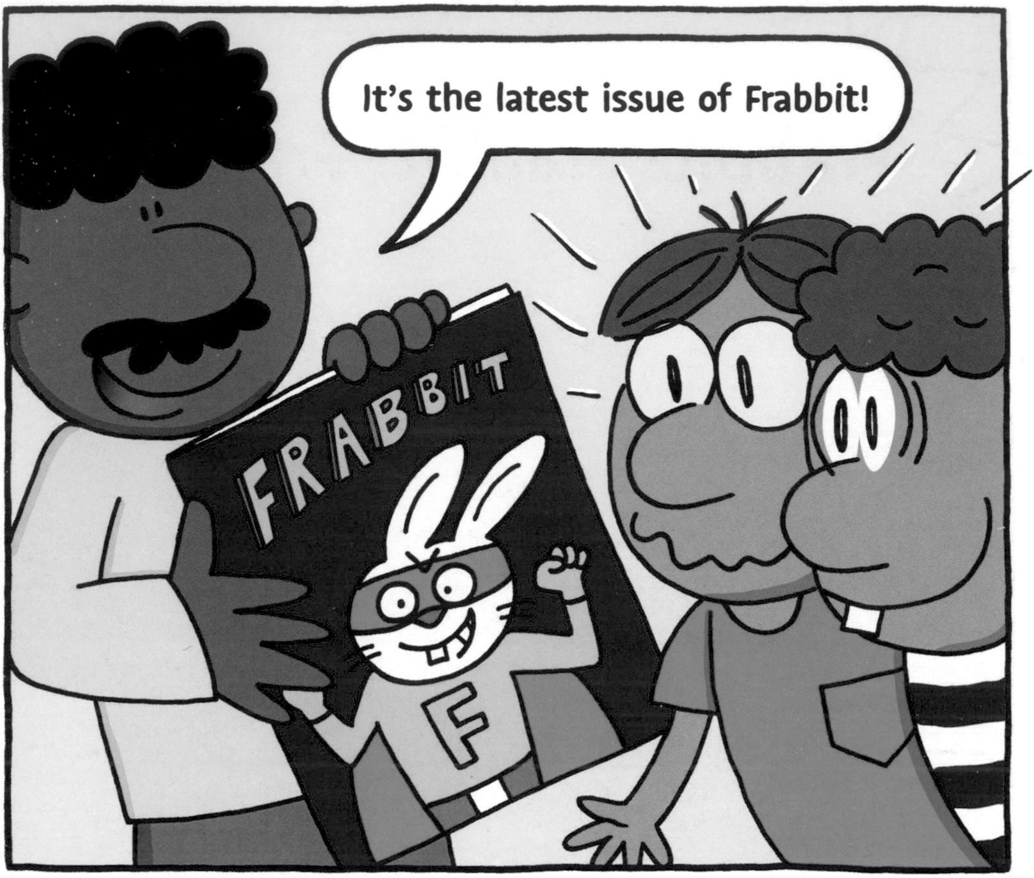
It's the latest issue of Frabbit!
FRABBIT
F

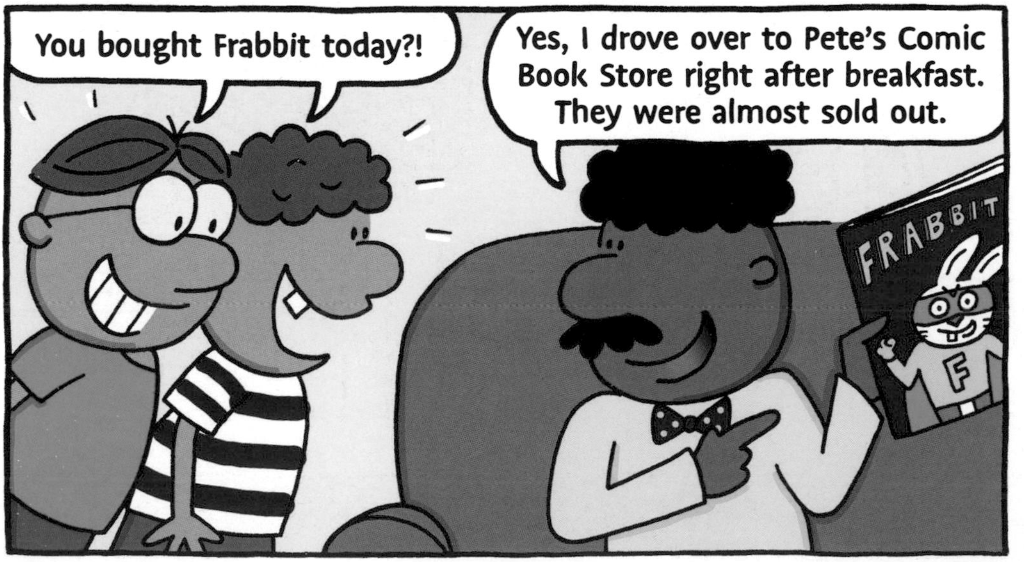
You bought Frabbit today?!
Yes, I drove over to Pete's Comic Book Store right after breakfast. They were almost sold out.
FRABBIT
F

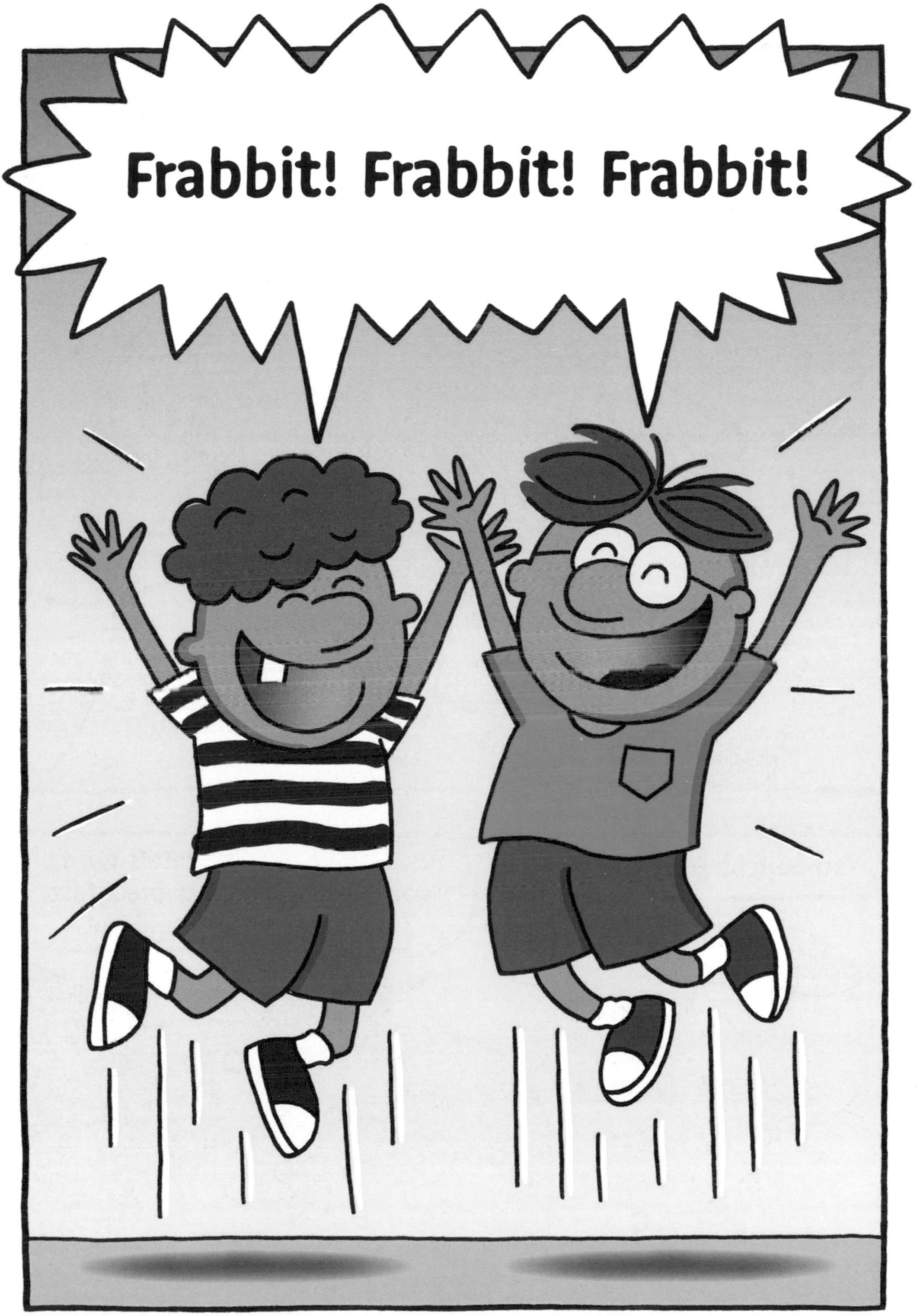
Frabbit! Frabbit! Frabbit!

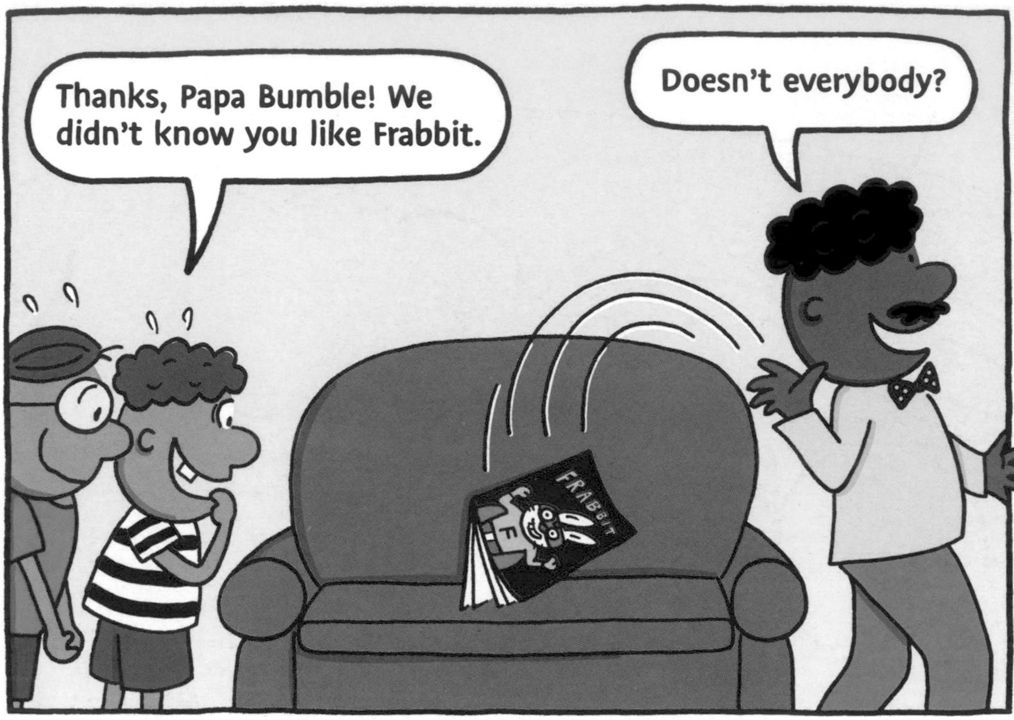
Thanks, Papa Bumble! We didn't know you like Frabbit.
Doesn't everybody?
FRABBIT

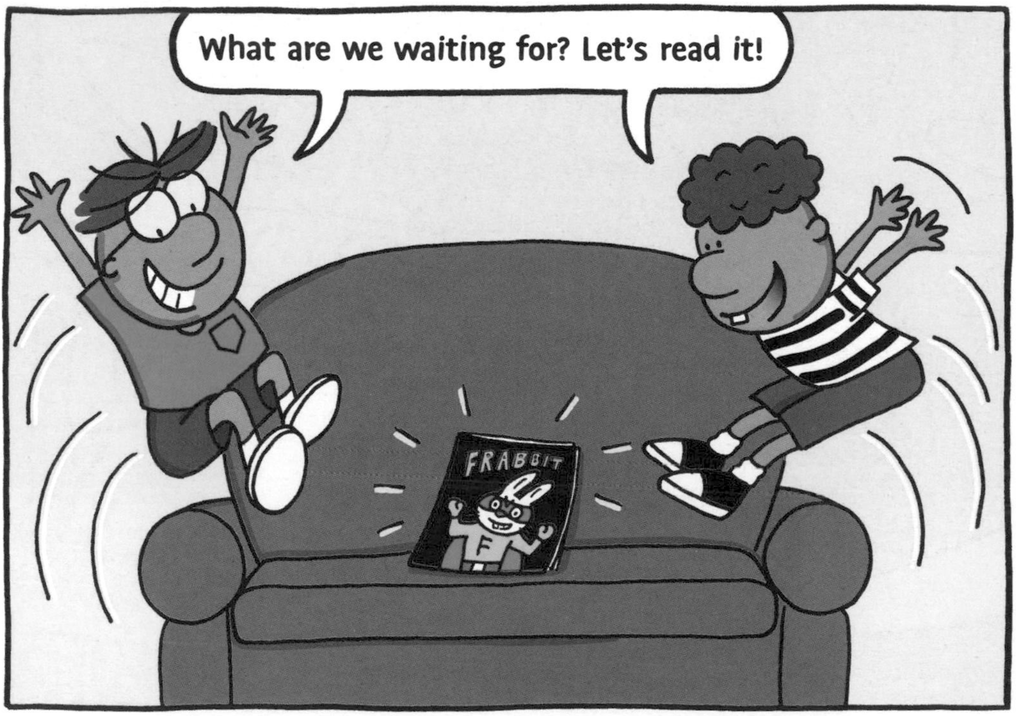
What are we waiting for? Let's read it!
FRABBIT

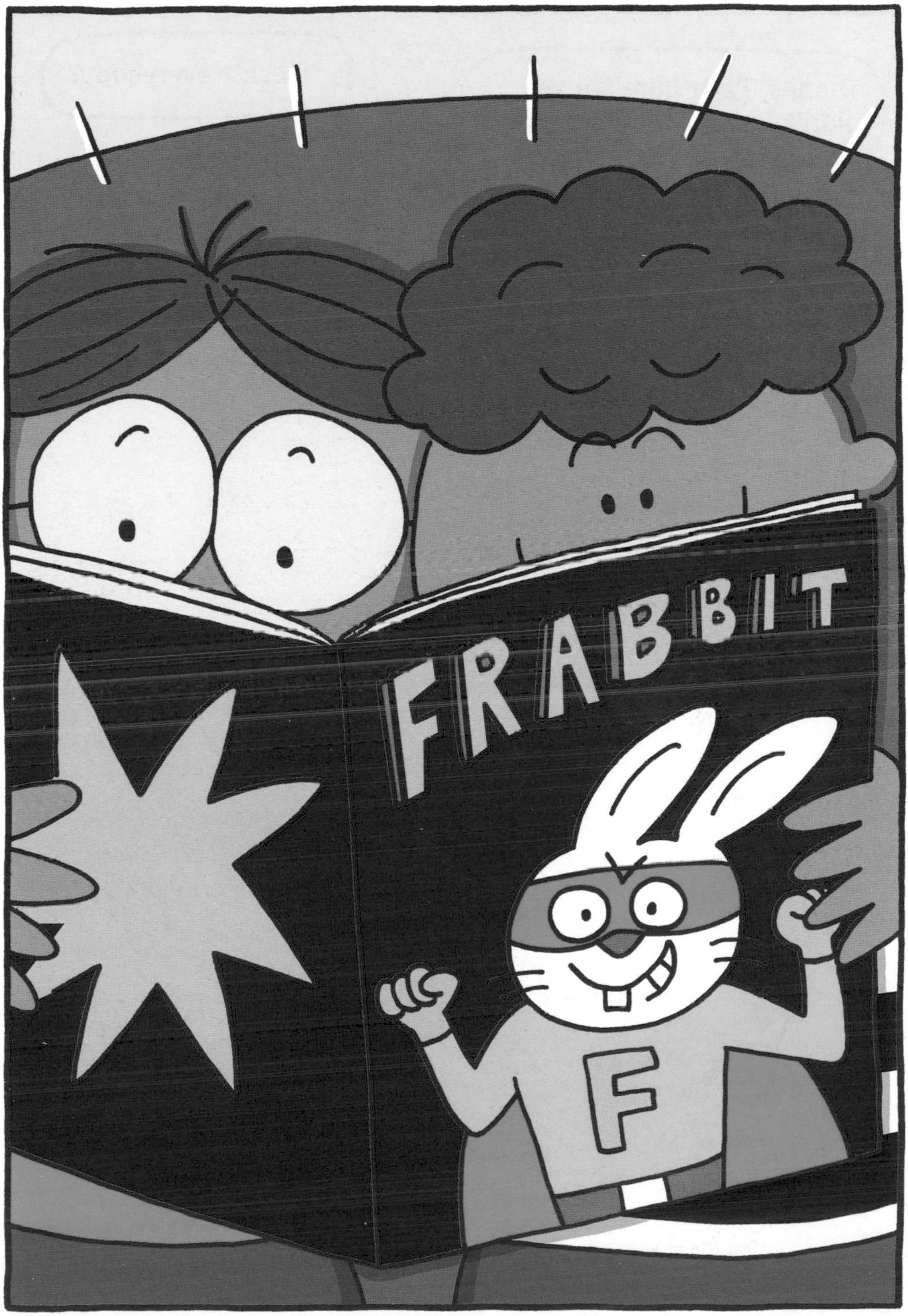
FRABBIT
F

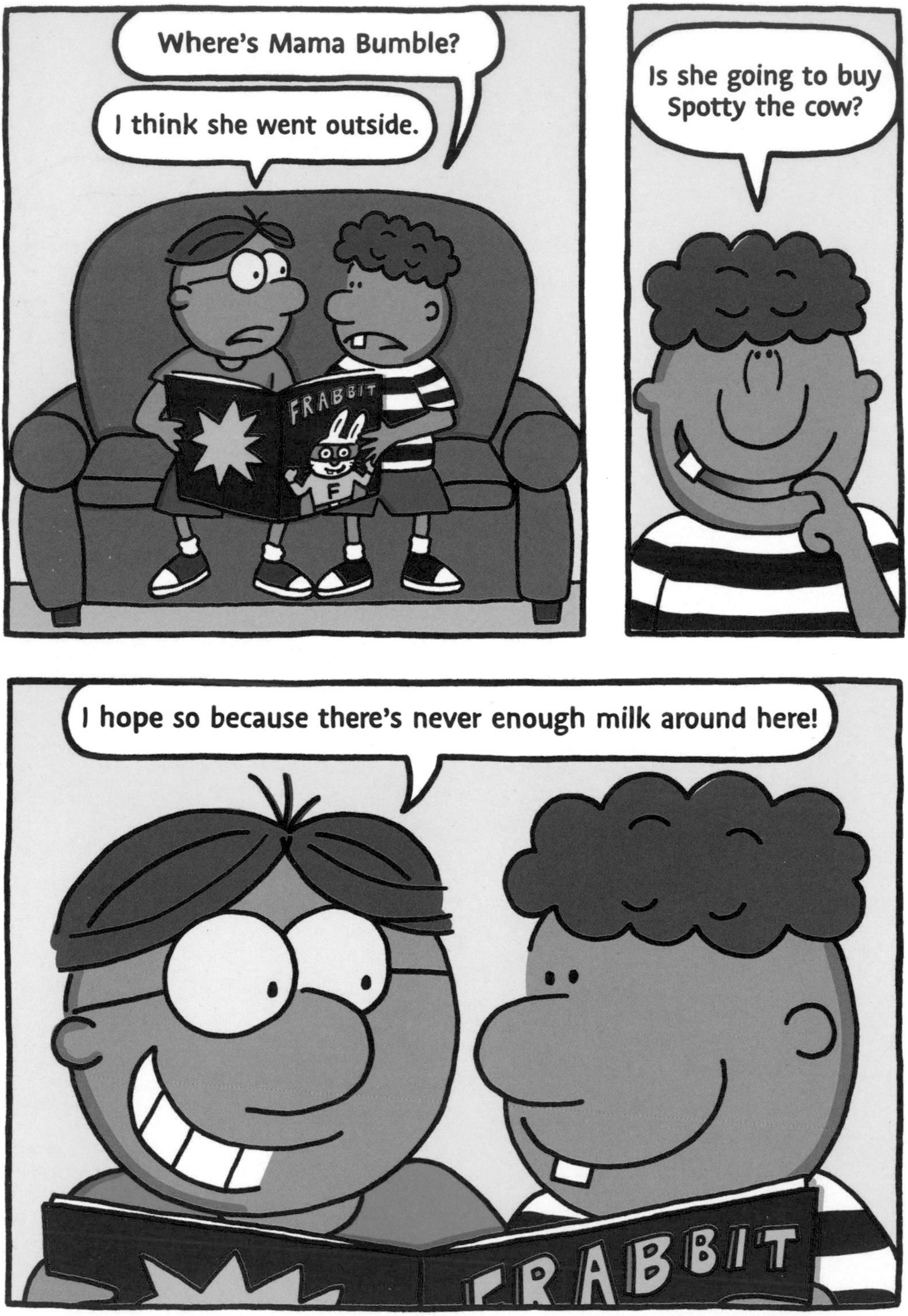
Where's Mama Bumble?
I think she went outside.
FRABBIT
F
Is she going to buy Spotty the cow?
I hope so because there's never enough milk around here!
FRABBIT

# The End

Steve Metzger is the bestselling author of more than eighty children's books, including *The Way I Act*, *Detective Blue* (IRA-CBC Children's Choice List. SLJ starred review), and *Pluto Visits Earth!* (ABC Best Books for Children). His latest book, *Yes, I Can Listen!* received a 2019 Eureka! Honor Award from the California Reading Association. Steve lives in New York City with his wife and daughter.

Brian Schatell has illustrated sixteen books for children, some of which he has also written. For many years Brian has chaired the Rutgers University Council on Children's Literature's annual One-on-One Plus Conference. He has also taught children's book illustration and writing at Parsons School of Design. Brian lives in New York City.

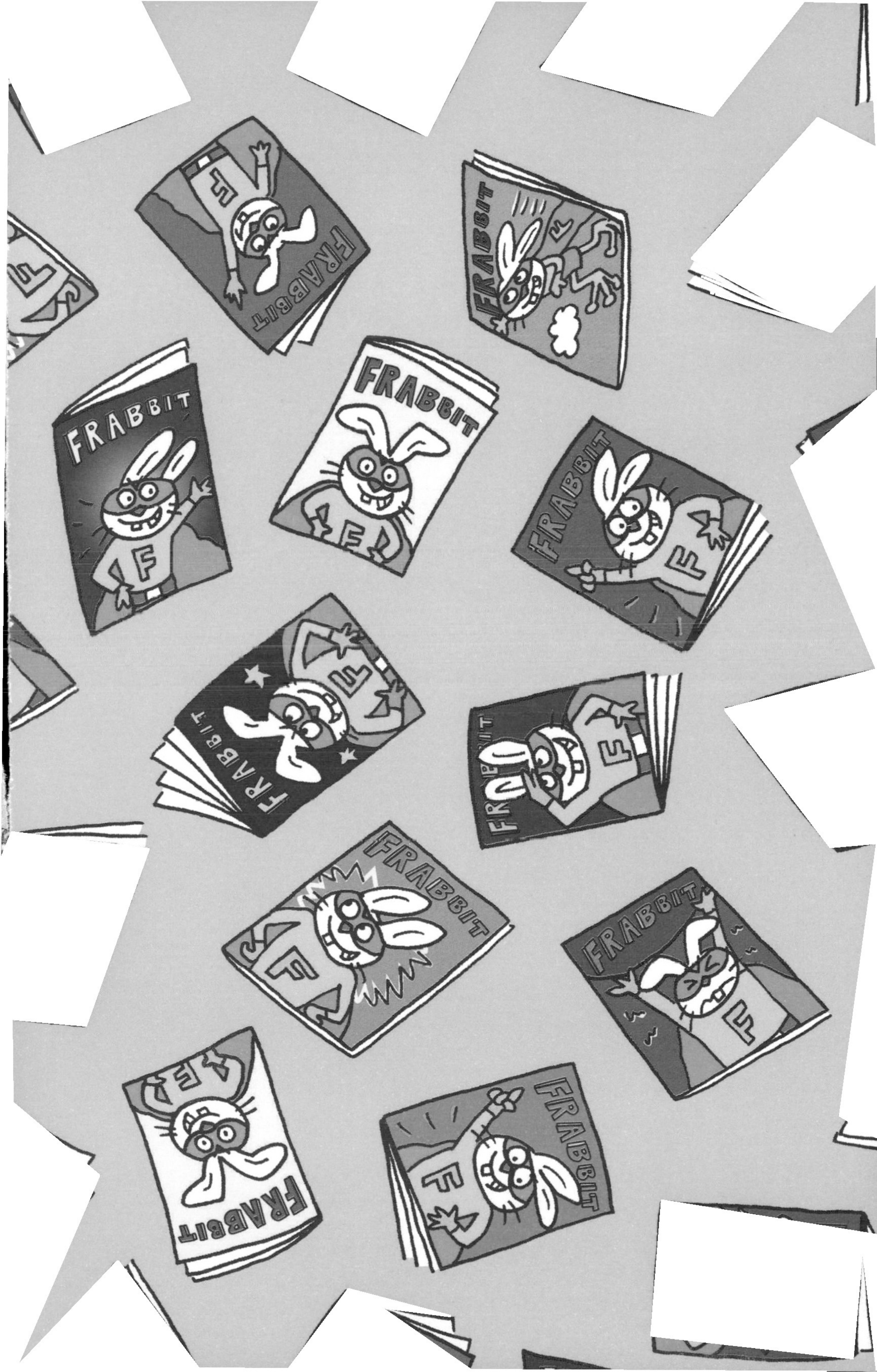
FRABBIT
FRABBIT
FRABBIT
FRABBIT
FRABBIT
FRABBIT
FRABBIT
FRABBIT
FRABBIT
FRABBIT

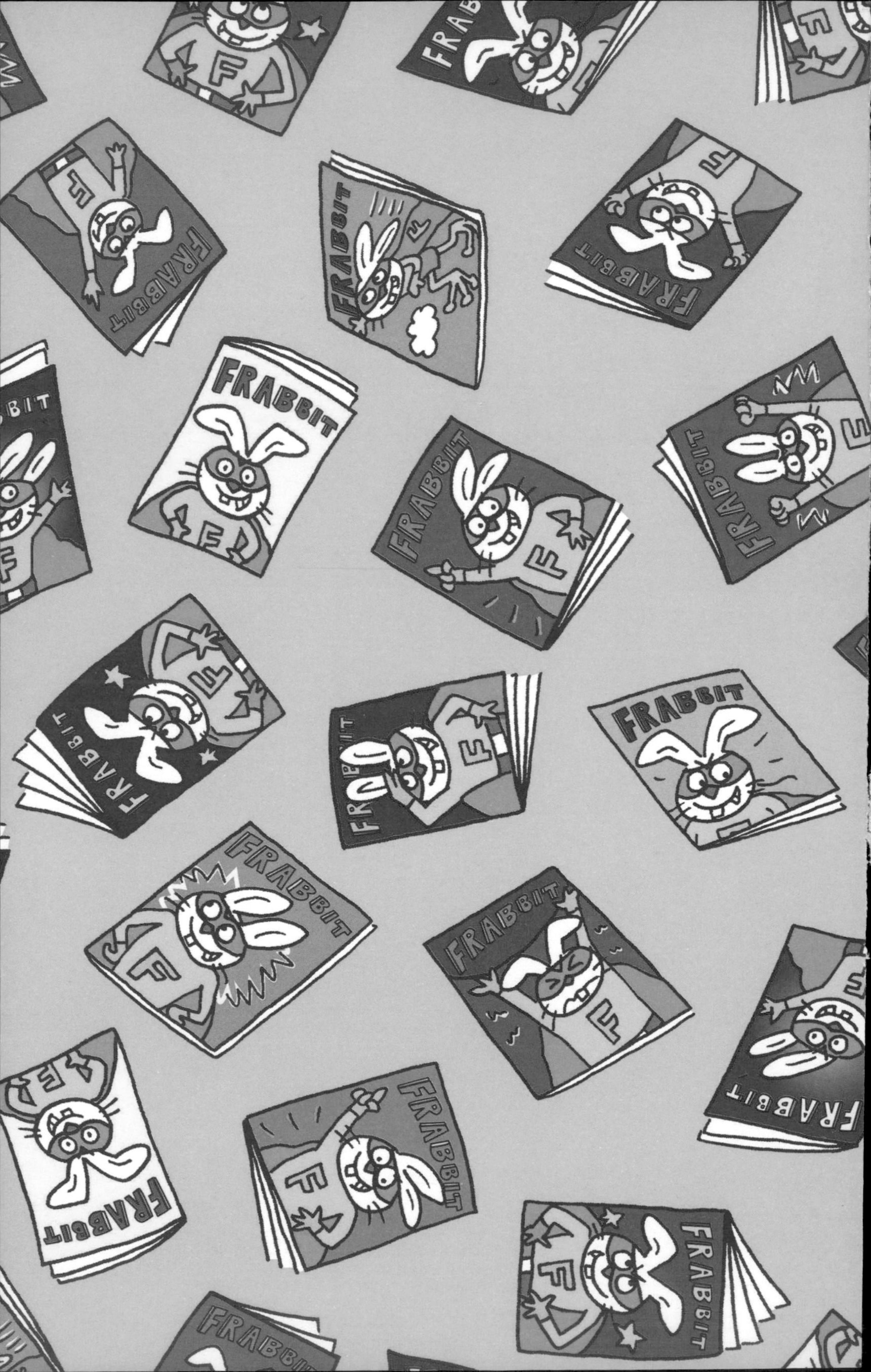
FRABBIT
FRABBIT
FRABBIT
FRABBIT
FRABBIT
FRABBIT
FRABBIT
FRABBIT
FRABBIT
FRABBIT
FRABBIT
FRABBIT
FRABBIT
FRABBIT